BEHIND ENEMY LINES

BOOK SEVEN OF THE EMPIRE OF BONES SAGA

TERRY MIXON

YOWLING
CAT PRESS

Behind Enemy Lines

Copyright © 2017 by Terry Mixon

Published by Yowling Cat Press ®

Digital edition date: 6/21/2023

Print ISBN: 978-1947376007

Large Print ISBN: 978-1947376304

Cover art - image copyrights as follows:

DepositPhotos/innovari (Luca Oleastri)

DepositPhotos/cobalt88 (Bozena Zuchowska)

Donna Mixon

Cover design and composition by Donna Mixon

Print edition design and layout by Terry Mixon

Audio edition performed and produced by Veronica Giguere

Reach her at: v@voicesbyveronica.com

ALSO BY TERRY MIXON

You can always find the most up to date listing of Terry's titles on his Amazon Author Page.

Note: the links below (ebook only, obviously) redirect you to my website where you can click a button to go to Amazon. This allows me to participate in Amazon's associates program and earn a little more. Sorry for any inconvenience.

The Last Hunter

The Last Hunter

Bonds of Blood

Alpha Strike

The Enemy Revealed

Command Authority

The Grand Conspiracy

Shield of Humanity

Fog of War

Ships of the Line

Operation Liberty

The Empire of Bones Saga

Empire of Bones

Veil of Shadows

Command Decisions

Ghosts of Empire

Paying the Price

Recon in Force

Box Sets

The Empire of Bones Saga Volume 1

The Empire of Bones Saga Volume 2

The Empire of Bones Saga Volume 3

The Empire of Bones Saga Volume 4

Humanity Unlimited Publisher's Pack 1

Humanity Unlimited Publisher's Pack 2

Want to get updates from Terry about new books and other general nonsense going on in his life? He promises there will be cats. Go to TerryMixon.com/Mailing-List and sign up.

DEDICATION

This book would not be possible without the love and support of my beautiful wife. Donna, I love you more than life itself.

ACKNOWLEDGMENTS

Once again, the people who read my books before you see them have saved me. Thanks to Alan Barnes, Michael Falkner, Michael Goad, Cain Hopwood, Jay Nedds, Kristopher Neidecker, John Naiser, Bob Noble, Andrew Olivier, Jon Paul Olivier, Bill Smith, Tom Stoecklein, Dale Thompson, and Jason Young for making me look good.

I also want to thank my readers for putting up with me. You guys are great.

1

"**W**hy the hell did you sneak aboard one of our ships?" Kelsey Bandar shouted once she had her mother alone in her office on *Persephone*. "We're at war!"

Justine Bandar sat without asking, smirking as she lounged in a chair in front of her daughter's desk. "I'm making certain that we have the opportunity to talk without you using your supposed duty as an excuse to avoid me."

She'd even had the nerve to use air quotes when she'd said "supposed."

Kelsey rubbed her face tiredly. "You've lost your mind. Do you even understand the situation you've inserted yourself into?"

Her mother made a pooh-poohing gesture. "I'm certain it's not nearly as dire as you'd have me believe. In any case, I refuse to let you go away angry. You're my daughter. I'm not going to allow you to deny me."

The woman leaned forward a little. "I've known you all your life, baby girl. You can't fool me. You're hurting inside, and you need your mother." Her expression allowed a little distaste to show through. "That has to be what's behind some of your more questionable choices recently."

Kelsey counted slowly to ten in her head before she spoke. "As hard as this may be to believe, you're not my biggest problem right now. Let me lay it out for you, Mother. While you've been hiding aboard *Audacious*, we've traveled deep inside the Rebel Empire.

"At this very moment, there's probably an enemy fleet trying to find and kill us. Let me emphasize that a little bit, just in case it's too subtle. They're going to try to *kill* us."

Her mother huffed. "Don't be so dramatic. I'm sure the situation isn't nearly as bad as you'd like me to believe. You're trying to distract me from this unhealthy mind-set of yours."

Kelsey slapped her hand on the desk and stood. As short as she was, that wasn't nearly as impressive as she'd prefer. Still, it would have to do.

"It's *exactly* that dire, Mother. Forget Jared Mertz. He's the least of your worries right now. We're currently behind enemy lines, and I just stole an entire Rebel Empire research station. One I'm sure they're desperate to keep out of our hands.

"Once they figure out how I did it, they're going to come after us. If they catch us, they're not going to politely ask me to give it back. They're going to start shooting."

For the first time since they'd discovered her mother hiding aboard the carrier, Justine Bandar looked a bit less certain. She squirmed in her seat. "What's a research station? Why are you taking it?"

"That's the kind of thing I don't have the time or patience to explain right now, Mother. The *only* purpose of this meeting is to tell you how badly you've screwed up.

"Until I have more time, I'm going to see that you get housing that's more suitable to your current circumstances."

Her mother smiled a little. "That little room *was* on the small side, and I can think of a few furnishings that would make life a little easier. These ships of yours are so... functional. Fleet should hire a few interior decorators. Add some soothing colors and make things a little more comfortable."

"I don't have time for this." Kelsey signaled for the marines through her implants. The door to her office slid open, and two hulking men stepped inside.

She pointed at her mother. "Justine Bandar is under arrest. Take her to the brig."

Her mother shot to her feet. "You can't arrest me! I'm your *mother!*"

"Oh, allow me to assure you, I can. Let's start with your unauthorized presence on a Fleet carrier. You've already admitted to that crime. I'm sure there are plenty of other regulations you've violated, but that will do for now.

"Once I'm certain we're in a relatively safe place, we'll have that little chat you so desperately want. Until then, you can contemplate your sins in a cell. If I have to, I'll send someone down to explain precisely how bad your situation is.

"In fact, that's a great idea. You *should* speak to someone in the Fleet Judge Advocate General's office. They can explain the severity of your crimes to you in exquisite detail. I'm sure the legal officer on *Audacious* can help you out. Marines, take her away."

The two men firmly grasped the ex-empress by her arms and dragged her gently from Kelsey's office. Her mother struggled and ordered them to release her until the hatch slid closed behind them. Kelsey was certain the woman would scream, demand, and promise retribution all the way to her new accommodations.

She slowly sat back down and rubbed the bridge of her nose. How in the hell had her mother even gotten on board the carrier? Obviously, someone had helped smuggle her aboard, but that didn't explain how she'd managed to stay hidden for two weeks. No, someone had been providing ongoing support.

It really didn't surprise Kelsey that some people in Fleet still saw her mother as an authority figure. After all, the woman had ruled the Empire at her father's side for decades. For many people, she still had that aura of command. Or they thought she could give them something in return for their support.

They needed to learn the error of their ways in the strongest of terms.

"*Persephone*, signal *Audacious* for me. I want to speak to Commodore Anderson."

"Signaling now, Colonel."

Kelsey's father—Emperor Karl Bandar—had decided that she needed to be a marine to command marines. So, he'd worked with Admiral Yeats to make that happen.

Her ship—*Persephone*—was a Marine Raider vessel from the Old Empire. Its computer would allow only someone with the appropriate codes and Marine Raider implants to command it. Kelsey was the only person in the New Terran Empire that met those criteria.

That wouldn't be true for very much longer, though. Her executive officer, Major Angela Ellis, was almost halfway through the implant procedures required to become a Marine Raider. She'd had the requisite cranial implants already. Last week, she'd gotten the pharmacology unit, ocular, auditory, and olfactory enhancements.

Over the next three weeks, she'd go through additional procedures to coat her bones with layers of graphene and weave artificial muscles through her natural ones. They'd start with her legs, and then move to her arms and upper body over two additional sessions. That would give the woman time to master her upgraded body.

Learning to use the new muscles was going to be challenging, but Kelsey had no doubt the marine would master them quickly. If a pampered little princess could do it, Angela Ellis could.

"This unit has Commodore Anderson on the line for you, Colonel," *Persephone* said.

"On my screen."

An image of Zia Anderson appeared on Kelsey's screen. The young woman smiled wryly. "Have you gotten your unexpected guest comfortably situated?"

"You could say that. I just had the marines take her down to the brig."

Zia's eyes widened. "Seriously? You locked your *mother* in the brig?"

"Damned right I did. She's got to learn that she can't just throw her weight around like that anymore."

"You mean she's got to learn she can't mess with you like that, don't you?"

"That too," Kelsey said with a grimace. "I'm going to put the fear of God into her. It'll do her good to sweat for a while.

"But that's not why I called. Someone on *Audacious* aided and abetted her. If they're willing to stash an ex-empress on your ship for two weeks, what else might they do?"

"That's a good question," Zia said. "I've already told Brandon to find them, though he has other things going on. He'll eventually get to the bottom of this."

Brandon Levy was a by-the-book kind of guy. Kelsey expected he'd find the people who'd hidden Justine Bandar. He'd make them suffer for it too.

"We'll let him take care that, then," Kelsey said. "I'd prefer administrative punishment."

"That pretty much sums up the orders I've already given him."

Technically, Zia was the senior Imperial officer in their task force, so that was really her call to make. Kelsey could make big picture decisions, but if she meddled in the details, Zia would have every right to smack her hand. Like she'd just delicately done.

"Right. Sorry. They're your people to discipline. I do, however, insist you leave my mother to me."

"You'll get no argument from me," Zia said solemnly. "I'd prefer not to tangle with her."

Kelsey nodded. "We have a deal, then. I want you to send your legal officer over, though. He needs to explain the regulations my mother violated and tell her the penalties she faces for breaking them. I think she needs a wake-up call."

"I'll talk to him as soon as we're done," Zia said with a nod. "He can come over with Carl."

She frowned. "Why is Carl coming over?"

Zia shrugged. "I'm not sure. Something about Ned Quincy."

"Maybe that means he's figured out how to relocate the program. That would be awesome. Having some privacy would be nice."

Ned Quincy had been an officer in the Marine Raiders before the Fall. He'd saved a lot of memories using an as-yet-unknown method devised by one of his people.

When Kelsey had taken those memories into her implants and allowed Marcus—the sentient AI in command of Jared's flagship—to change the operational program to enable her to search the memories, Ned had come to pseudo-life.

He wasn't quite a person, but he was far more than a computer program. He seemed to have genuine emotions.

Unfortunately, he lived in Kelsey's head. Which made going to the bathroom awkward, to say the least.

They'd come to an agreement about him accessing her implants, but it wasn't the same as being alone.

Carl had been working on some secret project to relocate the programs in a manner that kept them active. Perhaps his visit was to get that rolling.

"Ned is in hibernation at the moment," Kelsey said. "He doesn't sleep like a real person, but we found out that he had to have downtime every week or so. So, I can freely say that I'll be damned happy to have him out of my head.

"I like him, but no one needs to have someone potentially looking over her shoulder all the damned time. Or actually hearing the more focused thoughts in your head. That's too intimate."

"I can't imagine why it hasn't driven you crazy. Or Talbot."

Kelsey laughed. "Who says it hasn't? In any case, don't let my mother distract you from finding us a hidey-hole. That has to be your first priority."

She rose from behind her desk. "I'm certainly not going to let her distract me. Maybe I can help find us a weak flip point so we can get the hell out of here."

* * *

Major Russ Talbot tried not to hover as Carl Owlet hunched over the main computer in the captured research center. "What's taking so long? I thought you were the master of breaking into computers."

The young scientist glanced back peevishly. "I'd be done a lot faster if you'd stop asking me that every five minutes. This kind of work takes time under the best of circumstances. Which, I'll point out, this isn't."

Since Talbot really didn't know anything about computer hacking, so he couldn't dispute any of that.

"Why is this one so much harder?" he asked. "You've gotten into a lot of Old Empire computers before. Don't you have a bunch of tools to make this easy?"

Carl set the tablet he was using onto the locked console and turned to face him. "I *do* have tools, but I've had zero luck breaking into every military computer we've captured from the Rebel Empire. Whoever programs them is paranoid, and I mean that literally.

"I only got into the AI at Harrison's World because Kelsey killed its power so abruptly. It didn't have time to lock its memory. The storage was still accessible. If the AI had sent a command to lock it up, I'd be banging my head there too.

"This computer contains classified research the Rebel Empire doesn't want anyone to have. Not even its own people. Remember, the AIs don't exactly trust humans, particularly the ones they use as slaves.

"Honestly, the fact that they require humans to do this research in the first place tells us something very interesting about how they work. Or rather, how they don't work. I'm shocked they didn't shoot the researchers as soon as we attacked."

"I suspect that had to do with the fact we surprised them so badly," Talbot said. "We literally dumped a brigade's worth of marines onto them with no warning. First, we snuck into a system that they were certain they had locked down, then we used the transport rings to get our people onto the orbital without them having a chance to see us coming.

"Last, we set off your jammers and blew a nice big hole into their secure area. Our people were all over them before they had a chance to figure out what was happening, much less act on it. I'm sure that shutting down all the fusion plants within a couple of minutes had something to do with our success too."

The young man nodded. "Overwhelming surprise was the goal. I'm just stunned that it worked so well. Frankly, far too many of your wife's plans go astray for my comfort. Then she blows up a lot of things to make up for lost ground."

Talbot laughed. "A surprising number of things get blown up even when things go according to her plans too. I'll admit this mission resulted in less devastation than most. With discretion being the better part of valor, we'll just keep that opinion to ourselves.

"Maybe it would help to step back a bit and look at the big picture," he told the young scientist after a moment. "What precisely do we have our hands on?"

Carl sighed. "If we're just talking about the research facility, we've got five major labs doing work on various projects. One of them is some kind of missile-enhancement program. We're talking bigger warheads, faster drives, and more endurance. Possibly making them smarter and harder to hit. They're also looking at more powerful beams and stronger battle screens.

"Then there's the production area for the Raider implants. That's not technically research, but extremely restricted. I suspect the people running it are more like factory workers. They probably didn't know what they were producing.

"Stealing the orbital and the minds that made all this possible is going to have a profound impact on the Rebel Empire's research programs. We took their research, hardware, and the minds that made it happen. They won't be able to replace any of that very quickly, and this isn't the kind of knowledge the AIs want on the loose."

Talbot snorted. "They'd probably give any retiring worker a private send-off without a suit."

Carl winced. "Ouch. Based on the plans I saw on paper, it looks as though they only used the Raider implant equipment whenever they needed a fresh batch for the crazy AI on Erorsi.

"That points to the probability that the Rebel Empire doesn't have any attack forces outfitted with Marine Raider implants, which we already suspected. That's good news for us."

Talbot nodded. "Then there's the AI production line that Annette Vitter said was going to kick off soon."

The crazy fighter pilot had bluffed her way into the restricted area on the orbital and parleyed a case of mistaken identity into access to a briefing about the AI project. Talk about huge brass balls. The woman would've made a hell of a marine.

"Not exactly," Carl disagreed. "They already had a facility here to produce the hardware. The plans that Captain Vitter had seen there had revolved around expanding that. If I had to guess, I'd wager that this was a backup production center for AI hardware that they wanted to make more productive."

"Are you making any progress in understanding how to produce that hardware?"

Carl gave him a flat look. "In case it escaped your notice, there are a lot of competing priorities vying for my attention. It'll take several days just to figure out what we have our hands on, and if they find a weak flip point, I'll have to drop everything and work on that."

"I really wish we brought more of your people along for this mission," Talbot grumbled. "We're really short in the scientist department this time."

His young friend smiled wryly. "To be fair, we'd only planned on snagging some equipment and running for it. Nobody in their right mind thought Princess Kelsey would steal an entire orbital or run *away* from our support ships."

The untimely arrival of a Rebel Empire fleet had forced them to run in the opposite direction. All they had with them now was the carrier *Audacious*, the Marine Raider ship *Persephone*, a freighter whose contents they were still trying to pin down, and a recovery ship they were using to move the captured orbital along at a snail's pace.

Not enough force to deal with a determined pursuer, and circumstances had trapped them in a series of systems running deeper into the Rebel Empire.

The enemy would've already chased them down if they hadn't made it look as though the orbital had exploded. It wouldn't be long before the Rebel Empire commander saw through that ruse. Then he'd figure out that one of the battle stations guarding the system's flip points wasn't communicating. Neither were the destroyers that had been backing it up.

He'd likely assume that whoever had blown up the orbital had come in that way, killing the ships and station on the way in. Once they realized the orbital was gone, he'd be after them at top speed.

The New Terran Empire's forces only had one chance. They needed to find a weak flip point and slip away.

The Rebel Empire didn't know weak flip points existed. If his team found one, they'd get the breathing room they needed to solve their current problems. If not, well, things would get very, very ugly.

Carl proved his thoughts were roaming along those lines when he spoke again. "Any word on the search for weak flip points? All of this is going to be for nothing if we don't get off the path the Rebel Empire expects us to be on. Once they figure out that wasn't their orbital that blew up."

"Commodore Anderson hasn't mentioned anything. We still have probes and fighters out searching this system. No luck yet."

Their forces had fled through the first empty system without looking for weak flip points. Kelsey had wanted to be completely certain they'd gotten clear before any Rebel Empire ships came looking for them. They were in the second system now. If they didn't find anything here, they'd move onto the third.

"Well, do the best you can," Talbot finally said. "Once we have the prisoners settled into the area of the orbital we've cleared for them, I'll have you talk with the scientists. Perhaps you can form some kind of bond. You know, geek to geek."

Carl chuckled. "I'll certainly do my best. How long do you think that's going to take?"

He shrugged. "We're talking about roughly ten thousand people. Just determining who everyone is will take days. They're not exactly cooperating. It would help if we had access to the personnel files."

The young scientist picked up his tablet glumly. "I still have a few ideas to try. If all of else fails, we might be able to trick one of them into logging in."

Talbot considered that and smiled. "You know, that's a really good idea. I'll let you get back to work while I see if I can come up with a plan."

2

To Kelsey's joy, it turned out that Carl had indeed figured out how to extract Ned Quincy from her implants without harming him. The equipment the young scientist had brought over managed the task without incident, after she woke Ned and he gave his consent.

That didn't mean Carl was going to be putting Ned into something else right away, though. He had a lot of work remaining to design a computer that could correctly mimic having Raider implants.

When he managed that, Ned would be back in some form. She hoped that happened soon, but they had other things on their plates.

Such as the scanner readings from the far-flung probes. It only took a few hours after Carl had extracted Ned before one of them found something.

"I've found a weak flip point," Carl said from his borrowed console on *Persephone's* bridge.

Relief flooded through her. She'd been afraid they wouldn't find one before they had to flee this system. Now they had a chance.

"What can we tell about it?" she asked.

He shrugged. "Not much. The probe is still too far away from the flip point to take any measurements."

That's about what Kelsey had expected. "Have the task force change course toward the flip point. It might cost us some time, but I'd rather have everybody close by."

Time crawled as the ships slowly made their way toward the newly discovered flip point. It wasn't very far away from the regular flip point they'd need to use if this new one was unsuitable. They could resume their headlong flight with only a few hours lost if they had to.

"Is the flip point going to be large enough for the orbital?" she asked him once they'd drawn near the potential escape hatch.

"I'll need to send a probe through to get readings from the other side before I can be sure."

"I'm sorry if I seem a bit abrupt," she said, "but I'm worried we'll have company very soon. I'd really like to get away before they arrive."

"Couldn't we just move to the outer system? If we cut our power to standby, they'll go right past us."

"Yes, but they'd be in front of us then. If this flip point doesn't work out, we'd probably run into them when we try the next system. I'd rather avoid that."

The young scientist sighed. "I see your point. The probe is getting some better readings now. Once I've precisely isolated the flip point, we can send it through. When it comes back, I should be able to tell what the relative strength is and whether or not we can transit safely."

"What kind of timeframe are we talking about?" she asked.

"Half an hour or so. Maybe less."

Kelsey forced herself to wait. That involved an inordinate amount of pacing.

Twenty minutes later, he grunted. "The flip point is strong enough to allow the ships through, even *Audacious*. I'm not sure about the recovery ship while it's holding the orbital, though."

"We can't just leave it behind," she said. "This is a package deal. We all have to make it through."

He sighed. "I understand, but I can't command physics. We should focus on seeing what's on the other side."

"Send the probe. We also need to make sure we're not running into something like the nova where Omega lives."

"Good point. I'm sending the instructions to flip it now. It'll go over, take readings for about ten minutes, and then return. If you don't mind, I'm going to get a sandwich while it does that. It's been a while since I ate."

"That's something I can take care of." A quick message to the galley had food on the way for all of them.

The probe flipped out of the system just as their food arrived. Someone had made extra sandwiches for Kelsey, for which she was grateful. It no longer bothered her that she was always eating something to feed her enhanced body.

They had enough time to take the edge off their hunger before the probe returned and began transmitting data.

"The other side looks safe enough," Carl said after a moment. "It's a normal system with no obvious radio, grav, or power sources detected on passive scans. The probe didn't stay long enough to note anything subtle, so it might still be occupied in some smaller fashion."

"What about the flip point?" Kelsey asked. "Is it going to be strong enough to allow the recovery ship to make it through with the orbital?"

"It's close. The only way to find out for sure is to try. On the negative side, the far end is not as strong as this side. If we go across, the orbital is definitely too large to come back. Probably not *Audacious*, either. We'd be committed."

She sighed. "Tell me again what happens if the recovery ship comes apart midflip? Those arms aren't really all that secure, since the orbital is far too big to fit inside them in their normal configuration."

"I'm not really sure, but it can't be good. Best case, the recovery ship arrives in the other system but is unable to move the orbital any farther."

"What's the worst case?" She already had a fairly good idea of what it was, but she wanted to hear him say it.

His lips compressed. "Just about as bad as you'd imagine. The stress of flipping distorts the field generated by the arms, and the orbital comes apart. I'm not sure if that's preflip or on the other side."

Kelsey rubbed her face. If they passed this flip point by, they might not find another before the Rebel Empire caught up with them. On the other hand, if they tried to use the flip point and failed, thousands of people could die.

"Well, it's not as if we really have a choice," she finally said. "We'll go take a look around. If things look promising, we'll give it a try."

* * *

ANNETTE VITTER MADE a show of struggling against the two marines as they hauled her through the hatch. They weren't being gentle, so she didn't even have to act very hard.

"Let me go, you cretins!" she shouted.

Of course, they didn't release her. They had their own roles to play.

They manhandled her another few meters into the compartment and shoved her forward, just as planned.

She stumbled, turned, and shot a glare at their retreating backs as they marched back out. "I don't know who you bastards think you are, but you'll never get away with this."

The hatch slid shut and she turned with a huff to face the prisoners. She'd met most of them at the meeting she'd attended just before Kelsey and the marines had captured the orbital.

The only people she knew by name were Commander Edward Irons and Commodore Murdock. The former was friendly, and the latter was a droning bore. They, of course, knew her as Commander Violet Renner, a role she'd continue playing for the moment.

They'd stashed the real Commander Renner in a special holding cell. Princess Kelsey had decided early on to keep the woman isolated from everyone else so that Annette could use her identity if she had to.

Annette wasn't sure Talbot's plan would work, but she was willing to give it a try. He'd be monitoring the situation via a camera above the main hatch to the cafeteria they were using to house the senior prisoners.

Under other circumstances, they could've used her implants to see and hear what she did, but they had to jam everyone to keep the prisoners from communicating. In any case, the odds were good that no one was going to assault her.

If they did, she'd be able to handle herself until help arrived. One didn't fly marines around without picking up a few things.

Irons rose from the table where he'd been sitting and headed her way. "Commander Renner! We were worried. Are you all right?"

"I'm fine," she said, rubbing her forehead. "I've got a killer headache, though."

Stunners did that to people. They'd knock you out for a couple of hours and leave you with a splitting headache. Not that she'd been stunned this time, of course, but everyone else had. They'd know intimately what she was talking about.

He nodded sympathetically. "That's pretty much how the rest of us feel too. Did they question you?"

"Commander Irons," Commodore Emilia Murdock said from a table off in a corner by herself. "Please escort Commander Renner to me. You'll have time to chitchat later."

The woman's tone was one of irritation. Annette couldn't tell if that was because she was impatient because Irons was delaying Annette or if Murdock always sounded that way. Based on the meeting Annette had attended, she was betting on the latter.

Irons managed a contrite expression. "Of course, Commodore. Right away." He made a show of escorting Annette to the Commodore's table before returning to his associates.

Since the only chair at the table was the one the Commodore was using, Annette decided she'd just stand at attention. "Commander Renner reporting, Commodore."

"At ease, Commander. Report."

Annette allowed herself to relax fractionally. The older woman didn't seem to be the type that wanted her subordinates to be at ease.

"Yes, ma'am. I was on my way to my quarters when all hell broke loose. I heard explosions and then ran into a squad of marines in powered armor. They were shooting everybody in sight with stunners. I tried to get out of the way, but one of them hit me.

"I woke up in a small compartment with other Fleet personnel.

Once I was finally able to get someone's attention, I convinced them to bring me here with the other senior officers. All I know for certain is that there are a lot of marines and Fleet personnel among our attackers."

"I was able to get into my office and take a look at the monitors before they captured the primary control center," the older woman said. "There must've been hundreds of marines in armor. I have no idea where they came from, but their surprise was total.

"Whoever the traitors are, they had help smuggling people onto this orbital. Inside help. There's absolutely no way that many unknown personnel could've gotten past our security. Also, someone with the appropriate access codes had to disable their armor's self-destruct systems."

Annette made a show of agreeing without saying anything. She could see how it would be confusing to the older woman. The Rebel Empire didn't allow their marines to use powered armor or heavy weapons without strict supervision. Marines and enlisted personnel didn't have cranial implants, so the armor had to be manually controlled.

Which meant that an officer with implants had to unlock it for their use. Those same officers could remotely detonate explosive charges hidden inside the armor. She wondered if that engendered trust issues with the Rebel Empire marines.

"Whoever it was, ma'am, they knew what they were doing," Annette said. "The fact that we're still sitting here means they disabled all the self-destruct charges. They have everything."

"Not quite," Murdock said. "They're undoubtedly after our research, but it's not going to do them much good. The computers are locked down, and only our top people have the codes."

The older woman smiled. "And they're not going to have very much time to consolidate their gains. They don't know it yet, but they're going to have visitors very soon. Much sooner than they'd planned for, I imagine."

That would be the fleet of ships that had come into Dresden space right after Princess Kelsey had captured the orbital. They were still probably trying to figure out what had happened. Annette hoped they found a weak flip point so they could escape before those vessels came after them.

The senior Rebel Empire officer shook her head. "No, our captors aren't going to be pleased at all. Meanwhile, we need to come up with plans to escape our confinement and free our fellow officers. I'm not going to sit on my butt waiting for someone to come rescue me. We'll get out of here on our own.

"I want you to join Commander Irons and assist him in any way that he requires. He's much more familiar with the orbital layout than you are. After all, you've only been here a few hours."

The older woman sighed. "You're not seeing us at our best, Commander Renner, but that's about to change. Dismissed."

Annette came to attention and saluted. She spun on her heel and walked over to the table where Irons was sitting with several other senior officers. She'd seen most of them at the briefing, but hadn't learned their names.

Their conversation ceased as she stepped up beside the table. Irons gestured for her to take the open seat beside him.

"Everyone, this is Violet Renner. As you might remember, she arrived just before the current unpleasantness.

"Commander Renner, allow me to introduce the rest of the command staff. To my right is Commander Andrew Gomez. He's our hardware guru."

The slender Hispanic man inclined his head.

"Across from you is Jeannette Martin. She's the civilian computer specialist that oversees all aspects of our research computers. She'd normally have our chief scientist with her, but our captors have her somewhere else."

Martin was a somewhat overweight brunette woman with a darker complexion. She smiled at Annette shyly.

"Finally," Irons said, "the man you were here to replace. Commander Raul Castille is our senior security officer, of course."

The tall man smiled coolly. "Commander Renner. I'm sorry we didn't have an opportunity to get together before the Commodore's briefing, but I had other tasks that kept me occupied. I must say that the image in your personnel file doesn't do you justice."

Oh, crap.

3

Kelsey tapped in to the scanner feed as soon as they were through the flip point. As the probe had said, the new system seemed deserted at first glance, but they were only operating off passive scanners.

That meant they'd pick up active fusion plants eventually, if the people that built them hadn't shielded them well enough. If there were any ships moving out there, they'd spot them if they were moving fast enough.

That's where the risk came in. The system might have a Rebel Empire picket force that they wouldn't notice right away. They had to go slow and be careful.

"Take us out of the flip point," she ordered. "Launch a dozen stealthed probes and get them scanning the rest of the system. If there's something out there, I want to know about it."

The process of thoroughly vetting an unknown system could take days. They didn't have time for that, so she'd just have to do the best she could. If after three hours, they hadn't detected signs of people, she'd declare it safe enough for them to move forward.

"Colonel," Lieutenant Jack Thompson—her helm officer—said. "The computer has generally located this system in relation to the Old

Empire maps we have. If the estimate is accurate, the Old Empire wasn't aware of it."

Kelsey smiled at the man. "That's good news. It might mean we have some breathing room to get ourselves in order. It also means that the system might have flip points that lead somewhere useful. Like taking us partway home."

If they could avoid going into the Rebel Empire, that would be amazingly good luck. Now that they knew her people existed, it wouldn't be so easy to slip home again without them noticing.

"What do we know about the system?" she asked.

"It has a main sequence G-class star, and we're picking up indications of several planets," Angela said from her console. "We won't know for a while if any are in the habitable zone. It's roughly three hundred light years from the system we just left."

A habitable planet would be good. It would allow them the luxury of moving their prisoners to a location where they'd be both more comfortable and less dangerous. As long as they continued housing the prisoners on the station, there was always the chance they might stage a breakout.

"Take us into the system at half speed," she told Jack. "Continue scanning with passives. If you pick up anything unusual—no matter how small—I want to know immediately."

"Aye, ma'am."

While her ship and the probes began fanning out into the new system, she resumed considering how she was going to deal with her mother. Justine Bandar was a complication that Kelsey really didn't have time for, but the woman wasn't going away. Unfortunately.

From what Kelsey had heard, her mother hadn't stopped yelling at the poor lieutenant tasked with guarding her. *Persephone* was too small to have a brig. She'd used the word with her mother to make a point, but she'd really housed her in the smallest stateroom on the ship.

Having recently occupied several different cells, Kelsey knew her mother was just fine. A brig would only have a bunk, a desk, and a chair that didn't move. Oh, and a toilet that only barely protected someone's modesty from the guards.

Kelsey wondered how ex-Empress Justine Bandar would react to someone tossing her into a real cell. The mind boggled.

The next three hours proceeded without incident or unexpected discovery. *Persephone* edged deeper into the system, all her electronic senses straining to detect anything unusual. All they found was a seemingly empty system.

Kelsey drummed her fingers on her armrest and considered the situation. "We don't have time to search every corner of the system just now. Leave the probes in place, and take us back to the flip point."

"Aye, ma'am."

The Raider ship turned in a tight arc and returned to the flip point. When she was in place, Kelsey gave the order to flip. They appeared back in the original system without any problem. At least *Persephone* could flip back.

The latest information from Carl indicated that nothing much larger could go back. The weak flip point was one way for ships of any real size.

Kelsey opened a channel to *Audacious*. An image of Zia Anderson appeared. The other woman looked a little worn around the edges.

"Give me some news, Highness."

"Initial scans show the target system is probably empty."

Zia visibly relaxed. "Oh, thank God. I've been sitting here worrying that we were jumping out of the frying pan and into the fire. If this flip point had led to a heavily occupied system deeper inside the Rebel Empire, we'd have been screwed."

"I was a little worried about that myself," Kelsey admitted. "That doesn't mean all the news is good, though. The flip point is one way for ships larger than *Persephone*."

The other woman sighed. "It could be the other way around. That would suck."

"Agreed. Any sign of our friends?"

The Fleet officer shook her head. "The probes we left watching the flip point leading back toward Dresden are still clear. No sign of any pursuit. That won't last much longer."

That was true. They needed to get a move on, if they hoped to escape unnoticed.

"So, what's the plan?" Kelsey asked.

"We're going to take a chance and attempt to send the recovery ship through," Zia said. "I don't think we can risk hoping for a better option in the next system."

Kelsey thought so too. Sooner or later, their luck was going to run out.

"How are we going do this?" she asked. "Do we want to send some ships through first to wait on the other side, or send the recovery ship first? Also, what about the prisoners? Do we evacuate those we can, or does everyone take their chances together?"

The Fleet officer seemed to consider that for a moment. "I think we'll send *Persephone* through again, and then the recovery ship. We'll leave the prisoners aboard the orbital. We don't have room to house them anywhere else.

"Even if we could, moving them would take too long. We need to do this now. Head back over and wait for the recovery ship."

Cain Hopwood and his team of specialists were crewing the recovery ship for her. Their eclectic skills actually made them well-suited to handle it. If anyone could get the orbital through, they would.

"Roger that. We'll let you know as soon as the recovery ship arrives."

Kelsey killed the channel and turned toward her helm officer. "Take us back through."

It only took a few minutes to flip *Persephone* back to the other system and move away from the flip point far enough to be safe. The next few minutes were nerve-racking, but the recovery ship appeared without obvious signs of damage.

Kelsey let out the breath she hadn't realized she'd been holding, and then signaled the crew manning the recovery ship. A quick response indicated that everything looked good on their end.

She grinned. "We're going to pull this off. Send a probe back to *Audacious*. Let them know that everything went just fine."

Five minutes later, the rest of their ships appeared through the flip point. They'd escaped the Rebel Empire's clutches. Now all they had to do was find another way home.

* * *

RAUL CASTILLE CONSIDERED the woman sitting beside him. One thing was certain: she wasn't Violet Renner. If someone only had a basic description of Renner, she'd fool them, but he'd seen the real woman's personnel file.

From the look in her eyes, the imposter realized the game was up too. It would be interesting to see how she responded.

What had her plan been? Whom did she truly represent? Did he actually want to unmask her now?

After a moment's contemplation, he decided to keep his discovery to himself.

The revelation of her true identity would probably spark a small-scale riot. Her compatriots were undoubtedly ready to rush in and save her. His companions would likely attack her as well. Predictable and boring.

It would be much more entertaining to let this play out a little further. The life of a security officer was often one of drudgery. This was a rare opportunity for him to play at the top of his game.

"Yes, indeed," he continued coolly. "Your picture doesn't do you justice, Commander Renner. Then again, official pictures rarely do."

He smiled, being certain to show his teeth. "I can't begin to tell you how much I'm looking forward to working with you. Particularly under the circumstances we find ourselves in. This should be utterly fascinating."

The woman quickly regrouped and cleared her throat. "I agree, Commander Castille. This is going to be a unique experience."

"I couldn't have said it better myself. And I *insist* you call me Raul." He turned his attention to Irons. "I believe you were running down our options to escape confinement, Commander. Please continue."

Irons nodded, completely unaware of the byplay between Castille and the spy among them.

"Right. We can't be certain what conditions the rest of our people are being held in, but no matter how many marines they brought with them, these people can't have everyone covered as well as they'd like. All we have to do is look for an opportunity to escape.

"If we can get to one of the armories, we'll turn this around. Even a small number of armed personnel can free others. Once we start a breakout, they won't be able to stop us without killing everyone."

Castille allowed himself a small smile. "What makes you think they won't be willing to do precisely that? Obviously, these people planned long and hard for this operation. Simply acquiring the restricted weapons and powered armor must've taken years and an incredible amount of money. Surely they will kill to obtain what they want."

He glanced at "Renner" as he said the last bit.

Her presence actually argued against what he'd just said. If the enemy was willing to send a spy among them, they still needed something. Most likely access to the restricted computer systems.

"What are they really after?" he continued. "Considering the effort required to seize a classified research station like this, they must believe the return is worth a lot of blood and treasure. As we all know, the work we do here is not something one can sell on the open market.

"That means they have a backer. Someone in the upper reaches of the higher orders, I'd wager. Someone in a position of power that believes they can use this technology to advance their cause, whatever it is."

"I can't see that," Jeanette Martin said. "So much of what we're doing here is oriented toward Fleet. There's absolutely no way the lords will allow anyone in the higher orders to have that type of technology."

Well, that was certainly true, Raul conceded. The lords would not allow *anyone* to obtain the technical specifications for an artificial intelligence. Perhaps that was what the woman and her compatriots sought.

If so, it wouldn't do them one bit of good. They'd locked the information down tightly enough that not even he could access it alone.

Only Commodore Murdock, Jeanette Martin, and he acting in concert could access the computers controlling the manufacturing process for the artificial intelligence hardware. The lords had instituted that level of protection to be certain that this type of situation never occurred.

He suspected, however, that their attackers were unaware of this. They probably believed that they could just waltz in, take whatever they wanted, and escape before anyone noticed. That wasn't going to happen.

Truly, that was another reason to play this out and give them hope. He'd overheard Commodore Murdock mention the expected Fleet reinforcements to the false officer. She was aware their time was quite limited. What the woman didn't know was that the odds of her escaping were almost zero.

When the orders had come to send their protective force on their current mission, he'd argued against them. Not that he'd truly had a chance of amending the System Lord's instructions in any way. At least Murdock had arranged for a new protective force. They'd only been uncovered for a few weeks and that was coming to an end in the next day or so.

With the battle stations covering every exit to Dresden, these people would be pinned like bugs as soon as the Fleet vessels arrived. The longer he could delay them, the better this would work out.

"Well, they certainly came for something," he assured the computer specialist. "And they certainly wouldn't have brought the forces they did if they didn't expect to capture something worth their time. What else could they be looking for?"

"Perhaps they came for the restricted implant upgrades," Irons said. "That type of enhancement could prove very useful under certain circumstances."

Castille considered that. "Perhaps. That does seem to be the only technology that would be of use to someone in the higher orders, though I'm certain the lords would take drastic action to exterminate anyone that possessed it."

He turned his eyes toward the spy among them. "Do you think they came for the supplies on hand or the manufacturing equipment, Violet? I think your point of view would be quite helpful in this situation."

The woman shook her head. "I can't say that I'm familiar with the upgrades you're speaking of. Commodore Murdock didn't cover that during the briefing."

Raul nodded. It was possible she didn't know anything about the illegal upgrades. In any case, it would be educational to brief her on them and see how she reacted.

"Of course," he said smoothly. "The enhancements we're speaking of are restricted technology from the dictatorship. The old Emperor used illegal enhancements on his personal guard to increase their strength and combat ability to a mind-boggling degree. When the lords overthrew him, they banned this technology.

"It was quite invasive and irreversible. I'm told that it increased their strength tenfold and made them killing machines. It also used drugs that turned them into mindless monsters, forced to obey every command given to them.

"That dehumanizing aspect is perhaps why the lords have forbidden this technology. Would you ever want to see someone turned into a monster like that, Violet?"

"That sounds horrible. Of course I wouldn't. No one would. That said, these attackers had many armed marines already in their group. This technology would make them much more powerful."

The spy looked at each of them in turn. "What if they don't work for the higher orders? What if they're ghosts?"

Castille opened his mouth to reject the idea, but stopped. If one of their captors suggested the idea, he should at least consider it. Could they be ghosts?

No one really knew anything about the ghosts, but he'd read the classified briefings. They were undoubtedly some remnant of the dictatorship. No one knew precisely where they based themselves, but old ships occasionally attacked shipping or isolated warships.

What could someone like the ghosts gain from this research facility? Quite a lot, he decided. It wouldn't help them build more ships, but it might make the ones they clearly possessed deadlier.

"That's an interesting idea," he said after a moment. "I think it's worth exploring in more detail, but that doesn't really answer the question of how we can turn the tables on our captors. Tell me,

Violet, if you were leading us, how would you break out of this compartment?"

The woman smiled. "If you can't find an opportunity to overwhelm the guards, you need to manufacture one. Or you have to give up."

"Giving up is not an option," Irons said. "I refuse to sit on my ass until Fleet comes in and rescues us."

The woman shrugged. "I'm not sure what to tell you. We have no weapons and no real way to get any. Without them, we're stuck here."

"All true," Castille said. "I suppose it doesn't really matter. Fleet will arrive in force shortly. When they do, these people will run away like cockroaches in the light. All we have to do is wait."

He watched the other woman closely to see how she responded to that. She didn't seem concerned, which worried him a little. What did she know that he didn't?

4

———

Talbot watched Commodore Anderson as she monitored the prisoner's compartment with more than a hint of concern. He'd finally decided that he needed to tell her what he was doing. She'd arrived a few moments ago and now stood there shaking her head.

"This is insane," she said. "If Annette slips up, they're going to be all over her."

"There *is* a hint of risk," he admitted, "but we have a team of marines ready to rush in if there's any problem whatsoever."

The commodore looked unconvinced. "Did it ever occur to you to run this past me first? Hell, even Princess Kelsey would've told you no."

Talbot doubted that, but it would be impolite to burst the woman's bubble.

"She's been in there for over an hour, ma'am. If they were going to discover that she was a fraud, they'd have done so by now. She's convinced them that she's the real deal."

"All it takes is one slip-up," Zia disagreed. "We know next to nothing about these people. Not even the most basic things."

She sighed. "Okay, let's say that you're right. What is your endgame?"

"We want to engineer a breakout, but under our control. If we can make them think they're really escaping, I believe we can get them to give us the access codes to their computers."

"No way," Zia said. "You'd have to give them virtually complete access to the orbital so they could get there. This cafeteria is nowhere near the research center."

"It doesn't need to be. Once they're outside the compartment, they'll be able to use their implants to access the orbital's systems. We're almost certain they'll try to erase the restricted computers. If they do, the system will block them but capture the passwords."

She seemed to consider the plan, but shook her head. "Those computers aren't just isolated from physical access. They'll have made certain that no one can use implants to get into them."

"Carl said there were triggers to wipe the drives that can be accessed from anywhere on the orbital. I'd wager several people inside that compartment acting in unison could set them off."

"Let's say they do. I'm sure Carl's programing is good, but what if they somehow managed to get past the blocks? We can't risk them actually damaging the research computers. We *need* that data."

"Carl said the drives are heavily encrypted, but he's made multiple copies," Talbot said. "He also took the precaution of cloning the drives and putting the original cores on *Audacious*. The automated backups too. Even if the prisoners manage to wipe the drives, we've lost nothing, and we'll have their codes."

"I don't want to be the downer here, but I think you're underestimating these people. I'm willing to bet a dinner at any place you'd care to name that this plan fails."

"That's kind of negative," Talbot grumbled. "If we can't trick them, we're no worse off than we were before."

"You're not thinking of the big picture, Talbot. What if we missed a self-destruct device? What if they have a mad plan of their own?"

She gestured to the vid feed. "Obviously, it's too late for me to stop this harebrained scheme, but I'm putting my foot down about allowing them into the orbital's systems."

He rubbed his face. "I understand your concerns, ma'am, but if we can't get the prisoners to give us access, we might never be able to build artificial intelligences for ourselves."

"Well, you certainly won't be able to if you allow them to blow up the orbital. I'm not going to pull Annette out of there, but you're going to have to come up with some way to let her know your plans have changed."

"I suppose we could start pulling prisoners out to question," he said. "If we start with Commodore Murdock and work our way down, we should be able to get her in the first three or four people without raising suspicion. It also allows us to establish our bona fides with the prisoners. If we don't open a dialogue soon, they're going to get suspicious."

Zia watched the vid feed for a while longer. "What exactly do they imagine is going to happen? We popped out of nowhere and captured their orbital, but they think they have the Dresden system locked down tight. They've got to be wondering what we're doing."

"Surely they'll have figured that out now that they felt the orbital flip twice," Talbot said. "That's not easy to miss."

"Three times," Zia said. "We flipped into the new system an hour ago."

Talbot stared at her. "I didn't feel a thing. How is that possible?"

"It's probably the mass of the station," she said. "The larger the vessel, the less effect a flip has on the crew. You can feel them a little, even on a superdreadnought or a carrier, but this orbital is larger.

"Also, since the flip drives aren't actually inside the station, a lot of the disruption is channeled into the recovery ship. They get a pretty rough ride."

Talbot sighed. "Well, I suppose I need to start pulling the prisoners out for interrogation. Sorry, ma'am."

Zia clapped him on the shoulder. "It was a bold plan, Major. Your wife will be proud. Now, if you'll excuse me, I need to get back over to *Audacious*. This system seems empty, but we all know how quickly things like that can change."

* * *

COMMANDER VERONICA GIGUERE fought the urge to stalk her cell. The close confinement and isolation were getting to her. It had been three weeks, and her patience was long gone.

She understood that she didn't have any leverage, but she was going crazy. Ever since she'd surrendered, she'd had to do what her captors said. That changed now.

She was going to see her people, and she wanted answers to the questions that had been building up in her mind. Being locked into a cell certainly gave one time to think.

She'd presented her demands to the polite jailor two hours ago, and her self-imposed deadline was just about up. If someone didn't come to talk to her in ten minutes, she'd start her very own riot.

The hatch to her cell slid aside without warning. Standing on the other side was the officer that had separated her from the rest of her crew. After, of course, he'd done something to her head. Something he'd better be prepared to explain in detail.

"Commander Giguere," he said. "I understand you wished to speak with me."

"I demand to see my crew." She poured a fair amount of aggressiveness into her tone. She didn't want to sound like she was begging. This situation required strength.

He seemed to consider her request for a moment and then nodded. "That can be arranged, but I believe it's time we had a talk first. I'm certain you have many questions. You deserve to have some answers."

She eyed him suspiciously. "That's very accommodating of you, Captain Levy, if I remember your name correctly."

"I'm acknowledging the reality of the situation," he said. "You and your crew aren't going to get back to your people anytime soon, so it's not going to hurt if you understand the scope of what's happening.

"Quite frankly, I should've explained this to you weeks ago. Let's just say that I've had a lot on my mind. Now that we have time to take a breath, I'll rectify that."

"I'm not certain why, but that fills me with dread," she said suspiciously. "Fine. If you're going to answer my questions, let's start with this. Who the hell are you people?"

He smiled slightly. "We're Fleet."

"Bull. Fleet doesn't implant their enlisted personnel. You're rebels. Or something."

"I suspect it's going to take quite a bit of time for us to determine which labels are appropriate. In the meanwhile, allow me to suggest that we move somewhere that allows us to sit down more comfortably. Perhaps you'd care for something to eat or drink."

"To my shock, the quality of the food and drink has been more than acceptable," she said. "However, going somewhere with a little bit more leg room would be very nice."

He nodded sharply. "Then we'll do so. You'll forgive me if I'm not quite ready to accept your parole, so we'll have some marine guards to make sure that you don't wander off."

Levy stepped back and gestured for her to exit her cell.

The brig had a wide central area with a circular console. The lieutenant behind it watched her without expression. Four marine guards stood at varying points inside the compartment, each in unpowered armor and equipped with a stun rifle.

There were a dozen cells, each with their hatches closed. She imagined her senior officers were behind them. She itched to demand that Levy open them up right away, but she restrained herself. If he was going to give her some answers, she wanted to hear them first.

When the hatch to the corridor slid open, she saw two additional marines waiting for them. Unlike the others, these two were unarmored. They'd also exchanged their rifles for more discreet stunners on their hips.

Captain Levy gestured for her to precede him down the hall. He stepped up next to her, and the marines fell in behind them. Close enough to intervene if need be, but too far away for her to attack with any hope of success.

"What kind of ship is this?" she asked. "This is the big one, right?"

"She's a carrier," the man said. "The fighters you engaged are based here."

Those damned little things. Commodore Crabtree—the deputy fleet commander in charge of her portion of the task force—had dismissed them as a distraction. That proved a fatal mistake for him and far too many of her comrades.

Their part of the task force had started with six light cruisers and fourteen destroyers. By the time the fighting ended, they'd lost five light cruisers and five destroyers. Most of the rest were wrecked beyond repair, she suspected.

She'd never seen anything like the little bastards. They'd bob and weave, and then blast a ship with an intensely powerful short-ranged missile. Nothing like what a real ship carried, but more than enough —in sufficient numbers—to drop the battle screens on the cruisers. Without them, the larger ships were just as vulnerable as the destroyers.

The loss of life had been hideous. She'd spent the last three weeks grieving for the friends she'd never see again. Far too many of them had died at the hands of those little fighters. A type of craft that she knew Fleet didn't have.

"It's things like that that convince me you're lying," she said. "Fleet doesn't have anything like those devils."

"There lies the heart of our story. I'd normally take the lift, but the marines insist we use the stairs. The officers' mess is three decks down. We'll order something to eat, and I'll explain everything. Well, minus a few classified details, but you'll get the big picture."

"Why are you doing this?"

He smiled. "Because I need for you to understand just what your situation is. Everything you thought you understood is completely wrong. It's going to be very difficult for you to accept that. It would be impossible if I didn't give you as much information as I could."

"I have absolutely no idea what the hell you're talking about," she assured him. "Whatever game you're playing, I'm not buying."

"Well, then, lunch should be fascinating."

5
_____

Kelsey took a deep breath when she arrived outside of her mother's cabin. She'd rather be doing just about anything else right now, but she couldn't let this situation fester too long.

She smiled at the guard and opened the hatch to find her mother sitting on the couch and reading a tablet. She stepped inside and allowed the hatch to close. "I understand you wanted to speak to me. Start talking, but be pithy. I have zero patience for you right now."

"Haven't you ever heard of signaling?" Justine asked acerbically. "What if I'd been naked?"

Her mother rose from the couch gracefully and gestured at the compartment. "And couldn't you find a larger room? I can barely breathe in here."

"When is this going to sink in, Mother? You're a prisoner. You don't have a right to privacy any longer. The guard can come into this room at any moment without any notice whatsoever."

"You're being ridiculous," her mother huffed. "How long are we going to play this game?"

"You see, that's the problem. You think this is a trick. It's not. You broke the law and put people's lives at risk. There are consequences.

"I realize you haven't been subject to limitations on your behavior for a long time, but you've crossed the line. Unless you change your attitude, you're going to find yourself in front of a military tribunal. Did your lawyer explain the penalties you'd face?"

Her mother sneered. "Yes, that little stuffed shirt 'explained' it all to me. More like he droned on and on and on. Could you send someone with a personality next time?"

Kelsey sat on the edge of the couch. "You're a real piece of work. I don't think I've ever met anyone as full of themselves as you are. You think you can do no wrong, and that someone will provide everything you desire.

"Honestly, I've met rulers from an oppressive feudal society that treat people with more respect than you do. Since it's probably escaped your mind already, let me remind you that sneaking aboard a Fleet vessel could earn you a minimum of ten years in a military prison.

"In case it wasn't obvious, this cabin is not a cell. It's actually someone's quarters. Someone that had to move out so I could put you in here. A real cell is far smaller and significantly less comfortable."

Her mother snorted daintily. "Surely you aren't delusional enough to think I actually believe you'd do any such thing. This is just you trying to make a point.

"I'm your mother. I refuse to play. I've already wasted enough of my time hiding in that other room for weeks so that I could talk to you. All because you wouldn't take the time to sit down with me on Avalon. This is your fault."

"Amazing. Can anything get through that bulletproof skull of yours? Contrary to what you seem to believe, you don't get to disrupt everyone's lives because they don't dance to your tune. Not anymore. You gave that right up when you divorced my father."

Her mother threw her hands up. "And here we go. I was absolutely justified in divorcing Karl. Even if I weren't, that's between the two of us."

"Wrong," Kelsey said hotly. "You made it my business when you cheated on him like you did. When you dared to hold a grudge against Jared Mertz because my father cheated, just like you. A mistake he confessed and paid the price for, I might add.

"How many men did you cheat with while you were married? Let's see, at least eighteen that I'm aware of. You probably managed to sneak more in some other way. Or perhaps they were already there. How many Imperial Guardsmen have you slept with? Palace staff? Visiting dignitaries? Surely, the grand total is far greater than eighteen.

"You don't even have the threadbare cover of retaliating for Father's infidelity. According to the time stamps, you started cheating long before that. No, you don't get to shift the blame to other people this time."

"My sex life is none of your business," her mother said coldly. "As for Jared Mertz, the little toad thinks that because my ex-husband slept with the help, that makes him something special. Well, it doesn't."

"I agree," Kelsey said at once. "His parentage has nothing to do with him being special. He managed that all on his own, *in spite of* his parentage. And before you attempt to tell me how wrong I am, have you bothered to read anything about what happened on the exploratory mission?"

Her mother shrugged. "I wasn't really looking for news on the little bastard. I wanted to hear about my daughter, and let me tell you, there was almost nothing to learn. So, I came to see for myself."

Kelsey felt her jaw clench. "It's as if you're going out of your way to piss me off. I'm not twelve anymore, Mother. You don't get to declare whom I can be friends with. In fact, you don't get to dictate any part of my life anymore.

"Let me fill you in about a few facts. Jared Mertz isn't the only bastard in this family. So am I, but you already knew that. The more I think about it, the angrier I get. You're unbelievable. Are you even human? I ask because I've met an alien that has more human decency than you."

Her mother's eyes flashed. "How *dare* you speak to me that way? I should slap your face. I don't care how you feel. You don't get to disrespect me that way, little girl."

Kelsey grunted. "I've only begun understanding that you don't care how *anyone* feels. You also have peculiar expectations about the way the world works. You think you get to be a screaming jerk to whomever you like, but everyone else is supposed to be nice to you.

"Perhaps that's the way it used to be, but you have to *earn* my respect now. That isn't going to happen as long as you insist on being a selfish child throwing temper tantrums. I'm not a little girl that you can intimidate anymore, Mother. I've been through things in the last eighteen months that would make you run howling in terror. I mean that literally, by the way.

"I've survived things that you cannot possibly imagine. The kind of things that nightmares are made of. In fact, I still have far too many nights where I wake up screaming. That's my burden to bear, the price I pay for my own stupidity. My own arrogance."

Kelsey slowly stood. "When you're ready to speak civilly, tell the guard. If all you want to do is bitch, don't bother. If I come down here again and run head-on into your arrogance, I won't be so quick to come back again."

She walked out of the compartment without glancing back. The hatch closed in her mother's face.

"I want you to check on the prisoner at random intervals over the next shift," she told the guard. "Twice, I think. If she complains—which she will—ignore her. Stun her if she gets physical."

The man looked a shade uncertain.

"I'm trying to get her to understand the gravity of her situation," she added. "If I don't teach her some limits, she's going to be a jerk the entire time we're out here. Don't go overboard, but put her firmly in her place."

The marine nodded. "Aye, ma'am. She uses the door com to ask for you all the time. I've been ignoring that as you ordered. Should I start responding?"

"Yes. If she behaves civilly, tell her you'll pass along the message. If she's a jackass, tell her she can rot. If she's a monumental pain in the ass, I'll send her over to *Audacious* to spend some quality time in a *real* cell."

The man sighed. "This is harder than I'd imagined, ma'am. She was the empress when I grew up. The urge to obey is strong."

"Yes, and she uses that sentiment ruthlessly. Be strong. You're actually doing her a service. One she's likely to curse you for, but a real one nonetheless."

Kelsey started to walk away, but stopped and turned. "As distasteful as this is for me to say, she's probably going to try to seduce you. I don't want to come back later and find you tied up in her closet."

The man looked offended. "First, Colonel, I'd never do anything like that with a prisoner. Second, I'm a little harder to overpower than you seem to think."

"Probably," she agreed, "but don't play her game. I don't want to have to have that particular debriefing. There are some things a daughter doesn't need to hear about."

He chuckled a little. "I suppose not, Colonel. No worries. I'll keep everything safe and secure here, including my trousers."

"Good man. Carry on."

Carl was waiting for her on the bridge when she made it back. He sat beside Angela. The two of them had been speaking softly. He sat up straighter and waited for her to take a seat before speaking.

"I have bad news," he said. "There isn't another flip point in the system. A regular one anyway. We won't have finished searching for weak flip points for a few more days."

"That can't be possible," she said. "There has to be another flip point."

He shrugged. "Not that the probes have discovered. As far as I can tell, the only way in or out of this system is through the weak flip point we used."

She stared at the master plot. The various probes were filling in details about the system, but they still knew so very little about it. At least according to the icons she could see.

"I have a tremendous amount of respect for you, Carl, but how can you possibly know that? We've been here less than a day."

"I understand that. To be clear, this is only a preliminary status report. We might find a flip point buried in the data. I just wanted to alert you to the probability that there isn't one so you can plan.

"There are plenty of systems that have only one flip point. We call them cul-de-sacs. If that's possible with regular flip points, why would it be less likely with a weak flip point? Hell, there are undoubtedly many star systems that have no flip points of any kind."

She sighed. "It's more like I don't *want* to believe it. The weak flip point is too small to allow us back out. If there isn't something in this system, we're screwed.

"What about the theory Doctor Leonard had about using weak flip points for multiple destinations? Have you gotten anywhere with that?"

Carl shook his head. "Flip physics was never my specialty," he admitted. "I've read the papers, but I can't say I really understand the theoretical aspects. Not at the level I need to make that kind of breakthrough happen."

She scowled at the young man. "That's unacceptable. It would be wonderful to have Doctor Leonard here to figure out the answer for us, but he's not. You're going to have to buckle down and figure this out. If it's possible to utilize a weak flip point to go elsewhere—and with bigger ships—we need to know about it.

"I realize you've been trying to break into the research computers, but I want you to focus every bit of your attention on this problem. Take the theory apart and come up with something we can use. We're not going anywhere until you do."

He sighed. "I'll get right to work on it."

Kelsey watched him depart and worried. That was a lot of weight to carry on those young shoulders, but she'd seen him come through before. He was smarter than he thought. He'd find a solution to their problems.

Meanwhile, she needed to focus on their new home. While the probes had been unsuccessful at finding any other flip points, they'd gotten a good read on the normal matter in the system.

It was a fairly average place. Ten major bodies orbiting a normal star. Many of the outer ones were gaseous in nature, but the inner ones were solid. One of them was inside the goldilocks zone and might be habitable. They'd have to go a lot closer to be sure.

Nothing she'd seen had indicated there was any hostile presence inside the system. As far as she was concerned, the time for hiding was over. They needed to see what they were dealing with.

"Signal the other ships," she told Angela. "Set course for the planet inside the habitable zone. Let's go see if anyone is home."

6

Annette was more than a bit relieved when Talbot finally pulled her out of the compartment. The security man was creeping her out.

The marine officer eyed her. "You okay?"

"I'm am now. I was really worried they were going to jump me."

"You seemed like you were doing fine," Talbot said. "You must be hell at the poker table."

She grinned. "I can hold my own. Still, there's a guy in there that I wouldn't want to play against. Raul Castille, their security man. He made me right away."

The marine's eyes widened. "He *made* you? How could he have made you? You sat there and talked with them for hours."

"He was playing with me. He flat out said that he'd seen Violet Renner's personnel file. He knows what she looks like. He made several coy statements that the others never picked up on, but I knew he was poking at me."

"That is kind of creepy," Talbot said. "Well, it's pretty clear my plan isn't going to work. They have to know what we're up to.

"The commodore was down checking on you, too. She was pissed that I hadn't run this by her, and she thinks it's too dangerous. So, we're pulling the plug."

Annette nodded. "I was pretty much afraid of that. I saw that you pulled Commodore Murdock out for questioning. Has she said anything useful?"

The marine grimaced. "She's had plenty to say, none of it useful. I swear to God, I thought I'd never meet anybody more officious and condescending than Wallace Breckenridge. Boy, was I wrong.

"How the hell can that woman run a place like the research center? She'd be up in everyone's business. No one would be able to get anything done."

Annette laughed. "I suspect that most of the other prisoners would quietly agree with you. She's a real piece of work. If we're not going to get into the computers by trickery, how are we going to do it?"

Talbot shrugged. "Carl needs to find a tech solution. Or, he's just going to have to reverse engineer the manufacturing equipment based on the hardware we have. It might take longer, but he'll find a way."

"Speaking of finding a way, are we any closer to finding our way out of this system?" she asked.

"Last I heard they haven't found any other flip points. While they figure out that problem, we'll have to deal with the prisoners."

"Are we authorized to do that? I'm not exactly military intelligence."

"We're what we have," he said. "There are still a lot of questions we need answered. For example, why was the research facility located at Dresden, of all places? That wasn't precisely an easy-to-access location for the Rebel Empire. Why not somewhere more centrally located?

"And why did they send a fleet to take out the Erorsi AI now? Why not five hundred years ago? What was the trigger? Was it something we did?"

"Probably," she said. "I'd also like to know why they aren't using the Raider implants for themselves. Or are they? That kind of information is critical to our ultimate survival. Also, is this the only location that makes Raider implants? If it is, we might have caught a break."

"Where do you want to start?" Talbot asked. "The security guy?"

Annette smiled. "Surprisingly, yes. I think he might let some information slip. He seems to think he's smarter than everyone else. Maybe he is. If so, he won't be able to resist playing with us."

"How do you want to handle this?"

"I'm going to open up to him. Carl overwrote the viral code in the senior prisoner's implants while they were out, so there's no danger of a programmed reaction. If I give him some information, he may give me some back. If I answer some questions, so might he.

"Another thing I'd like to find out about is those ghosts they've mentioned. Who are they? What does the Rebel Empire know about them? What do they suspect? There's so much that we don't know."

"And even more that we don't know we're ignorant of," Talbot agreed. "We're using the compartment next to this one for questioning the individual officers. Commodore Murdock is in there now. Once my guy finishes with her, you can take his place, and I'll bring Castille to you."

* * *

Raul nodded toward Commodore Murdock as the guards took him out of the cafeteria and brought her in. She looked indignant. As though their captors had offended her by asking questions. The woman never ceased to amaze him.

Once into the corridor, the guards walked him to the compartment next door. Inside he found the fake Violet Renner waiting for him. Only now she wore captain's tabs.

"Goodness," he said with mock surprise. "Promotions happen without any warning around here."

The woman smiled thinly. "Have a seat, Commander. Since you took great joy in making sure that I knew you'd seen through my impersonation, I'm sure it won't shock you that I'm done playing that game. Instead, I'm going to ask you some direct questions. Ones that I'm willing to pay for."

He pulled out the chair and draped himself across it. The two marines stood in the back corners of the compartment. They were well positioned to restrain him, if he decided to become aggressive. He wouldn't bother.

"I must say I like this game better. I'm not a conventional man, Captain… I'm afraid we haven't been formally introduced. Whom am I addressing?"

"My name is Annette Vitter."

"So, you are a Fleet officer. I wasn't sure."

Her smile widened a little bit. "Oh, I'm a Fleet officer all right. Just not in the way you mean. I'm not a renegade officer. None of us are."

"Ah. I see. You're going to tell me that you're operating under orders."

"Absolutely."

"I find that difficult to believe. Let me tell you what I think. I believe you *are* Fleet, but a renegade. You're working for someone in the higher orders. Probably the coordinator of one of the major worlds.

"Somehow, you found out about the work we're doing here, and that coordinator wants it for him or herself. Your mission is to make that happen."

He grinned. "Unfortunately, that's very unlikely to happen. I'm sorry to have to inform you, but you're going to be trapped in this system."

If the news bothered her, she hid it very well. In fact, she looked completely unperturbed.

"I have some bad news for you. The fleet you sent to take out the renegade ship's computer and attack the holdout system it was keeping bottled up won't be coming back. As for the replacement fleet you're expecting, it's already arrived."

He laughed. "You'd like me to believe that you're part of the replacement fleet? Somehow, I doubt that very much. I'm not completely certain how you know where we dispatched the original fleet to, though. Perhaps you'd care to explain that in more detail?"

"As a gesture of goodwill, certainly. We were lying in wait for your ships. They won't be coming back at all, I'm afraid. You see, while I'm completely truthful in saying that I'm Fleet, it's not the same Fleet you serve. It's the one that came before."

Now he guffawed. "Please, tell me another one. I don't know what your game is, Annette, but this is *very* entertaining. You don't mind if I call you Annette, do you?"

"Feel free," she said with a magnanimous gesture. "You want to be entertained? Let's see if I can manage that. One of the things you manufacture here is for use by the computer at Erorsi. You did know that that's the name of the system where the computer is located, right?

"Back before the AIs overthrew the Old Empire, Erorsi was home to billions of people. Now it's a wasteland filled with savage human beings the computer enhanced against their wills using equipment produced here. Specifically, Marine Raider implants."

Raul sat up, all his amusement gone. "Where did you hear that name?"

Annette smiled. "From a different ship's computer. One on a Marine Raider ship. It confirmed many things we suspected about those enhancements."

He shook his head. "I'm sure you'd like me to believe that. You're fishing for information. It's not playing by the rules you set up, Annette."

"Ah, but I *am* playing by the rules," she said with a cool grin. "What's more, I'm willing to prove it. This compartment is shielded, so you can utilize your implants without me having to worry about you doing something naughty. Allow me to share with you what I know about Marine Raider implants."

When his implants received a connection request, he cautiously accepted it. As a security officer, he had special filters to be sure nothing malicious made it into his system, but these were interesting times.

The communication had a file attached to it. He opened it and was astonished to see a very detailed scan analysis of an individual with the implants they manufactured here on the orbital. It only took a moment to grasp that they were authentic.

"Where did you get this?" he demanded flatly.

The woman leaned forward and whispered conspiratorially. "I'll tell you that in exchange for a few answers of my own. Take a moment to examine what I sent to you. Are you going to try to tell me they aren't what we're speaking of?"

"No. It's obvious that you've somehow obtained extremely classified data. I'm not sure how you made them up to look as though they'd been implanted inside a real person, but that's very clever.

"Yes, these implants are manufactured here, and the old dictatorship called them Marine Raider implants. They're forbidden technology. Merely possessing knowledge about them is a death sentence. Which saddens me, since I kind of like you."

"That makes me feel all warm and fuzzy inside," she said. "I'm not worried about any death sentences. You see, I wasn't joking when I said I come from a different Fleet."

She leaned even farther forward. "Your precious lords missed a planet. That's all it took. Now we're back, looking to restore the Empire."

He eyed her suspiciously. This had to be a joke. One in admittedly poor taste.

"So, you're trying to tell me that you're a ghost? You really need to work on being more convincing."

"I can see that I'll have to do something drastic to convince you that I'm telling the truth. Very well."

She reached into a bag sitting beside the table and pulled out a headband with a chinstrap. She tossed it onto the table in front of him. "Put this on. Once you've secured it, it takes a special key to take it back off."

He examined it without touching it. "What is it?"

"An implant jammer. While you're wearing it, you'll be unable to interact with anything through your implants. As I said, I don't want you doing anything naughty. You have the choice of putting it on yourself or my associates will assist you."

Well, if those were his options, he'd do it himself. He picked the headset up and put it on. The chinstrap tightened comfortably, but wouldn't back off. By design, he supposed.

Annette rose from her seat, came around the table, and snugged the strap even further. "There we go. I don't want you slipping out of this unexpectedly. You seem very resourceful to me."

He gave her a toothy grin. "One does try. So, where are you taking me?"

"On a sightseeing tour. Take my word, the view will be *very* educational."

The two marines gripped his arms as she exited the compartment. She might be willing to pretend to trust him a little, but they weren't taking any chances. He'd have no opportunity to tear loose from their grasp. Certainly not after he noted the other marines that trailed them at a distance in the corridor.

She led him down to the docking level where an unfamiliar small craft awaited them. It had aggressive lines and only two places to sit. One of them was situated far forward on the craft and the other was immediately behind it. Both had raised canopies.

He stopped and examined the craft closely. He'd never seen anything like it.

"What is this?"

"This is a Mark Five Raptor," she said. "A space superiority fighter. You'll be in front. Normally, we'd both be in flight suits, but I'm not going to do anything fancy. Just a little stroll in the park. Get in."

He had to admit, this was not where he'd expected things to go. He utilized the handholds built into the side of the little craft and climbed up to the acceleration couch. He didn't have very much experience with small craft.

In fact, he'd never been inside the cockpit of one before. He'd expected more controls, though. As in more than blank, featureless panels.

The canopy above his head lowered and locked into place. He heard the woman climb into the area behind him, and her canopy lowered as well.

The small craft came to life and lifted off the deck. It turned and flew through the protective field into space at a gentle pace.

As soon as they cleared the bay, he noticed there was something attached to the orbital's hull. Some type of metal band. A large, thick one.

"What is that?"

"You ask a lot of questions without giving me any interesting answers of your own, but I'll let you put them on account. Keep watching. It'll become obvious in a moment."

As the fighter craft drew away from the orbital, he started getting a better look at the metal band. It was attached to a ship that nestled against the orbital. One that looked vaguely familiar.

"Is that…"

"The recovery ship you've been using to transport ore? It is, indeed. It took a little bit of modification, but it managed to move your orbital just fine too."

A chill ran through his body. He turned and scanned the heavens.

"Are you looking for a planet?" she asked helpfully. "I'm afraid we've left Dresden far behind."

The small craft began rotating slowly, giving him a look at everything around them. There was no planet. They had taken the orbital out of Dresden orbit.

"I'll grant you that's clever," he said, "but it's not going to make any difference when Fleet arrives. They'll keep looking until they find us."

"I'm certain you're right. Unfortunately, they'll still be looking in the Dresden system for a while. We're no longer there."

The chill became ice that settled at the base of his spine. "What do you mean?"

"I think you can piece it together. That ship is more than capable of flipping with a huge cargo. It was designed to move superdreadnoughts and larger freighters from system to system in the Old Empire.

"It took a little bit of work to expand the arms to encompass the orbital, but we managed. We've departed and taken the entire orbital with us."

"That is quite a claim. One that I'm not willing to believe. Even though there weren't many ships in this system, each of the flip points is guarded. You didn't just sneak out with our orbital in tow."

Annette laughed. "We absolutely did. Though, I admit it took some force to get past the battle station and three destroyers at our target flip point."

The little craft turned again. What it exposed took his breath away. It was a Fleet warship unlike any he'd ever seen. Sitting near a large freighter of a class that seemed familiar, it looked much bigger than the rare heavy cruiser that had passed through Dresden. Certainly larger than the light cruisers that normally led their guard forces.

"What you're seeing is our flagship," she said before he asked. "That is the Fleet Carrier *Audacious*. She's a modified superdreadnought hull. I realize that the AIs aren't forthcoming about larger vessels, so you might not have seen one before."

He eyed the ship worriedly as it grew larger in front of them. "Superdreadnought? What is a superdreadnought?"

"Let's just say that it's the next size up from the battlecruiser," she said with some amusement. "And if you haven't heard of those, they're significantly larger than heavy cruisers. *Audacious* dates from before the Fall. We've put her back into service, and that's where this fighter came from.

"Full disclosure, my actual duties are to command the fighter wings aboard that ship. You see, Raul, I'm not lying to you. We've come to retake what's ours. If you want to know more about that ship and us, you're going to have to answer a few questions on my terms."

As the massive vessel grew larger before them, he decided that he had no choice but to believe she was telling him some version of the truth. If so, this wasn't a game anymore. Or perhaps it was. Just a significantly more dangerous one.

He allowed himself a small smile. Well, he'd always told himself that he could play at any level. Now was the time to prove it.

7

"The probe is starting to pick up readings from the planet," Angela said.

Kelsey turned her attention away from the system schematic she'd been studying. According to the latest update, they still hadn't found any flip points in the system. That was worrying.

She could've checked the scanner readings for herself, but what was the point of having a crew if you did everything? She was forcing herself to delegate.

"What have we got?" she asked.

Her XO threw a scanner image up on the main screen. "I think there might be a ship in orbit."

That made Kelsey sit up and take notice. She tapped into the feed the probe was sending back. The new object might be a ship, but if so, it wasn't under power. There were no detectable fusion plants.

It could just be a captured asteroid, but she didn't think so. Not with their luck.

"I assume there's no indication of scanners from the bogie?" Kelsey asked.

"No. If it's looking, it's only using passive scanners."

Kelsey knew the odds of any vessel detecting one of their probes with passive scanners was insignificant, but that didn't mean impossible. She'd best be cautious.

"Launch two more probes and bracket the planet. I want to be sure there aren't any other surprises in orbit."

The probes approached the planet slowly and carefully. Once the first had made it into close range, it was apparent the object *was* a ship in a stable geosynchronous orbit. Still no fusion plants. The ship was probably a derelict.

One that certainly seemed to have discovered the weak flip points long ago, if there truly were no other exits from this system.

"Bring us into orbit, Jack. Keep us on the other side of the planet from the derelict. Can you identify what kind of ship that is, Angela?"

"It's in the Imperial database," she said. "It's a Capella-class cruise liner. Top of the line back in the Old Empire. She could move ten thousand passengers in style. Maybe twice that if you packed them in. Even more if you strained life support to the breaking point."

That wasn't what she'd expected to find out here. The stories of the ghosts had led her to expect an Old Empire Fleet ship.

A few minutes later, they had a visual. It looked undamaged and unpowered. The probe's passive scanners indicated that it was cold and lifeless. Its passengers and crew had either died or departed.

"What can you tell me about the planet?" Kelsey asked.

"It looks as though it might be habitable, if you stretch the definition a bit. Somewhat cold for my taste, but beggars can't be choosers, I suppose. At the moment, most of the planet is experiencing heavy winter.

"Only the equator is relatively warm. We don't have enough information on the planet's orbit to determine if it goes closer during part of the year or perhaps even farther away, but there's almost no axial tilt. If the orbit is relatively circular, this place is an icebox"

Kelsey watched the images of the planet slowly rotating beneath them. There was some green—mostly around the equator. She didn't know what temperature was more prevalent closer to the poles, but it certainly looked cold.

"Any radio transmissions or power signatures?"

"No, ma'am. Everything quiet on that front."

"Okay," Kelsey said. "Task two probes with mapping the planet. If there's something man-made down there, I want to know about it. Keep the third probe watching that ship.

"Then I want you to take a team over to examine the ship. I want to know how it got here and what happened to the passengers and crew."

Angela raised an eyebrow. "I'm shocked that you aren't insisting on leading the expedition yourself."

"Oh, I want to, but I just can't justify it. Being an adult sucks. As boring as it sounds, I need to keep an eye on the big picture."

Somehow, someone on that cruise liner had figured out how to use the weak flip points. If they'd had good luck, their descendants were living on the planet below. If not, then they'd all died in orbit.

"How long until we know if the planet is habitable?"

"I can give you a little bit more information now. The atmosphere seems breathable. It looks as though the equatorial temperature is above the freezing point of water. I suspect most places on the equator are pretty comfortable right now."

"What about the poles?"

"Damned cold. We're talking Arctic freeze. There's evidence of glaciers coming pretty far down into the two hemispheres. If I had to make a wager, I think the money is on this being a chilly place to live."

Kelsey nodded slowly at the picture. "You don't think it gets much warmer than this?"

"Further observation might change that, but I'm not inclined to think so."

"How much landmass on the equator are we talking about?"

Angela shrugged. "There are a number of scattered islands—some of them pretty big—and one sizable continent. Plenty of room for survivors."

"Focus your attention there, then. I want to know if we have any people living down there."

"The continent is heavily forested. We may not be able to easily spot them."

"Do the best you can."

Kelsey composed a message to Zia Anderson and attached the

scanner readings they had of the cruise liner. By the time they had more information, the other ships would be to the planet. One way or the other, she hoped the ship had an interesting story to tell.

* * *

VERONICA GIGUERE TRIED to listen to Levy without calling him a liar to his face, but it was hard. He kept insisting on telling her nonsense stories about survivors of the old dictatorship and how the artificial intelligences behind overthrowing the dictator were evil.

Please. She was a Fleet officer. She knew who the lords were and how they maintained and nurtured the Empire. That didn't mean they kept humanity in a state of slavery and ignorance. That was simply bull. They kept society orderly and efficient.

Were there problems? Of course. Where human beings lived together, there were always problems. For the most part, the lords kept humanity from eating its own entrails. One only had to look at the dregs of society to see that.

"How can you say any of that with a straight face?" she asked when he'd finished. "I'd call it propaganda, but even someone from the lower orders would recognize that stuff couldn't possibly be true. Those are the paranoid ravings of a lunatic.

"Why don't you tell me the truth? Someone subverted Fleet. Which world is funding your little outing? More importantly, what do you actually hope to accomplish by ambushing your fellow officers like this? You know I'll never rest until I take you down."

The man shook his head. "To be honest, you're something of a long-term project, Commander Giguere. You've lived in your society your entire life, so I don't expect change to come easily. In fact, I suspect that convincing you I'm telling the truth is going to be a long and difficult process."

He sipped his coffee. "Why do you find it so difficult to believe me? I can present any number of my fellow officers that will tell you exactly the same thing. I can even find crewmen that will tell you so. Thousands of people. Surely we're not all deluded."

She looked around the officers' mess and once again examined the men and women dining around them. They looked so normal, but she knew that was a lie. They couldn't be. Every single one was a traitor.

How had Levy or his masters convinced so many people to betray their oaths? Was Fleet really that rotten?

Veronica knew Fleet wasn't perfect. There was entirely too much politicking and currying of favor for her taste. Add to that the fact that larger commands were rare, and you had an environment that was almost toxically cutthroat. About the only thing off-limits was actually planting a knife in someone else's back.

Yet that was life. Nothing worthwhile came without fighting for it.

The man shrugged when she said nothing. "As I said, I don't expect this process to go quickly or even to be successful in every case. All I can do is try. My intention is to expose you to the truth and let you draw your own conclusions."

She gave him a cool smile. "That seems a little difficult considering I'm locked away in a cell all by myself."

"That changes today. I'm relocating you and your senior officers to new quarters. They may not be much more spacious than the brig, but they'll allow you to interact with each other in a more comfortable environment. I'm also giving you access to the ship's computer. The library is quite extensive."

She sighed. "So you're going to give me unfettered access to your propaganda? Why bother? We can't trust anything you people say or the documents you provide."

"Once you see the sheer volume of information, I think you might change your mind. If nothing else, perhaps it will be entertaining for you to dissect the 'propaganda' I'm providing for you.

"With the exception of military secrets, I'm also going to make certain you have an opportunity to question either myself or someone else of your choosing about what you find. You'll have complete access to your crew to be certain that we're seeing to their needs, too. Surely that's better than sitting alone in your cell twiddling your thumbs."

She couldn't very well argue with that. Three weeks being by herself had almost driven her mad. Of course, she was also familiar with Stockholm Syndrome. The longer he kept telling them his story, the more likely that some of them begin believing parts of it.

Not that she was certain how anybody could give any credence to the story he was putting out.

"Since you're going to be answering my questions, I have one for you," she said. "I saw several of your people with implants pretending to be marines that first day. Why would you have your officers pretend to be crewmen?"

"We're not pretending. Every single human being on our ships has implants. Crewmen, officers, and civilians. Only one person that I'm aware of doesn't have them, and she's a special case. Does that sound like your Fleet to you?"

It sounded like insanity. Only idiots trusted the lower orders with a loaded weapon, and she included implant access in that list.

"I can question anyone I like?" she asked.

"Pick anyone in this compartment or we can walk anywhere you'd like on board this ship. You can stop anyone you like and asked them whatever strikes your fancy. If it's classified, I'll make the decision on whether or not they can answer, but I won't put words in their mouths.

"In fact, I suggest you ask unusual questions. What they do for living. Why they're fighting against the Rebel Empire. That's what we call you, by the way. It's because we consider ourselves to be the true Terran Empire."

Well, if he was going to be so forthcoming, it shouldn't be very hard to trip someone up. All she needed to do was get away from the people he had groomed to give his false answers. Someone from the lower orders—as the crewmen would be—certainly weren't sophisticated enough to deceive her.

"Very well. Let's play your game."

8

Talbot stuck his head into Carl's lab and knocked on the frame of the hatch. "How's it going?"

The young scientist looked a bit frazzled when he turned from his screen. He held up his fist. "I swear to God, the next person to ask me that is going to catch this on the nose."

Talbot laughed. "So that's the way it is. They told you we found a ship, right?"

Carl's expression brightened. "They did? That's excellent news, though I'm certain Doctor Leonard is going to be very disappointed to learn that someone else discovered weak flip points."

"It doesn't count if you don't make it back," Talbot said. "Your girlfriend is searching the ship right now, but it certainly doesn't look as though anyone is living there. Either they're living on the planet, they died off, or they went back where they came."

"No. I'm just about certain these weak flip points actually do lead to other locations, but not without technology the Old Empire didn't have. Do you understand anything about how flip drives work?"

The marine nodded. "A little. The engines express energy along a certain frequency that triggers a weakness in the space-time continuum. The ship moves from one end of a wormhole to the other."

"That's right, as far as it goes. What Doctor Leonard suspects—and what I've come to believe is probably true—is that we can focus the energy even more precisely along certain wavelengths. That may open up other potential destinations. In effect, a weak flip point is actually one with multiple wormholes terminating in the same volume of space."

He cleared away a spot on the table. "Think of it this way. This cup is a weak flip point. If we come along and express energy in a broad spectrum as we currently do, we can trigger it to take us to my stylus. If we do the same at my stylus, it will take us back to my cup.

"However, there might be other wormholes present, and the distorted gravitic reading comes from some kind of harmonic dissonance as they try to express themselves. If we can narrow the energy frequency to most closely link to one of the secondary wormholes, perhaps it will open a wormhole leading to this data chip."

Talbot sighed. "I hear you talking, but it doesn't make sense to me. How is that even possible?"

Carl's face told him that he wouldn't understand the answer, but the young scientist gamely tried to tell him anyway.

"I could give you lots justifications, but it boils down to an educated guess based on the evidence. The only way to be sure is to make it work. Tell me about this ship."

"At this point, we only know that it's some kind of passenger liner. It's cold and dark, so nobody's been on it for a while. Maybe we'll be able to salvage its computer and figure out how they got here, though."

"That would be good. It would be even better to know how they discovered the weak flip point in the first place. I suppose we need a better name than weak flip points. If the theory is correct, that's an inaccurate term. Maybe I should call them multiflip points."

The marine smiled. "It doesn't really matter what you call it, so long as it works. Another angle they're looking at is the planet. One of the continents and several islands sit on the equator. From what they tell me, it's a cold place. Even living on the equator would be hard going if it gets colder."

"If the ship really did come through during the Fall, none of the people down there is going to be able to tell us anything first hand. Civilians with nanites have long lifespans, but that potential gets much shorter under primitive conditions. You'll lose people to accidents and violence. It's probably a safe bet that none of the original survivors lasted more than a hundred years."

Talbot shrugged. "People tell stories. We'll find out something about how they got here, though it might be garbled. If, of course, there's anyone here in the first place."

"How did playing a spy work out for Captain Vitter?" Carl asked.

He grimaced. "Not so well. Apparently, somebody figured out who she was right away. The guy spent two hours tormenting her with innuendo. If we're going to get the specifications and manufacturing techniques for the artificial intelligence systems and Raider implants, you'll have to come up with another plan."

The younger man sighed. "I was afraid of that. Given enough time, we'll eventually work out the specifics of creating each individual part. Just having the equipment itself will make that a lot easier."

Talbot clapped his friend on the shoulder. "You'll figure it out. I'll leave you to your work and go find some other trouble to get into."

He'd barely made it into the corridor before he received a message from Commodore Anderson.

"Yes, ma'am?"

She smiled at him through the implant feed. "We have good news, for once. The probes have picked up signs of primitive settlements on the equatorial continent. Somebody's down there. I want you to gather up a scouting team and check it out."

He grinned. "I'll get rolling."

* * *

Raul felt as though he were stumbling along when the marines put him back into the mess compartment. The events of the last few hours had shaken him to the core.

"Commander Castille," Commodore Murdock said sternly. "Where have you been?"

He shook his head in a futile attempt to clear it. "I've been getting an education on precisely how screwed we are, Commodore."

The woman frowned. "Get your ass over here and explain that to me."

The confused jumble of feelings in his gut narrowed to irritation. Murdock was the worst choice for a senior officer in a situation like this. Not only was she completely clueless, she was going to make any action the rest of them took that much harder.

His annoyance grew when he saw that she still didn't have another chair at her table. That was just the kind of petty nonsense the woman had a reputation for.

Well, perhaps he should do something about that.

He came to attention. "My apologies, Commodore. The information I just obtained is shocking. Our situation is graver than we'd believed. I need to brief all the senior officers so that we can coordinate an organized response to this new threat."

Her frown deepened. "I'll make the decision about who needs to know what, as well as what our response will be, *Commander*." She emphasized his title, no doubt to remind him that she was a flag officer and he was not.

"Are you familiar with the security protocols for the research station?" he asked politely.

"It's a little early to start a court of inquiry into how you should've stopped this attack before it ever started, Commander. Let's focus on turning the tables first."

He smiled blandly. "While I no doubt hold most of the blame in this, you're right this isn't the time. My point is that the security of the Empire is at stake. I'm declaring a state of emergency and assuming command of this facility and its personnel so I can effectively deal with it."

Commodore Murdock surged to her feet. "I will not tolerate you attempting to usurp my command, Castille. You're under arrest." She raised her voice. "Commander Irons, come here."

The other officer hurried over from his table. "Yes, Commodore?"

She pointed at Raul. "Commander Castille is under arrest. See that he is secured in whatever manner you see fit."

Raul smiled at Irons. "That won't be necessary, Commander. Under the research facility's emergency security protocols, I've just assumed command of this facility and all its personnel. I assume you're familiar with them?"

The other officer nodded. "Of course. What are your orders, sir?"

"What the hell are you doing?" Murdock demanded. "You will do as I instructed, or you'll find yourself under arrest as well, Commander Irons."

The man looked contrite. "I'm sorry, Commodore. The security protocols give Commander Castille the authority to assume command."

He turned to Raul. "We don't have access to more private accommodations for a prisoner, sir. Particularly one of flag rank. What you have in mind?"

"This is mutiny," Murdock snarled. "I'll have you both shot for this."

"I suppose we'll need to keep her at this table for now," Raul said, ignoring her. "It's not as though she's been mingling with anyone else up to this point. Find a pair of officers that will obey your instructions and make sure that she stays here and behaves herself."

"That shouldn't be too difficult," the other officer said with a glance at the fuming Commodore.

A few minutes later, two scowling officers flanked the Commodore. Raul supposed they would keep her in line, but if they didn't, he could deal with her more harshly.

He joined Commander Irons and Jeanette Martin at their table. He then filled them in on the things he'd seen when Annette Vitter took him on her little tour of the carrier *Audacious*. He wrapped up with the revelation that they weren't in the Dresden system any longer.

Jeanette held up a hand. "Hold on. You're telling me that they *stole* the orbital? As in, they've absconded with us?"

Her choice of words made him smile. "I'm afraid that's exactly what I'm saying. As the imposter was bringing me back, we were just entering orbit around a planet.

"I saw this world with my own eyes. It's in the habitable zone, but it wasn't Dresden. I haven't got the faintest idea where we are, but our assumption that Fleet was coming to rescue us is incorrect."

Irons rubbed his forehead. "That changes everything. This is a disaster, and this is all my fault."

"That's an epic declaration, Commander. Considering the number of ships and those fighters they brought with them, I'm somewhat at a loss as to how you bear any responsibility. Perhaps you'd care to explain it to me."

The other officer slumped dejectedly. "I brought her into the restricted area. I thought she was Renner, and I bypassed every bit of security we had in place to keep hostile personnel out."

Raul laughed. Not a little chuckle, but a fuller laugh. "Frankly, Edward, I don't think it made the slightest bit of difference whether you brought her to that meeting or not. They were still on the station, and they had overwhelming force.

"No. If you'd realized you were dealing with an imposter—which has to be the ballsiest move I've ever seen—then the most you'd have been able to do was force them to advance their timetable. That would've changed nothing."

He considered telling them the woman's ludicrous claims about being minions of the despot that escaped the revolution, but decided that would only muddy the waters. The ploy had to be a bizarre disinformation campaign anyway.

After a moment, he sighed and leaned back in his chair. "What's obvious to me is that this operation was meticulously planned and took advantage of weaknesses in our security that we didn't even know were there.

"Frankly, I'm convinced this had to be some kind of inside job. Someone smoothed the way for these intruders. There's just no other way to explain how they got so many people on board the orbital without being discovered."

"What do we do now?" Jeanette asked. "We can't get to the computers to purge them, but they're not going to break into them by brute force, either. They're going to have to dissect every bit of equipment in the research area to gain any kind of advantage.

"Do we have any idea which world is financing this operation? Or is it some type of mutiny inside Fleet itself?"

Raul shrugged. "I'm not sure. We need to stymie them in a way that won't provoke them into torturing us. They have us completely at their mercy."

Whatever the enemy's plans were, he felt certain they'd be coming along to execute them before very much longer. Once they had more information, he and his compatriots could formulate a plan to resist them.

While Raul would never have willingly chosen for these events to occur, he felt invigorated. This was going to be the most fun he'd had in years.

9

K elsey exited the pinnace into the cruise liner's landing bay. The magnetic boots of her armor clicked on the deck as she walked. Angela had portable lights scattered about, so the compartment was not in total gloom.

She could've used the miniature grav drive her armor boasted, but for such a short distance, it didn't seem worthwhile.

It had taken her executive officer less than an hour to determine that the derelict was completely lifeless and harmless. In fact, it probably hadn't been fit for occupation in centuries.

The evidence was all around her as she made her way toward engineering. The deck plans in her implants guided her past stripped compartments. Even the hatches and grav plates were gone.

The ship would never be useful as an interstellar vessel ever again. It probably wouldn't ever support life on its own. They'd even taken a number of hull plates, exposing the interior to open space.

She found Angela and several engineers standing in the gloomy cavern that had been engineering. At least it was gloomy until the rear end lit up with bluish light. The aft quadrant was gone, and Kelsey could see the planet they were orbiting.

Someone had ripped all of the consoles out. The only notable object in the room was the flip drive. For some reason, they'd left it behind.

"What have we got?" Kelsey asked as she stepped up beside her executive officer.

The marine's expression was wry inside her helmet. "We've got a whole lot of nothing. In fact, we have so much nothing that it means something. Someone stripped this derelict of anything useful, and when I say anything, I really mean *everything*."

Kelsey gestured toward the flip drive. "That doesn't look like nothing."

"I'll let Jake explain that."

The engineering technician took that as his cue. "That might look like a flip drive, Colonel, but it isn't really. At least, not anymore. It's completely fried. As far as I can tell, there's not a single salvageable part left. Seriously, it actually caught *fire*."

"Any idea what might've caused that?" Kelsey asked.

"Whatever it was, it happened a long time ago. Based on the age of the scorch marks, probably sometime around the Fall."

Kelsey nodded. "It's always possible this happened when they used the weak flip point. Our military drives are more robust than civilian models. What about the rest of the ship? Is there *anything* useful left?"

"Someone spent a lot of man-hours stripping this ship down to the decks, and then taking most of the decks too. The computers are gone, and every bit of electronics is missing. They even took the wiring. Basically, this liner is ready for the scrapyard. There's nothing we can recover from it that will tell us anything."

Kelsey sighed. "Well, that's disappointing. Somehow, this ship used the weak flip point, arrived here in orbit, and then the crew and passengers vanished, taking with them anything that might tell us something useful."

"Maybe that's intentional," Angela said. "If I wanted to be certain that no one could figure out where I'd gone, I'd either strip the ship down or destroy it. Frankly, I think these folks probably needed every bit of technology they could get their hands on, so dumping it into the sun didn't make as much sense."

"Talbot is almost ready to check out the inhabited area we spotted below," Kelsey said. "Basically, all we can see from orbit is the fact that they have some cultivated fields. The area is heavily forested, so any dwellings are probably underneath the trees."

"If I had to guess," Angela said, "they're not intentionally trying to hide from anyone. Otherwise, they'd have destroyed the ship. They'd also be a bit more cautious about hiding any cultivated areas."

Kelsey agreed with that assessment. Whoever was down there—if anyone was down there—wasn't concerned about someone spotting them. Not really.

The fact that they didn't have any high-tech dwellings might very well mean that the descendants of the survivors were living a very primitive lifestyle. Probably nothing like the Pale Ones, but definitely something more agrarian.

"I'm going to have Jake ship the flip drive over to Carl," Angela said. "If anyone can figure something out with this piece of junk, he can."

"Did the ship even have a name?" Kelsey asked. "Maybe it's in our databases."

"*Radiant Dawn*. We only know that because it's written on the hull. Our databases have listings of Fleet vessels, but not civilian ones. We've got nothing on this ship."

Kelsey grunted. "Pity. Maybe Talbot will be able to find out something. We'll just have to keep working with what we have up here."

"Speaking of working with what we have, how are things going with your mother?"

Kelsey gave the tall woman a sour look. "I went down and talked with her. Things did not go well. Did you know that her picture is in the Imperial dictionary next to the word 'entitled'? That woman thinks that the universe revolves around her. It's maddening."

"This should not be a shock to you. You've known her your entire life. Surely, she behaved the same way when you were growing up."

Kelsey sighed. "Of course she did. It's not that I expect her to be different, but I've changed. I don't have the tolerance to deal with her bull. I have so many other priorities that I just want to leave her down there in that little cabin until we get back home, however long it takes."

Angela laughed. "That's a nice pipe dream, but you're going to have to deal with her sooner rather than later. That is one situation that won't be improved by putting it off."

"I don't know what to say. I've been through things that she will never understand. Her petty prejudices make my teeth hurt. I just want to shake her."

"Maybe you should, if you think it will serve your end goal. Since she's here and you have to deal with her, what is the optimum outcome of your interaction with her?"

Kelsey thought about that. "I want her to respect me for who I am. I want her to respect Jared as my brother. And I want her to recognize how bad her behavior is."

Angela shook her head. "One of the things they taught me when I became an officer was that some things are outside your control. If your mother is ever going to realize that what she did is wrong, it's going to have to be on her own time.

"Kelsey, she's been behaving this way longer than you've been alive. One thing everyone needs to understand about relationships is that you can't change the other person if they don't want to change."

"So I should dial back my expectations and just let her get away with it?"

"I wouldn't say you're letting her get away with anything. You're accepting that it isn't your problem to fix. Give her the cold shoulder all you like, just don't expect it to make her change who she is unless she wants to.

"As for Admiral Mertz, that's also tied up in her past with your father. Nothing you do is going to change how she feels. Maybe one day she'll be forced to sit down with Jared and learn what kind of person he really is. If so, that's Jared's fight. You need to focus on what's critical for you."

Kelsey smiled a little. "So it's all about me, then?"

"Yes, it is. The only thing you can work out with your mother is your relationship. If she doesn't respect you, grind her face into it. Make her decide to change."

"I suppose that's true," Kelsey said slowly. "I just don't want to talk to her right now."

"Putting something painful off only makes it more difficult. When you find yourself having to do something difficult, grit your teeth and do it. Every time she disrespects you, yank her up short. If she wants to discuss your life, make it clear that you have the final say in all the decisions about your personal life. If she doesn't like that, tough."

"I kind of started that already."

Angela clapped Kelsey on the shoulder. "Then go finish it."

* * *

VERONICA WALKED around *Audacious* for almost two hours. To her shock, Levy allowed her to dictate their direction of travel and didn't even deter her from going into sensitive areas.

For example, when she wanted to go to engineering, he allowed it. He had to know she was looking their engines over and seeing how they powered the ship, but he didn't seem concerned.

She had to admit the big ship intimidated her. As a junior officer, she'd served aboard a heavy cruiser. At the time, she couldn't have imagined a more powerful warship.

Audacious could swat that ship down with zero effort. Hell, it could do the same for several of them, even without its fighters. Her little destroyer wouldn't have had a chance.

It didn't take her long to forget about their surroundings, though. The more people she spoke with, the more confused she became. She followed Levy's advice and asked a wide array of questions about people's backgrounds and origins. She asked them what they knew about the fall of the dictatorship.

Their answers were not what she expected. As with any group of people, there wasn't a lot of consistency in the wording they used, and some even made contradictory statements. Just like she'd have found asking people back home about the fall of the dictatorship.

Yet these people all seemed to believe that Levy's version of the truth was what had really happened. More chillingly, even the lowest ranking of the crewmen spoke like someone born to the middle orders.

They seemed educated and bright. Even more unusually, they didn't have the general fear of officers that Fleet seemed to inoculate them with. Everyone she spoke to seemed reserved, but unawed by her, or even Captain Levy.

It was surreal and more than a bit frightening.

He allowed her to see her crew. He didn't take her in to speak with them, but he did show her the large cargo spaces his people were using to hold them. They seemed to have everything they needed and were in good spirits.

After watching her people interact with one another without interference from Levy's people, she allowed him to lead her back to her new accommodations without comment.

Two marines with rifles stood outside the hatch. They stepped clear to allow her access while still covering the doorway.

She turned to Levy before she entered the suite. "I'm still not certain what you're playing at. I'll tell my officers what you've said and what I've heard, but I don't expect any of us to believe this pile of horse manure."

He shrugged. "I can't control what you believe. All I can do is make sure that you have enough data to make an informed decision.

"Once you've slept on it, you might consider looking at some of the records available in the ship's library. Then we can speak again."

She nodded and went into the suite. The hatch slid closed behind her.

They'd already relocated her senior officers to the suite. They gathered around her and started asking questions.

She held up a hand. "Let me sit down for a second. I need to get this straight in my head, and then I'll brief you on what happened. The good news is that our crew is safe. I've seen them, and they're in good spirits."

A lot of senior Fleet officers didn't care how the lower orders fared, even under good conditions, but she'd surrounded herself with men and women who cared about the people under them. She was convinced that was why her efficiency rates for ship performance were so high.

Someone brought her a cool drink, and she took a sip. After a moment, she set it on the coffee table and launched into a concise description of everything that had happened while she was gone.

It would take a while, but the discussion afterward should be damned interesting.

10

Talbot guided the pinnaces down to an isolated spot. He'd sent drones ahead to be certain their landing zone was clear, so all he had to do was redirect them toward the cultivated fields after the pinnaces landed.

The temperature outside hovered somewhere between cool and cold. There were no crops currently growing in the fields, but there was evidence that someone had tilled them recently. There were people around somewhere.

He dispatched two squads to set up a perimeter around the pinnaces and then sent the drones farther afield.

It only took twenty minutes to locate a village. The people were dressed in rough, homespun cloth. Their grooming was on the unkempt side. Definitely not an advanced people.

The only people in sight were male. That seemed somewhat odd. Perhaps the women were inside the buildings, such as they were.

The locals had used roughly hewn logs and stone to build their dwellings. A few of them looked somewhat lopsided. Definitely not put together by professionals.

The drones were low profile, so he didn't expect any of the locals to notice them. That gave him plenty of time to record them in their natural setting.

That's when the first of the incongruities appeared. Once he had the long-range microphones on them, he realized that their basic conversation didn't match the technological level at which they were living. They spoke standard and occasionally mentioned things that were technological. Tablets mostly. They seemed to miss them.

Talbot eventually decided that he wasn't going to learn any more without approaching them. He weighed the pros and cons of appearing on foot or bringing one of the pinnaces in for a landing near the village.

Since they seemed to have some understanding of high technology, he decided on the latter. There were fewer chances for misunderstandings that way.

He did take the opportunity to relocate his marines closer to the village beforehand. If one of the locals tried something, he wanted his snipers in position to take them out safely.

Once everyone was in position, he had the pilot bring his pinnace around and landed beside one of the fields nearest the village. He dropped the ramp and walked down it slowly.

The air smelled of vegetation, and the wind bit at him through his uniform. He should've brought a jacket.

The people in the village noticed the pinnace landing, of course. It only took a few minutes for a small delegation of men to approach. Their expressions were closed, their faces hostile. This didn't look promising.

"What do you want?" one of the men asked. "You've already collected your damned bounty for the year."

"I just want to talk," Talbot said, his hands out to his sides a little. "There's no need for trouble."

The men glanced at one another in evident confusion. The man who'd spoken seemed to consider Talbot's words and then stepped forward. "Very well. Talk."

"Whoever you think I am, you're mistaken. I just want to find out who you people are."

The man blinked in obvious surprise. "You know who we are. You come every year to take the crops you demand we raise for you. Why are you playing this game?"

Talbot shrugged. "I don't know what to tell you. We just arrived in this system and found the derelict ship in orbit. I have no idea who you people are."

His words caused more consternation amongst the men. They had a brief, emphatic discussion in hushed tones before the first man once more turned to face Talbot.

"You're telling me that you're not one of those rebel bastards?"

"Maybe if we start with a simple question. How did you people get here?"

For the first time, Talbot saw something that looked like interest or excitement on the man's face. "You're truly not one of them? Are you with Fleet?"

"I'm Major Russel Talbot, Imperial Marines."

The man took two steps forward and fell to his knees. "Thank the gods. We thought no one would ever rescue us."

Talbot smiled. "Well, we've found you now. Who are you, and how did you get here?"

The man wiped tears from his face. "My name is Arthur Craig. I was a civil servant on Gibraltar before those bastards captured the freighter I was traveling on. They banished me here. They said all the higher orders were banished here."

Talbot checked the man. He had implants. They all did. Based on what he'd just heard, they were nobles from the Rebel Empire. Or at least wealthy families. They sure didn't look like it now.

The princess had chanced across a planet where someone—likely the ghosts—were putting their high-ranking prisoners. These people wouldn't be at all happy to learn whom he represented. In fact, their corrupted implant code would force them to attack him if they knew.

"I see. The people that captured you live somewhere else but force you to grow food for them. Is that right?"

"Yes," the man said. "It's those damned ghosts. The gods only know how long they've been doing this. We've had contact with other villages where none of the original prisoners is still alive. Some of the villages claim they've been here since the despot was overthrown.

Have you come to take us home? Please tell me you've come to take us home."

Talbot hedged his bets. "Since we've just found you, I can't speak for my commanding officers about what's going to happen next. We never expected to find anyone here, so they'll need to devise a plan. I feel certain that they'll wish to speak with someone to get more information."

The man surged to his feet. "I'll go with you. I'll explain everything. I even have some information about the ghosts. Critical information." The desperation in his voice was painful to hear.

The marine nodded slowly. "Very well. I can take you up to our ship, but I can't say when you'd be coming back."

"I hope I never come back," the man snarled. "This place is hell. A frozen hell."

Talbot sent instructions for the marines to regroup at the other pinnace and then gestured for the man to come with him. "I'll take you up now. If your people have any specific needs that we might be able to meet, such as medical care, I'll see to it as soon as we get to the ship."

"Thank you," the man said, tears streaming down his face. "I thought this nightmare would never end. They make us live like animals just to feed them. They make sure to tell us about the warm, beautiful worlds where they take the women and the lower orders just to torment us."

The ghosts sounded like a bunch of asses. Or pirates.

That explained why Talbot wasn't seeing any women. The marine kept an eye on the rest of the men as he led Craig into the pinnace. He didn't want them to rush him. He only spoke again once he'd safely closed the ramp.

"Well, I can assure you that we'll get to the bottom of this," Talbot said. "Let's get you strapped in and start up, shall we?"

* * *

ANNETTE WALKED into a compartment and eyed the researchers gathered there. It had taken her a while to figure out where the marines had stashed them. With over ten thousand people under lock and key, it wasn't easy to keep track of specific individuals.

Unlike the last set of people that she'd dealt with, these were all civilians. In fact, she couldn't imagine a more diverse set of people. They ranged from young to old, male and female, and any number of body types. Many of them reminded her of Carl Owlet. She supposed that wasn't surprising.

This compartment had originally been a storage area, but they'd moved all the crates against the bulkheads. Someone had scrounged up a few tables and chairs to go with the bedding on the floor. They really needed to come up with a better way of housing so many people.

She cleared her throat. "May I have your attention? My name is Annette Vitter, and I wish to speak with the most senior person."

A middle-aged woman with dark skin and curly hair rose from one of the tables. "I suppose that would be me. Jacqueline Parker. Is someone finally going to tell us what's going on?"

Annette gestured for the two marines at her heels to stay where they were and walked forward with her hand extended. "Yes, ma'am. I'll do what I can to explain everything and try to reduce the stress that you're undoubtedly under. Might we sit somewhere?"

The woman gestured to the table that she'd risen from. "Join me. Who are you people? What's going on?"

Annette verified the woman had implants as she sat. She couldn't tell her the unvarnished truth until they'd scrubbed the code. "I just need to verify some facts first. Once I've done that, we'll give you an examination to be sure you're healthy. Then I'll explain why we're here and what we intend to do.

"Let me begin by assuring you that we mean you no harm. We are not going to hurt any of you. In fact, we'd prefer to be your friends."

The woman gave her a lopsided smile. "You certainly have an odd way of showing friendship. Well, it seems I have some time available in my schedule, so go ahead and ask your questions."

"Are you all scientists and researchers?" Annette asked.

"Yes, though not all of the researchers are here," the woman said, her expression strained. "Are they all right? No one's been hurt, have they?"

"No one has been harmed," Annette said. "We just didn't have room to place everyone together, and I'm afraid we didn't realize we had missed some of you. If I could get a list of names, I'll have them moved here so that you can all be housed together."

"That would be good," Parker said. "It would take a lot of the strain off of my shoulders."

"What precisely do you do here?" Annette asked.

"I work in the gamma lab. I'm responsible for the people there and the research that we conduct."

"What are you researching?"

The woman smiled wanly. "It's classified. I may be your prisoner, but I still can't reveal the secrets of what we're working on."

Annette smiled. "We're going to find out one way or the other. Why don't you make it easy on yourself and just tell us?"

"Because I'd like to live," the woman said.

"It may not be readily apparent, but you're safe now. No one is going to harm you."

"I don't think you understand," Parker said. "We physically cannot tell you any aspect of what we're working on. To even attempt to do so would mean death."

Annette gestured around them. "No one can get to you here. You're safe."

"You definitely don't understand. We have explosive devices implanted in our skulls. If any one of us attempts to speak about classified projects with someone not cleared to hear the information, the explosive device will quite literally blow our heads off."

That information flabbergasted Annette. That was a new low, even for the Rebel Empire.

Now she was afraid to ask the woman any further questions. She couldn't risk someone with critical information blowing up in front of her very eyes.

"I assume that it's somehow linked with your implants," Annette said. "Would it object to a medical examination? In other words, can we look at it?"

Parker shrugged. "No one has ever had problems with an examination before, but these are new waters. None of us is particularly happy to have devices like that ready to snuff our lives at a moment's notice. I'll volunteer on one condition."

"What's that?" Annette asked.

The woman smiled widely. "I want us to get better food and some strong drink. It's been a tough couple of days."

11

K elsey stood in *Audacious*'s landing bay as the cutter transporting the senior prisoners from the orbital landed. She'd decided it was time to relocate them. She had to admit she really wanted to meet this Castille. He sounded like quite the character.

The marines escorted the prisoners off the cutter and herded them into a small group in front of her. She stepped forward and cleared her throat.

"May I have your attention, please? My name is Kelsey, and I'm going to see you situated. I'd welcome you aboard *Audacious*, but that feels a little pushy. You didn't exactly have a choice about coming over."

Commander Raul Castille stepped forward to meet her with his hand extended. "My name is Raul. I'd say it's a pleasure to meet you, but the circumstances are less than ideal. In any case, I suppose we're at your disposal."

"Has anyone told you that you're refreshingly honest, Commander?" Kelsey shook his hand. "Well, we might be enemies, but there's no reason we can't be civil. Perhaps even cordial."

He inclined his head. "This is also true. What do you have in mind for us? Forgive me, but I don't know your rank. Or even your last name."

She smiled. "We'll get to that in due time. First, let's get you to the suite of rooms we've set aside for you. I assure you, they're much more comfortable than the officers' mess on the orbital.

"Also, since you're no longer aboard the orbital, we can remove the jamming devices that were blocking your implant access. The unclassified portions of our ship's library are now available to you."

The other male senior prisoner stepped up to join them. "Forgive me if I seem to be butting in. My name is Edward Irons, and as the operations officer in charge of—or formerly in charge of— the Dresden Orbital, I must ask what you intend to do with the remaining prisoners.

"The conditions that they're being kept in are not conducive to good health. They need to be able to get out and move around."

Kelsey inclined her head toward him. "Commander Irons. We find ourselves in agreement. I want to move all the prisoners that we can, but it will take time to prepare accommodations that are more spacious.

"I can assure you that our medical personnel will continue examining them and make absolutely certain that they are in the best health possible as we work on that."

The third member of the senior officers' cabal stepped forward. "My name is Jeanette Martin. What are you going to do with us? How long are we to be your prisoners? When can I see the people I'm responsible for?"

Kelsey held her hands out. "I will answer those questions as soon as we get you settled into your new quarters."

She looked over to where Commodore Murdock stood glaring at them. "It's my understanding that you have placed some type of restriction upon Commodore Murdock. While it's unusual for prisoners to have prisoners, we've decided to allow that.

"One set of rooms in the suite can be secured from the common area. So long as you do not attempt to harm the commodore, we'll continue to allow you to restrict her movement."

Kelsey gestured for the marines at her side to lead the way. The prisoners fell in beside her while the other guards brought up the rear.

Once they arrived at the suite of rooms, Kelsey went inside, but instructed the marines to wait in the corridor.

Castille raised an eyebrow. "Don't you think you're being a little too trusting? We are, after all, your prisoners. What if we seize you and present a set of demands?"

Kelsey smiled. "I suppose that's part of the conversation that we need to have. I'm not concerned that you're going to take me prisoner. You might try, but you wouldn't succeed.

"Perhaps you should examine your accommodations? Then we can settle in before I broach the subjects. I suspect this is going to be an intense conversation. If you don't mind, I'd rather do it over food. I'm feeling a bit peckish."

He laughed. "Considering that we were living in a cafeteria, I feel confident that these rooms are significantly better than what we had." He glanced at Commander Irons. "Edward, please look everything over."

The other man nodded and began walking through the rooms attached to the common area.

Kelsey pointed at the far door. "That's the compartment reserved for Commodore Murdock. You can secure the manual lock from the outside. Over on the right, you can see the communal kitchen. If you want to continue this conversation, that's where I'll be."

It only took Kelsey a few minutes to make some iced tea and put a selection of meats and cheeses beside stacked bread. The condiments were on the side. Everyone could build a sandwich to their taste.

Once she was ready, the four of them sat at one of the tables. Kelsey put together a sandwich with a little bit of everything on it and dug in.

Castille waited for her to finish her sandwich before he spoke again. "We appreciate your seeing us to better-quality quarters. However, I believe it's time we put our cards on the table. Who are you, and what do you want with us?"

Kelsey smiled. "I believe you know who we are. Captain Vitter said that she was very clear about it."

Irons and Martin glanced at one another, confusion evident on their faces. Castille inclined his head toward them.

"I didn't think her story truthful, so I didn't pass it on to my associates. If that's going to be your official line, perhaps you should restate it. My apologies, Jeanette, Edward."

"I can see where this would be hard to accept," Kelsey said. "Our story isn't easy to believe. That doesn't make it untrue, however.

"I'm sure you've all heard about the Empire's civil war. I'm not going to get into the weeds about it, but what you've been taught is incomplete."

Commander Irons frowned at her. "Incomplete in what way?"

"It doesn't take into account the fact that some of the people your ancestors fought against escaped. They got away and settled a world outside your reach. Over the last five hundred years, those people have gathered their strength. I should say, my people. Now we've returned."

Jeanette shook her head. "That's preposterous. The lords completely overthrew the old dictatorship. Surely, you're not going to try to convince us that we're still fighting that war. It's settled."

"That's where things get complicated," Kelsey said. "My full name is Kelsey Bandar. I have two titles. The first is colonel because I'm the senior officer in the newly reconstituted Marine Raider division."

Castille laughed. "That's ridiculous. You expect me to believe that you command detachments of unstoppable war machines? I can bend you into a pretzel with one hand. If there is anyone less likely to be a warrior in this compartment, I do not see them."

"I can understand your reservations," Kelsey said. "I agree that I don't look very intimidating, but that doesn't change the facts."

She dabbed at the corners of her lips to make sure she hadn't left any mustard and dropped her napkin onto her plate. Then she rose to her feet, stepped over to the couch, and picked it up. It took a moment for her to find its balance, but she raised it almost to the ceiling.

Everyone stared at her, their eyes wide and mouths open. Silence ruled.

Once she was certain that she'd made her point, Kelsey set the couch back onto the deck. She brushed her hands off and returned to her seat.

"Commander Vitter told me she showed you a scan of someone with Raider implants. That was me."

Castille's mouth snapped shut. "This is an unexpected and somewhat frightening turn of events. How is this even possible? We control the manufacture of those things. How could you possibly have them if you've been separated from the Empire for so long?"

Kelsey smiled without humor. "Do you remember the computer you sent that fleet to destroy? Well, you've been sending it Raider implants for centuries. It followed the same instructions given to all the other subverted ships during the civil war.

"In case you don't know, they took anyone that they captured, corrupted their implants, and forcibly made them into fighting machines. They became prisoners in their own bodies, compelled to slaughter their friends and family.

"How do I know this? Because until very recently, it was still doing exactly that. I had the very great misfortune of straying into its grasp, and that computer put these things inside me. I still have nightmares about it, and I probably always will."

She took a deep breath and forced the terrible thoughts back into their mental lockbox.

"I believe that establishes my credentials on the Marine Raider front," she said brightly. "Let's get my other title settled. It's actually more relevant to our current discussion anyway.

"My father is the sitting emperor of the New Terran Empire. His lineage goes all the way back to Lucien, the boy emperor who escaped your grasp. Marcus's son. So, in nonmilitary settings, I have to deal with people calling me Crown Princess Kelsey Bandar, heir to the Imperial Throne."

Kelsey smiled at their shocked expressions. "We're not some greedy group from inside your Empire trying to take all of your secret research for profit. We're the people your ancestors failed to exterminate. You see, Commander, the war is far from settled."

Needless to say, they didn't believe her. She answered their questions and argued with them for a while, but finally hit her limit an hour later.

She stood slowly. "I think we've accomplished as much as one can reasonably expect. As I said earlier, you have access to the ship's library. I urge you to explore it deeply. You'll certainly learn a lot. Perhaps even understand what really happened all those years ago. We'll speak again soon."

Kelsey exited the compartment and gave the marine guards more detailed instructions. Once she was satisfied things were well in hand, she headed for Carl's main lab on the carrier.

Surprisingly, he wasn't sitting at his computer. He stood beside the recovered flip drive from the liner.

He smiled at her as she stepped up beside him. "You look tired."

"I feel tired. Give me some good news."

Carl gestured toward the drive. "I've just finished looking this over. It's just as fried as they'd said, but it has a nonstandard modification. It has a frequency tuner."

She eyed his satisfied expression warily. "You say that as if it means something. What is a frequency tuner?"

His expression fell. "What is with the education these days? A frequency tuner is a device that restricted the flip drive to a certain range of output. Or perhaps one of several ranges."

"You think they used it to refine their destinations through the weak flip point? Like what you were discussing as an option for us?"

"Yes," he said. "It's not possible to determine which particular range of frequencies the device might once have preferred, but that's what it did."

"How difficult will it be to duplicate?" she asked. "And how dangerous? Something burned out this flip drive. We absolutely cannot afford to have something like that happen to us."

"This is a civilian drive, built to far less robust standards than what you'll find on our ships. Even the recovery ship has military drives. I can't say for sure that it's completely safe, but we can be careful. Since there isn't another flip point in this system, we're going to have to take chances."

"You're sure of that?"

"I'm afraid so," he said softly. "The probes have scoured the system. There are no other flip points. The only way out is the way we came."

12

Talbot knew he probably should run this visit past his wife, but he wanted to have an unmonitored conversation with her mother. This was likely to get ugly, and he'd rather spare Kelsey that. This conversation needed to happen no matter how nasty it got, though.

The marine guard nodded at him as he instructed the hatch to signal his presence. Perhaps a little bit of common courtesy would make this easier. Talbot wasn't going to hold his breath, but one never knew.

The hatch slid open, and Justine Bandar stared up at him imperiously. Her already sour expression took a turn for the worse.

"Well, that just about makes this day perfect. What do you want?"

"I'd like to talk about your daughter. Believe it or not, it's in my best interest to see the two of you reconciled."

He figured the odds were about fifty-fifty that she'd close the hatch in his face. He could see the calculation behind her gaze.

She stepped back and gestured for him to enter. "Well then, by all means, come in. This should be fascinating."

Her quarters were standard Fleet issue. She undoubtedly saw them as a step down.

His mother-in-law walked to the couch and sat. "I'd offer you some refreshments, but I don't believe you'll be staying that long.

"Why would you want to see my daughter and me reconciled? In case it escaped your notice, I am not in favor of your marriage."

While the woman hadn't offered him a seat, he took one anyway. Standing while she sat gave her too much power over him.

"We've never been formally introduced," he said. "I'm Major Russel Talbot, Imperial Marines. Call me Talbot. Everyone does."

"I know your name. Russel. You left out a few titles. Let me be clear. Your position doesn't change one thing between us. You're a commoner trying to climb the ladder into high society, and I will not allow it."

He laughed. "I couldn't give squat about my position in society. Frankly, I thought the knighthood was far too much. The rest of those titles? If you can convince your ex-husband to take them back, I'm perfectly fine with that. I have no desire to see myself included in the nobility. Bunch of puffed-up stuffed shirts."

Justine raised an eyebrow. "That's the first interesting thing you've said. I'm shocked that we find ourselves in agreement about anything."

"I don't know why," he said. "In any case, I'm not here to talk about me. I'm here to talk about Kelsey."

The woman sneered at him. "What can you possibly tell me about my daughter that I don't already know? She thinks something has changed that makes her incomprehensible to me. She's wrong. And if you think you're going to take me to task for my sex life, you'd better think again."

"I couldn't care less about your sex life. Bang whomever you choose. Knock yourself right out. As far as how Kelsey feels about that, that's between you two. All I'm here for is to give you some information that your daughter isn't going to give you."

The woman's eyes narrowed. "What information might that be?"

"The fact that she's been through hell. Literally, through hell. She's changed in ways both mental and physical that you cannot comprehend unless I explain it to you in words with less than three syllables."

He held up a hand when she started to respond hotly. Miraculously, she shut up.

"Rather than argue, why don't you let me explain it to you? If you have questions, then you can ask them. If you don't, then I can leave. I'm not here to fight with you. That's your daughter's job."

Justine leaned back and crossed her arms over her chest. "Why do both of you think that I cannot understand my daughter has been through something terrible? I'm sure the mission she was on was ghastly. Just look at the company she had to keep."

"Sometimes ignorance is bliss," he said. "It's going to give me great pleasure to educate you. And by company, I assume you mean Jared Mertz. He's also outside the scope of our discussion.

"Focus on your daughter. Kelsey went through something horrific. Something that has changed her irrevocably. Not just mentally— though it has certainly given her nightmares—but physically.

"Let me stress that again. It's been more than a year since the events in question, and she still has nightmares almost every night. She wakes up screaming in terror and pain. Is that getting through that thick skull of yours?"

A look of unease flitted across the ex-empress's face. "Nightmares? What could possibly have happened to her to give Kelsey nightmares?"

He leaned forward. "The information I'm about to pass on to you is classified. Your ex-husband has declared it an Imperial secret. Technically, I'm in violation of quite a few laws in mentioning this to you, but I suspect he'll grant me an exemption.

"Your daughter was captured by a group of individuals we call the Pale Ones. They implanted machines in her body. Not just the implants you might've heard about. I'm talking about much more significant changes, and this was not a voluntary or painless process."

He used his implants to send a signal to the vid monitor on the wall. It began playing one of the marines' helmet videos from the rescue. He'd selected the clip from after they'd arrived aboard *Courageous*. The team was on their way to the medical center.

He froze it so that Kelsey's face was framed on the monitor. The terrible red scars of the implant surgery cut across her face.

Justine Bandar sucked in a horrified breath. "Oh my God."

"They didn't use anesthesia or any form of regeneration. She had scars just like that across her entire body. I was a prisoner in the next compartment while they did it. I could hear her screaming for over an hour as they cut her open."

He made the image go away. "I could show you everything they did to her, but I'm going to do you a kindness that I'm not sure you'd do me under similar circumstances. I'm not going to show you something you can *never* forget.

"They coated her bones in a substance called graphene to strengthen them. They wove artificial muscles through her normal muscles. They implanted equipment to dispense combat drugs into her. They turned her into the deadliest killing machine that Imperial science could build."

His mother-in-law stared at him in horror. "No. That's not possible. She doesn't look like that at all."

"Regeneration fixed the physical scars, in combination with something called medical nanites. She has millions of tiny machines scattered throughout her body to repair damage. The only lingering injuries she has are inside her mind.

"And that brings me to the second half of her situation. She's had to kill people. Not just by giving orders, not just with guns, but also with her bare hands. I'm not sure I can put a number on how many lives she's ended to save her friends and herself. Oh, and the Empire. Let's not forget that."

He started the second video. The one taken at the Parliament building on Pentagar. He didn't watch the events on the monitor. He'd seen those innumerable times. Instead, he watched his mother-in-law's expression of horror grow deeper.

When the video finished, he allowed the silence to drag on. When she continued to stare at the monitor as though it were still playing, he continued.

"While your daughter isn't a murderer, she's most assuredly a killer. She's one of the deadliest fighters I've ever seen. All of this trauma has brought out one factor you've never seen in your daughter. One that's been hiding in plain sight all this time.

"Kelsey has a will of steel. She will do whatever is necessary for the Empire. The little girl that you could bully around died in an operating theater on board a space station that no longer exists. The woman you see may look like her, but she won't knuckle under to bullies. Not even to you."

He rose to his feet. "I'll leave you to think about that in whatever peace you can find. I'll also give you some free advice. If you want to reconcile with your daughter, you're going to have to give up any thought of dominating her. Trust me, the worst you can do doesn't even come close to what she's been through."

Talbot left her in the compartment, still staring at the blank monitor. He hoped she could come to grips with this information and change how she interacted with her daughter. If she couldn't, well, he'd done his best.

* * *

ANNETTE STAYED with Jacqueline Parker throughout the entire process of scanning the woman's implants. She could see the woman's nervousness.

Audacious's chief medical officer, Zac Zoboroski, walked the scientist through the process without explaining any of the details that would have caused a negative reaction. Annette was impressed with his bedside manner and soothing voice.

The process of overwriting the corrupted code took several hours. The doctor passed this off as a deep scan mapping out the explosive device and how precisely it was placed.

He stepped over beside Annette while the machine in the medical center overwrote the corrupted code. "That's a despicable device. I have no idea what the software triggers are, but the amount of explosive is easily enough to completely shatter her skull and sever her spine."

Annette grimaced. "She said that the programming monitored them and what they said. If they knowingly revealed classified information to someone that wasn't cleared to hear it, it would set off the device. There has to be some extra code inside the implant that monitors that somehow."

The man shrugged. "I've captured the code, and I'll pass it on to Sir Carl. He'll be able to figure out precisely what's different. Under normal circumstances, the device would be relatively simple to remove, but I'm pretty sure it has an antitampering device. Without the appropriate codes to disarm it, I suspect it would go off if I tried."

Annette considered that. "Is there any kind of remote activator?"

The doctor nodded. "Almost certainly. Overwriting the implant code will probably make it safe for her to speak, but I'm not sure what to do about remote signals. Those will continue to be a danger."

"Something else for Sir Carl to work on. Who knows? We might be able to get the researchers working on fixing the problem themselves. There's a kind of symmetry in that."

She went over and exchanged small talk with the scientist for the next two hours. That was challenging, considering she knew very little about the woman's society as a whole or the life of a restricted researcher in particular.

The theme that emerged was that while Jacqueline's education was quite broad and, in specific fields, very deep, she didn't get out much. It seemed that she and the other scientists kept each other's company more often than not.

Basically, they were prisoners. If Annette was right in her guess, this had been true for the woman's entire life. Considering that they hadn't found any retired scientists, the Rebel Empire probably disposed of them once they couldn't work. Dead women told no tales.

Annette excused herself and went for sandwiches and tea. She figured the other woman would be hungry by the time this was all done.

The procedure was complete by the time she returned. She set up the food in the closest break room and brought Jacqueline Parker to join her.

"Okay, let me start off by telling you what we were really doing," Annette said.

The other woman smiled a little. "I figured that was taking too long for any kind of realistic scan."

"Since the device is rigged to be controlled by your implants, we overwrote the code with the base version that doesn't have the interfaces to do anything with it," Annette said. "In other words, the code running your implants now has no idea the explosives are there or what should set them off.

"The doctor is uncertain if they can be safely removed, but nothing we discuss should pose any danger to you at this point. One other piece of bad news is that they may also be remotely controllable. While we have everyone on lockdown, I think it might be best if we bring all of your people off the orbital just to be safe."

"I think that's a great idea," Parker said. "You have no idea how it feels to have them watching you all the time. To know that if you made a mistake, you'd be dead before you realized it."

"I can't imagine how they recruit people for this kind of job," Annette said. "If they don't let you out to talk to anyone else, the whole concept of pay seems ludicrous."

"We aren't paid for our work," the woman said bluntly. "We never had a choice about what we wanted to do with our lives. All of us were brought in as children and trained for this work. But even with all the negatives, it's still better than where we came from."

Annette frowned a little. "I don't think I understand."

"We all came from an exceptionally primitive society. One where we were taken as very young children and separated from what amounted to savages. Thankfully, most of our memories of that time aren't very clear, but it was a brutal life."

Everything suddenly clicked, and Annette knew where these people came from. The tithes of children the computer at Erorsi had been trading for the high-tech gear from the Rebel Empire. That had to be where the scientists had come from.

She wondered if the Rebel Empire had done so because no one would miss those people. Now wasn't the time to ask, but it did call for some deeper research later.

Based on what she'd seen, Annette thought the woman was understating the benefits of living on the orbital in comparison to being a Pale One. The woman didn't even know what was done to those that stayed as they grew older.

"I might be able to provide a little information about where you came from," Annette said. "If my guesses are correct in any case. What I need to know is if you're willing to have a frank discussion with me about what you were working on. Now that it's safe to do so."

Jacqueline Parker smiled coldly. "I've been under a death sentence my entire life. I'll tell you everything I know if you can get my people out of this place."

13

Veronica sat alone in her quarters trying to wrap her mind around just how screwed they really were. She and her people had stayed up late into the evening discussing their situation and looking through the massive library of data that their captors had made available to them.

It hadn't taken long to realize the sheer volume of information available—exabytes of material—meant that not all of it could be fake.

The library dated back literally centuries. Millions of hours of vids, news shows, and more. Billions of articles, books, textbooks and academic journals for restricted research subjects, and more.

And a mind-boggling amount of virtual-reality porn stashed in various hidden repositories. Even some ancient pieces which looked to be live action with actual participants. Which begged the obvious question. Why would anyone include something like that?

She'd set her people to reading different articles about the war against the old dictatorship.

After a few hours, a disturbing trend appeared. What they were reading did not match up with what she had learned in school. Of course, this could all be propaganda. If so, someone had invested an incredible amount of work to trick people that couldn't do anything about it in the first place.

It made no sense. These people had already demonstrated they had enough firepower to take out an entire Fleet task force. Why try to convince her the lords had been playing some kind of game with humanity?

She stayed awake late, picking random historical areas to poke her nose into. It made her sick to her stomach, having to read the lies about the old dictatorship. And they had to be lies. She refused to believe that the lords had overthrown humanity and now oppressed them in a slavery so pervasive they couldn't even recognize it.

It was later than normal when she woke. She dressed and ate breakfast with her senior officers in the little kitchen their suite shared.

Many of them had burned the midnight oil as well. All of them seemed uneasy.

She laid out the areas she'd researched more closely and listened to them as they detailed their own finds.

Her chief engineer, Lieutenant Graham Bakersfield, summed up her thoughts in his usual blunt manner. "Something stinks."

Lieutenant Commander Armand Fuller, her executive officer, glared at the engineer. "Watch yourself."

The younger officer raised an eyebrow. "About what, Commander? It's all laid out for anyone to see. They don't have any reason to lie to us. It's not as though we can do anything. They destroyed our entire task force."

Veronica rapped the table with her knuckles. "Let's restrain ourselves. We don't have any idea what their true plans are. Let's not make assumptions."

She added her helm officer, Lieutenant Candice Wells, and her tactical officer, Lieutenant Brent Kowalski, into her instructions with a pointed glance.

"What I want each of you to do today is divide up the various areas we've already looked at and start reading everything you can about them. I want an assessment of how authentic these documents look. As Graham said, there's far too much material here for them to have just created everything out of whole cloth. I want to know if it feels consistent."

She gave them all a stern look. "What I don't want is for there to be any fighting amongst ourselves. We're already in enough trouble."

After sending each of them off to their own corners, she again dug into every bit of information she could about the dictator, Marcus Bandar. From everything she'd learned in school, the man had been a monster. Surely, they couldn't whitewash him so completely.

By lunch, she was feeling much less certain of that viewpoint. Of course, she'd been certain going into this that they would censor anything negative about the man. The narrative she'd learned as a child didn't suit this story at all.

Yet she found plenty of criticism. Any number of people seemed to object to some aspect of the man's rulings. It seemed, based on the record she had in front of her, that anyone could criticize the man about anything. Not just privately, but on what passed for news programs.

Diving down the rabbit hole of watching news programs to see if they seemed real had caused her to question everything she'd believed. Just one of the news programs went back many decades before the rebellion against the old dictatorship. She had copies of every evening newscast.

There was absolutely no way that someone had spent the time to fake everything in it, not even the lords.

She picked dozens of news items at random. Both good and bad. Most times, she was able to verify through other sources that the events the news programs covered were consistent with what was being presented in them.

Oh, the opinions of the people on the shows might be at odds with the facts, but it wasn't difficult to discern their individual agendas. Anyone that served in Fleet had to play politics, even if they detested being anywhere near the higher orders.

By the time her stomach informed her that she needed something to eat, she wasn't sure she wanted to. She felt ill. No wonder Captain Levy seemed so confident and serene. She was finding it difficult to refute the evidence.

That still didn't mean it was true. It could be some elaborate ruse used to dupe Levy and his people. If so, someone had gone to an insane amount of trouble to fake the historical record for these people. That seemed even more far-fetched. Why?

She wasn't sure what to believe anymore.

Rather than dine with the rest of her people, she decided to see if she could get another trip to the officers' mess. She signaled at the hatch and smiled at the marine who opened it.

He stood far enough back that he wasn't in danger of being rushed, and his companions had them covered from farther down the corridor.

"Yes, ma'am?"

"I was wondering if it is acceptable for me to take lunch at the officers' mess, Corporal."

The marine nodded. "Captain Levy left orders that allow it, ma'am. If you'll stay inside, I'll summon two marines to escort you. Do you want me to notify the captain to join you?"

She shook her head. "No, Corporal. I think I'd rather dine alone. I just want to see and hear the people around me."

"Understood, ma'am. Please step back into your quarters."

Ten minutes later, the hatch opened again. Two new marines stood waiting for her. "This way, ma'am," one of them said politely. The woman gestured for Veronica to precede her.

They escorted her to the officers' mess. It looked pretty much as it had the last time she'd been there. A fairly chaotic room of people dining and talking.

One person stood out, however. A man with commander's tabs dining at a table against the wall, with a pair of marine guards of his own.

She stopped and eyed him. She knew all the senior officers of her task force. He wasn't one of them.

"Who is that man?" she asked the marine at her side.

"One of the new prisoners. They just came aboard yesterday. He's from the orbital at Dresden."

Veronica stared at the woman in shock. None of them had

explicitly said where the task force had come from. This had to be some trick to try to get information from her.

Only, how was that supposed to work?

"I've changed my mind," Veronica said. "I think I'll dine with him. Unless of course, you have an objection." She stared challengingly at the marine.

The woman shrugged. "Nothing in my orders precludes that, ma'am. After you."

* * *

RAUL WAS ABOUT HALFWAY through his meal when he saw the woman stalking toward him with a determined step. She was new. Her rank tabs indicated she was a commander, and marines flanked her.

Under other circumstances, he might think she was coming to arrest him. That seemed somewhat redundant at this point.

He put his fork down and focused his attention politely on her. "Yes?"

"Might I join you, Commander?"

He gestured toward the seat across from him. "Be my guest. Might I suggest the steak? It's quite good."

Once the woman had seated herself, the marines that had been accompanying her joined those watching him. Curious.

"I don't believe we've met. I'm Raul Castille."

She extended her hand. "Veronica Giguere. Commanding officer of the destroyer *R-7322*."

That prompted him to check his implant storage. That was one of the destroyers formally assigned to guard Dresden. It was one of the ships that had departed a few weeks before the intruders had showed up.

As the orbital's security officer, he had files on all the senior officers assigned in the system. Indeed, he had hers.

It only took a few moments for him to conclude she was the real deal. Her personnel file had a number of images that his captors would not have been able to alter.

He smiled. "I'm actually familiar with you, Commander. I am—

rather, I used to be—the chief security officer for the Dresden orbital. We never personally met, but I have reviewed your file. I'm surprised to see you here."

"I'm not even sure where here is, Commander. My crew and I have been prisoners aboard this ship for three weeks. Are we at Dresden?"

"I'm not certain where we are, either," Raul said. "The only thing I can say for sure is that I don't believe we need to be so formal with one another. We're both prisoners together, you and I. Call me Raul. May I call you Veronica?"

"I suppose so."

The same man who'd taken his order stepped up to the table and offered Veronica a menu. She shook her head. "I'll take what he's having."

Once the server had departed, she stared at Raul. "How did they get you? Were you traveling on some ship they ambushed? They seem to be quite good at ambushes."

He gave her a wan smile. "On that point, I believe we agree. No. They captured the orbital entirely. Then they proceeded to steal it. What about the task force you were with? Did they only get your ship? Were some of the others able to get away?"

Veronica stared at him, her mouth open for a moment before she snapped it shut. "You've got to be kidding me! How could they possibly steal the Dresden orbital? The system is guarded! There are battle stations at every flip point. Surely you saw them coming."

He laughed. "Yes, well, I'd imagine my next performance evaluation is going to be a trial. Probably quite literally. I'm still not certain how they managed it, but they snuck into the system without anyone being the wiser. It was as though they magically appeared on the orbital. There were marines in powered armor *everywhere*.

"We never had a chance. Once they were inside our guard, they stunned everyone with the orbital's antiboarding weapons. They took the ship we used for moving ore, modified it to hold the orbital, and somehow got away with it. I was unconscious at the time, so I'm not sure how they managed that, but they did it. What about your task force? What happened?"

Veronica sighed and sagged a little in her chair. "We made it to the target system. The one with the crazy computer. Commodore Wilson split the task force and led the smaller portion to ambush the computer. Commodore Crabtree—his deputy—led the larger portion to take the system next door. My ship was with the latter group.

"Only they were waiting for us. They took out the pickets we left behind to keep the exit open, and then ships inside the computer's system jumped the freighter and its escort. Commodore Wilson went after them, but they took him out."

She rubbed her forehead. "I didn't see it happen. Commodore Crabtree pushed forward and flipped into the other system. They were supposed to be primitive, relatively speaking. Only they weren't. They had a fleet bigger than ours waiting on the other side. Huge ships. Modern ships. A lot of them.

"They had old battle stations guarding the flip point that absorbed our initial fire. I think they were decoys. Only two light cruisers and six destroyers made it back out."

He let that sink in. "I see. And what did you find when you got back to the computer's system?"

"They destroyed Commodore Wilson's section of the task force. They were waiting for us too. Commodore Crabtree died during the assault on that third system. The two remaining light cruisers died trying to take out this carrier.

"All six of the destroyers that were left were damaged and obviously outclassed. When they offered to accept our surrender, I gave in. As a security officer, that's probably not what you wanted to hear."

He allowed himself to shrug. "I'm not precisely in a position to judge. Only six destroyers survived? That's terrible. You mentioned other ships. How many and of what classes?"

"They had a fifty percent numerical advantage," the woman said, pain written across her face. "They also had a number of significantly larger ships. Not only heavy cruisers, but also things they call battlecruisers and two monster ships the same size as this carrier they called superdreadnoughts. We never stood a chance."

Raul leaned back in his chair masking his shock. The carrier had been a terrible surprise to him, but this news undercut everything he thought he knew. He'd been toying with the idea that his captors were lying to him. Now he could no longer afford to delude himself.

If they possessed fleets of that caliber—ones they hadn't felt the need to use at Dresden—then their story must be true. Some version of it anyway. They must actually be a splinter group of the old dictatorship that escaped the rebellion.

The Empire was in serious trouble. He wasn't sure what he could do, but he had to come up with some kind of plan. He couldn't just sit back and let them get away with this.

The classified research they'd stolen not only helped them, but its loss hurt the Empire. As far as Raul knew, Dresden was the only place that manufactured Raider implants. Those would be terrible in battle.

Worse yet, while other locations were probably able to produce the hardware required by the lords, allowing lackeys of the dictatorship to build lords of their own would be a catastrophe.

He leaned forward. "This is shocking, terrible news. I'm afraid that I'm going to add to your sorrows."

Raul proceeded to tell her about some of the things the enemy had stolen with the Dresden orbital. With any luck, the two of them could come up with some kind of plan to turn the situation around.

Considering how isolated they were, that seemed unlikely, but he had a duty to try.

14

_____

Kelsey rapped her knuckles on the briefing room table. "If I could have your attention, we need to get this show on the road."

She'd gathered all her top people to get an update on the various threads they were each working on. They'd been in this new system for a full day now.

"Zia, what's the status of the prisoners?" she asked.

"The ones on the orbital or the ones on the planetary surface?"

Kelsey grimaced. "Let's stick with the ones that we brought to the party."

Their surveys had located dozens of farming and ranching villages. Based on the testimony of the one man they'd brought up from the surface, everyone below was likely to be either someone from the higher orders of the Rebel Empire or descended from them.

These ghosts—whoever they were—occasionally dropped off new people, but mostly left the prisoners to whatever lives they could build for themselves. Not exactly kind considering the climate, but not brutal, either.

They'd finally pinned the planet's orbit down. It was deep winter for the inhabitants now, but it appeared that everything would warm up to an acceptable level for summer. So, as long as they didn't leave the equator, existence wouldn't be overly harsh.

"We finished going through everyone and getting names," Zia said. "We've isolated the purely civilian side from the Fleet crewmen and officers. The vast majority of them are still on board the orbital, and there's no way to change that. We don't have the space to house them anywhere else."

There had been over ten thousand people on the orbital when they'd captured it. She really needed to come up with something else very soon. Just guarding the various areas were straining their manpower to the very limit.

"I've been thinking about that," Kelsey said. "I think we need to tear out every bit of equipment that we're interested in and turn them loose."

Brandon Levy looked skeptical. "With that many people together, they're going to come up with some kind of mischief to get into. Is that really what we want?"

"Do we have a choice? How long are we going to drag them with us? Once we take the manufacturing equipment and the research computers off the orbital, we don't need it anymore."

"So, you're just planning on leaving it here?" Annette Vitter asked. "Isn't that just asking for trouble? If they get back through the weak flip point, then the Rebel Empire will know all about the hole in their maps. That would be a disaster."

"So, let's tear out all the manufacturing capability," Carl said. "If they have no way to build a flip drive, it doesn't matter what they do."

"That's too risky," Zia said. "People are more resourceful than you give them credit for. Maybe somebody on the planet's surface used to be a whiz at manufacturing or is a flip drive physicist. We can't know what would happen, other than to say the chances would be unacceptably high."

Kelsey sighed. "You're probably right. All it would take is them cobbling together some type of probe with a makeshift flip drive. I guess that's off the table."

"Maybe not," Carl said. "To build a flip drive requires several extremely rare and hard to refine elements. That's what kept us on

Avalon for so long. Yes, I understand that we didn't know how to build one, but the refining process took decades to perfect once we actually located enough of the exotic elements.

"Pentagar had knowledge of how to build flip drives, but because their system didn't have any of these elements, they were trapped. Basically, it doesn't matter what these people know if we can keep them from accessing any of those exotic elements."

"That's all fine and good," Kelsey said, "but you haven't said whether or not those elements are present here. Are they?"

He shrugged. "We'd have to look a lot harder—and in many more places—for me to answer that question. I think the takeaway from this should be that we could make it impossible for them to build a flip drive.

"There's a lot of similarity in how they build the AI computer systems. The basic manufacturing gear that they have outside of the research facility just isn't capable of performing the tasks required."

Zia slowly nodded. "Add in the fact that they don't even have detectors to find the weak flip points, and that should keep them pretty well pinned down for a long time. Besides, somebody else is responsible for the people in this system. They'll be back long before the new guys figure out a way to escape."

Kelsey wasn't convinced. "I'm going to have to think on that for a while. It might be better to shuttle them down to the surface. We can move some limited manufacturing capability down and allow them to build a higher tech civilization without giving them access to a space-based platform."

She looked over at Annette. "What about the research scientists? How goes the process of making friends?"

"Exceedingly well. Now that we've disabled the explosives in their heads, they've become a very friendly bunch. *Very* helpful. I have a list of all the research projects they were working on and access to their files.

"Unlike the two manufacturing units, the chief researcher has access to her people's computers. We've already copied all the files. Of course, I'm not a scientist, so I have no idea how useful it's going to be, but it sounds promising. Virtually everything is aimed toward some kind of improvement on Fleet vessels and weapons."

"I've glanced over some of it, and I think a number of items are revolutionary," Carl said. "They were working on upgraded computers for the missile systems. The potential increase in targeting ability and range are going to be more shocking to us than the Old Empire missiles were to our compatriots back on Avalon."

"That's quite a statement," Kelsey said. "I look forward to hearing about it."

"One other thing," Annette said. "I found out what happened to the children from Erorsi. The Rebel Empire brought them to Dresden, and they became researchers."

Kelsey blinked. "You're telling me that the scientists here are all kids taken from the Pale Ones? That's amazing."

"I couldn't agree more," Annette said. "I haven't told them all the details, yet. I figured there'd always be time to have that conversation when you decided the time was right."

"Excellent. I think that can wait until we get the hell out of here. Speaking of getting out of here, what's the status on your research, Carl?"

"I've already begun modifying some of our probes. The frequency tuner that I'm installing onto their flip drives should restrict the power output to ranges similar to what that liner used.

"I suggest that we send one of *Persephone*'s stealthed probes back to the system that we came from before we test these. There's always a possibility that one of them will flip into that first system, and if the drive malfunctions, it might be detectable by ships there. So, let's be sure no one is home before we start playing around with this."

"Agreed," Kelsey said. "We'll wait until we're certain the other system is empty before we test any of your prototypes. Let's set this up for tomorrow morning. Can you be ready by then?"

"Absolutely."

Kelsey turned her attention to Brandon. "I have a few questions for you. First up, have you located who helped my mother?"

One side of his mouth quirked up. "They weren't nearly as clever as they'd thought they were. Once I identified who was bringing her food, it was child's play to get them to turn on one another.

"It seems that there were four of them. Someone in Fleet Personnel convinced them that he could give them orders to do this. I'd imagine Admiral Yeats will strenuously disagree once we get home."

"What's going to happen to them?" Kelsey asked.

"While I could bring them up on charges, I've decided to handle it administratively. I figure a year or two of scut work will satisfy me."

Kelsey laughed. "Perfect. The other question is about Commander Giguere. I understand that you've been trying to ease her into the mindset that the AIs lied to them. How's that going?"

He shrugged. "She's fairly closed-mouthed. All I've heard her express is skepticism. As I recall, you said it took months for Commander Richards to come around. I don't think we'll benefit by rushing this situation, either.

"There has been one interesting development. She's linked up with Commander Castille from the Dresden orbital. They've had their heads down over lunch for almost two hours now."

Annette chuckled. "Man, I'd love to listen in on that conversation. That guy is devious. I'm not sure that allowing them to mingle is going to help our cause."

"Probably not," Brandon agreed. "It might convince him that we're telling the truth, though."

"Come again? He's a hard-core Rebel Empire officer. What makes you think he's susceptible to being turned?"

"I'm not certain that he'll be turned into a supporter. More like a believer. Even if we convince him that he's been lied to his entire life, he has a lot invested in their system. He might just continue supporting it. In any case, the discussions will be fascinating."

Zia sighed. "This is all getting very convoluted. Let's say that we do leave the majority of our prisoners here. Who are we keeping with us and why?"

"We need to keep the researchers," Kelsey said. "We also need to have the top management people from the orbital, both civilian and

Fleet. All of them might have useful information. Given enough time, some of them will come over to our side.

"Here's what I think we'll do. We need to strip out the equipment and computers we intend to take with us when we leave. Then we can pick an area down below and start setting up housing for the prisoners. We can turn construction over to them.

"Considering that everyone else here has been getting by with only primitive tools, these folks should be able to make perfectly serviceable and comfortable housing. They could then trade those skills with the other prisoners to get food and knowledge. The technology would spread to the other villages eventually. A win-win situation."

Carl stared off into space. "It will take us a couple of days to strip the orbital of all the useful equipment. Moving the manufacturing gear is going to be the most time-consuming. Then we have to parse out what equipment is acceptable to move to the planet's surface. That'll take longer."

"Indeed, it will," Zia agreed. "Transporting that many people is going to take a while. I figure at least a week."

"Then we'd best get started," Kelsey said. "Round up some of the civilians that have the most construction experience and take them down to select their new home. Get them started building the initial shelters.

"I want to keep their population sizes similar to what we're seeing now. Spread them out. Separate the Fleet people from the rest. I'd imagine the Fleet personnel will still manage to dominate them in the end, but that's not our problem.

"I want to complete the relocation of prisoners and stripping the orbital within seven days. That might be tight, but let's try to make it happen."

Once she saw the agreement in everyone's eyes, Kelsey stood slowly. "When we find a way out of the system, we'll drop the orbital into the sun. That'll keep anyone here from being able to use it, even if they eventually get off the planet's surface."

"I think that's a bad idea," Zia said. "Why don't you save it as a bargaining chip? Once we finally locate these ghosts, I'd imagine they might be able to find a use for an orbital like that and a ship to move it around. We're going to need to build some goodwill."

Kelsey considered that and slowly nodded. "Okay. Once we've stripped it clean of things we're taking with us, we'll relocate it into the outer system. That way they can't just come back here and locate it while we're out searching for them. Keep me informed about all these projects. Dismissed."

15

The next morning Annette stopped by Carl Owlet's lab just after breakfast. She found the young scientist already hard at work.

From all appearances, he and his people had disassembled the flip drive that they'd found on the disabled liner. It lay scattered across several tables with the remainder sitting in a pile at the rear bulkhead.

She'd brought Jacqueline Parker with her so that the two could become acquainted. The woman looked around the lab curiously.

"What are you researching here?"

Annette smiled. "We'll get to that. First, I want you to meet someone."

She led the woman over to where Carl was furiously typing on a keyboard, hunched over a large monitor. She cleared her throat. "Good morning, Carl."

The young man looked up, apparently startled by her voice. He rose to his feet. "Sorry. I didn't hear you come in."

Annette wasn't surprised. By all accounts, the scientist was very single-minded.

"Carl Owlet, allow me to introduce Jacqueline Parker. Jacqueline is the lead researcher from the Dresden orbital. Jacqueline, Carl is our senior researcher."

The woman looked a little skeptical. "Forgive me, but you seem a little young for the lead position."

Carl smiled. "I get that a lot. Frankly, I'd be a lot more comfortable with someone else in charge too. For some reason, they've decided that I'm the best guy they're going to get for this position. Particularly on this mission."

"Don't let him fool you," Annette said. "This is the same man who discovered and perfected faster-than-light communication."

Jacqueline's eyes widened. "That's impossible. Nothing goes faster than the speed of light."

Carl gave Annette a look. "Isn't that supposed to be classified?"

"Actually, I've already spoken with Princess Kelsey and Commodore Anderson. Jacqueline and her people were prisoners on the orbital, forced to work against their will. They've cooperated fully with us, and the computer is satisfied that she is a free agent willing to work with us.

"In fact, I would suggest that she and her research team might be of great use to you in figuring out our current problem. Nothing against your assistants, but we didn't bring a large scientific contingent along with us on this mission. You can use all the help you can get."

She turned to Jacqueline. "I wouldn't let his youth lull you into a false sense of who he is. He's very humble, so he'd probably never tell you this, but he won the Terran Empire's highest award for scientific achievement: the Lucien Prize. The emperor knighted him for his contributions to science."

The older woman searched her face for a moment, as though she were trying to determine if Annette was pulling a prank on her. "Well, if you say he's done all this, then I suppose I best learn a little bit more about him."

The woman focused her attention on Carl. "Faster-than-light communication? Exactly how does that work?"

Carl stood. "Basically, the communication device uses entangled photons in large numbers to transmit information from one place to another. That unfortunately means that the units are paired.

"That results in information passed from one unit to another at faster-than-light speed, regardless of the distance between them. In fact, the effect works through a flip point.

"Not more than one hop, but once is enough. That means we can place units on either side of the flip point and get real-time information sent from one to the other without a vessel having to traverse the flip point."

Jacqueline looked skeptical. "You're talking about Einstein's theory, right? Spooky action at a distance? You've actually managed to build hardware that utilizes this principle reliably?"

"I have," the young scientist said. "When I have time, I intend to work on FTL buoys we can sit at flip points scattered throughout the Empire. They'd be linked with ones on the other side of flip points, with main worlds in the system, and any Fleet installations.

"If it works as I hope, someone on one side of the Empire could send a message from their world to the flip-point buoy, which would then retransmit it through the flip point and across to any destination. If it were a multisystem jump, one buoy would communicate across to another buoy that would then send the information along.

"Theoretically, a person on one side of the Empire could send a message to a friend on the other side with a transmission delay measured in minutes.

"It would depend on the load of the buoy. If no one else was using it, or if its processing power was strong enough, the actual transmission of a single message could span the distance in less than a minute."

Silence reigned for a moment. "I want to see this."

"We're not in a position to devote the resources to that research right now," Annette said. "We've got higher-priority work that has to be done first. That's why I brought you down to meet Carl. Or perhaps I should say, Sir Carl. The emperor did knight the man, after all."

Jacqueline considered them both. "Okay, I'll bite. What projects are you working on now, if I can ask? How could my people or I help you? Does it revolve around some of the research we were doing at Dresden?"

Carl shook his head. "It doesn't. While all the work you've done appears fascinating, this revolves around flip-point physics. Have they explained to you where we are or how we got here?"

"No."

"You might as well pull up a chair. This is going to take a while."

Once the women had seated themselves, he continued. "One of the first things that we discovered when we explored the old Empire was that there was a different kind of flip point. One that was extremely difficult to detect but led to places that we'd never visited before.

"We've utilized one of them to get to a place that is safe for the moment. However, we believe that these new flip points have a special property that potentially allows for transit to multiple destinations, depending on the specific frequency of the output."

He gestured toward the disassembled parts. "Someone utilized this flip drive to do exactly that. We have to figure out how they did it and where they went from here."

"I'm not a flip-point physicist, but what you're saying is impossible."

Carl grinned. "Not really. In fact, we're going to send some probes through to verify the theory very shortly. Let me explain this in more detail. Get ready to have your mind blown."

Annette sat back and listened as he began explaining the physics behind the weak flip points to the disbelieving scientist. While much of the explanation was going to fly far over her head, she was pleased to see that the two were already working together. This was going to work out.

* * *

TALBOT ESCORTED a civilian survey team from the Dresden orbital down to the surface of the planet. To keep things simple, he chose a large island a good distance from where the other prisoners lived. Perhaps "prisoners" was the wrong term. "Unwilling colonists" might be more appropriate.

Since he was feeling a bit puckish, he dubbed the island Atlantis.

After all, it was going to be the home of the high-tech civilization among the primitives.

The civilians doing the survey were a surly lot. He couldn't blame them. They were completely uprooting these people and stranding them on an unknown world. Likely for the rest of their lives.

Considering what the Rebel Empire stood for, his sympathy was limited. If his side won this war, they'd come back and relocate these people. If they didn't win, well, at least they'd survive.

Once he had the construction people surveying the island to find a location for their new home, he set out to get detailed scans of the entire island and its surroundings. He'd chosen a large harbor as the primary city location for Atlantis. That way, when they built oceangoing vessels, it would be handy.

Commodore Anderson had ordered him to get decent scans of every island within striking distance of Atlantis. Other teams were busy scanning all the other potentially habitable landmasses. They wanted to be sure that they knew the location of every single group of colonists. It wouldn't do to have some folks isolated and left to suffer.

It only took a few hours for something to pop up as unusual. They were flying over a moderately sized landmass centered on an extinct or dormant volcano when the scanners read something artificial. This place was far away from where any other colonists had been located, so he was curious.

Talbot ordered the pilot to bring them around for a closer pass. The target was camouflaged fairly well.

Sitting along the western side of the island were the remains of a moderately large town. The vegetation had encroached completely into the area, making it look like a wilderness. He could see why he hadn't seen it from orbit.

He zoomed the scanner in and examined one of the buildings. It was roughly done, but obviously made of modern materials. Imperial materials. The style was also one he was moderately familiar with from his time on Harrison's World. He'd seen similar structures when visiting some of the small towns.

"Find us a good place to land near that town," Talbot instructed the pilot.

"Aye, sir."

The cutter pilot brought them down into a clearing about half a kilometer away from the ruined town.

Talbot knew that he should probably let someone know where he was going, but he wanted to take a good look at the place first. No one had occupied this place for a very long time, so it should be relatively safe.

He dug out some unpowered armor from one of the storage bins and verified that he had plenty of flechettes for the pistol he always carried. Just to be safe, he grabbed the flechette rifle kept with the armor. He doubted there were any wild animals that could hurt him, based on their previous scans of the planet, but he'd play it safe.

"Take the cutter back up over the town and circle around," he told the pilot. "I'll stay in communication with you every ten minutes. If you can't get ahold of me, call for backup."

He exited the cutter and headed toward the town. The vegetation he was crossing through was very similar to what he'd found on the other islands. All of the separate landmasses must've been connected at one point. Everything was too homogenous to have developed separately.

With the rough terrain, it took him about twenty minutes to get to the outskirts of the town. Some buildings were made of plascrete, though roughly done. Barring serious damage, they'd last a long, long time.

Not all the buildings around him were that sturdy, though. Many of them were made of local materials and had collapsed. He could see trees growing out of what had once been buildings made of wood or stone.

Talbot resisted the urge to go inside any of them. He'd save that for the larger ones near the center of town.

Large was a relative term. The tallest structure looked to be about eight or nine stories. Maybe ten, at most. It was also made of plascrete, but someone had taken the time to make it actually look good.

Even after all this time, the walls were still bright white, and he could see inlaid pieces in the plascrete that gave it darker accents. It looked very sleek and completely out of place in this wilderness.

The doors leading into the front of the building were closed but not locked. With his pistol in hand, he cautiously went inside. The bottom floor appeared to be mainly a large lobby. A wide desk with places for half a dozen people stood in front of the bank of elevators.

The wall behind the desk had the Fleet emblem across its entire width, with the almost-unnecessary words below it: Fleet Headquarters.

It seems he'd found where the ghosts had set up shop after they'd fled through the weak flip point.

16

Raul Castille looked around to see if anyone was sitting close enough to overhear what he was about to say to Veronica. Realistically, he knew that the enemy could be monitoring them closely, but the other diners were making enough noise to perhaps shield what he was about to say.

"I think I've come up with an escape plan."

She raised an eyebrow. "Where would we go? Are you planning to steal one of the flip-capable warships? That seems a little bit of a stretch."

"No. I'm smart enough to realize we don't have the manpower or access for something like that. I'm talking about hiding until these people are gone. They're not going to stay here in this system forever. Once they've left, the Empire will eventually come and find us."

The woman gave him a look that said she was not convinced. "I'm not sure that's the best idea. In fact, I'm not sure of anything at this point."

He frowned. "What does that mean?"

She gestured at the people around them. "My people and I have been doing research on what they say happened during the revolution.

I went into that project with the full expectation that we'd quickly find the forgeries. Now, I'm not so sure."

"Of course they're feeding us lies," he said derisively. "You can't possibly believe that fiction they're spouting. That the lords have enslaved us? You are a Fleet officer. You should know better."

"We've done a lot of reading," she said quietly. "Their library of books is quite extensive. I'm talking exabytes of data. It can't all be faked. Looking back at the time of the revolution, none of what they have indicates anything like what they taught us in history class."

Raul rubbed his forehead. "I can't believe we're even having this conversation. How could you possibly believe anything you're reading?"

She shrugged. "One of my officers picked a few books that he'd read before. Heirlooms handed down through his family since the revolution. Actual, physical books.

"He was only passingly familiar with a few of them, but some he knew by heart. There's no way these people could know which books to leave in the same condition as what my officer had read. None."

"And you're saying that these books your officer knew were precisely as he remembered? Please. No one has that good of a memory."

"His memory is pretty good. If he says that he can't find anything in that particular volume that looks different, I believe him. If one book is accurate, I have to wonder how many others are."

He shook his head strongly. "That kind of talk is treason. I suggest for your own well-being that you reconsider what you're saying."

"Don't be an idiot. I'm not disloyal to the Empire. The problem is that I'm not a rubber-stamping yes woman, either. If we ever hope to understand who these people really are, we have to understand our own history, and we need to be sure that it's true. At this point, I'm not convinced it is."

He stared at her coolly. "So you're saying that you have no intention of trying to escape with me?"

"That's not what I'm saying at all. We have a duty to escape. If you have a plan with a reasonable chance of success, I'll do whatever I can to make it happen."

He relaxed a little. He hadn't realized he'd tensed up. "Good. Good. I've overheard a number of people talking about the planet we're orbiting. Apparently, it's where the ghosts have been keeping the people they've captured during their raids. Mostly the higher orders.

"They've also located the island used by the ghosts before they departed this world. Details are sketchy about both groups, but if we can escape to the surface of the planet, we can hide among the people that are already down there. They will help us.

"Eventually, someone will come looking. When that happens, we can all get off this planet and take the knowledge we've gained with us. The lords need to know what we've found out about these people."

Her eyes turned toward the guards leaning against the wall. "How do you intend to get past our armed watchers?"

He smiled. "That's all a matter of timing. You see, my guards keep watch on me, and your guards keep watch on you. They're not working as a concerted whole, but as two separate entities. We can use that lack of communication to our advantage."

"Sounds tricky. As soon as we attack, alarms will go off throughout the ship. How are we going to get to the docking bay, steal a cutter, dodge the fighters these people have, and land on a planet without them knowing where we've gone?"

"That sounds like defeatism. You need to trust that we're going to have some luck fall our way."

She grunted. "The problem with luck is that it comes in two flavors: good and bad. I'm certain we're going to have some kind of luck. I just suspect some of it is not going to be the kind we want. How do you want to do this?"

"Here's what I have in mind…"

* * *

KELSEY LOOKED around the massive lobby with amazement. "How in the world did people running for their lives build something like this?"

Talbot shrugged. "I have no idea. They had the liner with them, so they might have had some skilled construction people they could tap. Maybe even some equipment. Or they could have built this place a hundred years later.

"I've had my people sweep the building from top to bottom. The previous occupants stripped all the computers out. We haven't found a single electronic device of any kind. Nothing with any writing at all. Someone scrubbed this building."

"Surely they couldn't have done that to the whole town."

"You might be surprised. We selected a few buildings at random and turned up very similar results. The town appears as though they abandoned it in a very orderly fashion.

"They swept it from one end to the other looking for anything they'd missed. If it were me, I'd have had multiple teams. One group to sweep behind the first. Perhaps even a third."

"It's not very helpful," she said sourly. "This is obviously where the survivors from Fleet set up shop. The thing is, I'm not really sure why. They had their ships. They're obviously using them to harass the Rebel Empire. This world is okay, but why pick it?"

"I'm going to bet it took time for them to figure out how to use the weak flip points," Talbot said. "If they didn't have someone like Carl along, it might have taken them years to grasp what they were dealing with. Fleet engineers are pretty bright people, but there are limits to what they can do.

"If I had to wager a guess, they used the liner to test out their first-generation flip modulator. It failed spectacularly. That would make them slow down."

That made sense. If they didn't have someone to work out the theory, it might have taken them decades to work it out. That more than explained the town they were standing in.

"Well, we need to be thorough," she said. "I want you and your people to search every building that seems safe to enter. Leave no stone unturned. Pick a few that aren't safe and see about having the engineers help move the rubble. Perhaps something was left there."

"I'm not holding out too much hope," he said. "These people were pretty damned thorough."

Once he'd left, Kelsey stared up at the Fleet emblem on the wall. What must it have been like for those people? They'd obviously fled during the height of the rebellion. This place must've seemed like a godsend. No pursuit and a chance to live out their lives in peace.

But at some point, they'd made the discovery they could use the weak flip point to travel to other systems. Ones not occupied by the Rebel Empire.

They'd relocated. From the rumors that she'd heard, these people attacked the Rebel Empire where they could and then vanished as if they had never been.

It had to drive the AIs nuts.

They'd undoubtedly lost ships along the way. They'd probably never had very many to begin with. If she had to guess, the ghosts probably came from a single task group assigned to escort the liner, and perhaps a few other vessels they'd picked up along the way.

She imagined that the discovery of multiple destinations through the weak flip points had inspired them to move on and then to use them to attack their enemies. Guerrilla warfare.

Now they lurked in the dark, striking out at their enemies from the shadows, and then vanishing without a trace. No wonder the Rebel Empire called them ghosts. The supernatural overtones were almost inevitable.

It fell to her and her people to find out where these descendants of loyalists lived now. They'd obviously decided to use the first world they'd discovered to house the prisoners they'd captured. The ones they didn't like anyway. That meant they'd found more desirable worlds that they lived on now.

They took the lower orders elsewhere. Hypothetically, there were probably several other strata to the society that had formed around these ghosts.

Based on this building, Fleet service might be one of them. Certainly, it had to be important to them. Even more important than it had been for the Old Empire. Fleet was all that stood between them and death.

Kelsey sighed. This wasn't getting them any closer to solving the mysteries. If they were going to find a way to track these ghosts, then it was going to fall to Carl and his people. There were obviously more destinations to be discovered using the weak flip point. Her friend just needed to find them.

She supposed she needed to stop using the phrase "weak flip point." Carl had been tossing around a new name. Multiflip point. That was a hell of a lot more descriptive, so it was time for her to endorse its use. She'd spread the word once she got back into orbit.

Finding this town had excited her so much. She'd figured that they could finally get answers to some of her questions. Yet the people they were following had proved cautious and thorough. It was going to take a lot more work to track them down.

Once she did, then the delicate dance would begin. These people had no reason to trust anyone. They'd been at war for five hundred years. It would be all too easy for them to assume that her task group was a Rebel Empire unit and attack.

Whenever they found these people, she was going to need to proceed very, *very* carefully. They needed allies, not more enemies.

These ghosts had absolutely no reason to trust her people. She needed to come up with a reason why they should. So far, that had eluded her.

After taking one last look at the wall, Kelsey headed toward her cutter. It was time to get back to work.

17

_____

E ven after thinking about Castille's plan overnight, Veronica still thought he was insane, but she really didn't have a choice. He was a security officer. If she didn't follow his instructions, the end result would not be pretty. Once the lords found them again—which they would—it would be the end of her. Perhaps literally.

Timing was going to be key in making this work. If the two of them were not precisely where they needed to be at exactly the right moment, it couldn't happen.

Thankfully, cranial implants made keeping precise time a simple task. She gathered her officers and informed their guards they were going to eat lunch as a group.

Even with the larger number of prisoners, the two guards still felt they had control of the situation with their stunners. They followed along somewhat behind Veronica and her officers to keep them at a safe distance.

On a ship of this size, with as many people as were around them, that would normally be perfectly adequate. Unfortunately for them, Raul Castille had taken this behavior into account. At a predetermined cross corridor, he stepped out at just the right moment to surprise her guards.

She had to admit he made quick work of them. They had no chance to stop his explosive attack.

Not that she had time to watch. She whirled and threw herself at his guards. All of her hand-to-hand training came to her rescue with a spinning back kick that caught one of them in the head. He dropped without a sound.

Two of her officers took out the final man just as quickly.

Veronica expected the overhead alarms to begin screaming, but they were silent. The guards had not gotten an alert out before they'd gone down. That was an unexpected bit of good luck. The original plan had called for them to retreat as quickly as possible while the ship searched for them.

Castille shot all four men with the stunner he'd appropriated. They quickly stashed the unconscious marines in a handy compartment. He'd chosen a section of the ship with less traffic, and fortune had favored them with no inconvenient witnesses.

"Where is the Commodore?" she asked.

"She won't be joining us. She and the rest of the orbital staff will be staying here. Don't worry. They'll keep their mouths shut."

That might mean a number of different things. Veronica hoped it was just mulishness on the commodore's part and not something more sinister.

Still, she had to admit that she felt some relief at avoiding close quarters with the obnoxious woman. A single visit had convinced her that she wanted nothing to do with Murdock.

Since they all wore Fleet uniforms, no one raised an eyebrow as they headed for the landing bay. She could only barely suppress her paranoia. Everyone they passed seemed to be staring at them.

Castille stepped next to her. "That went well."

"Better than I'd expected," she admitted. "I hope we're able to appropriate a cutter before they discover we've escaped."

"Me too," he admitted. "From everything I've heard they're busy exploring the planet below us. There are a number of cutters going up and down. We should be able to insert ourselves into the traffic without too much trouble."

"I love your confidence."

Unfortunately, she didn't share it. The odds of them being able to hijack a cutter without the pilot giving an alarm were low. In that case, they'd have to make a run for it anyway, but they'd have other ships in pursuit. There would be no chance to hide themselves on the planet's surface.

The landing bay was just as large as she'd remembered. It obviously serviced a lot of small craft.

It only took a moment to pick out a cutter that was just coming in for a landing near them. She gestured for the pilot to open the boarding ramp as he settled down, and he nodded.

She led her people up the ramp as if she belonged there. Two marines stood in the center of the cutter, bracketing a well-dressed woman. Based upon the restraints, she was a prisoner.

Interestingly, Veronica didn't detect cranial implants in the woman. She was obviously of the lower orders. Why was she here? What did she know?

One of the marines pushed the woman a step forward. "We'll turn her over to you, Commander."

"Yes, you will." She shot him with her stunner.

Her executive officer took out his partner before the first man even finished collapsing.

The woman opened her mouth to say something, but Veronica shot her too.

Castille sprinted toward the cockpit and stunned the pilot. A quick search of the cutter verified that no one else was aboard.

Veronica stepped back out to the cutter and looked around. No one seemed to be paying any attention to them. Excellent.

She made her way to the cockpit as they secured the prisoners and closed the cutter up. A query of her implants revealed the cutter wasn't locked.

"It's not secured," she said through the open hatch. "The good luck just keeps coming. I've accessed the communications log. I have their call sign."

With a deep breath, she initiated communications with flight control.

"Control, this is foxtrot seven five two requesting departure."

"Stand by, foxtrot seven five two."

For a moment, she worried the man had realized it wasn't the same person speaking to him. Then he continued. "You are cleared for outbound departure, foxtrot seven five two."

"Copy that. Thank you, Control."

She deftly lifted the cutter off the deck and turned it toward the exit. A gentle application of acceleration slid them smoothly outside of the ship. They were in space.

Other cutters were moving back and forth between the ships and the planet. It seemed that their destination was on the other side of the planet. That was good enough for her. She fell in behind one of the other cutters and followed it around.

Many of the cutters headed toward a series of islands, but she saw one rising from a much larger island that was significantly farther away from the first cluster. Perfect.

Based on the level of traffic, that other location would be a much better hiding place. It also had a large volcano near the center of the island. It must've been inactive, because there was a large lake filling it.

Even better.

Once the cutter she'd seen departing the island was out of scanner range, she changed course and darted toward the volcano.

It had experienced a significant eruption at some point in the distant past. One side of the caldera had blown out. The lake that filled the interior came up right to the edge.

Her scanners couldn't detect how deep the water was, but that was kind of the point. Once she submerged, no one would find them that easily. They could hide out at the bottom and wait for their enemies to depart.

The interior of the volcano was interesting. It seemed as though they were not the only visitors. Someone had taken the time to carve a deep ledge at the base of the caldera near the water line.

With the missing side, the water would never rise high enough to flood it. Interestingly, the pocket was deep enough to land a cutter in. With all the stone all around it, no external signals would be able to reach the cutter.

That meant their enemies would be unable to detect or control the cutter remotely. It only took a moment for her to make the decision to change their course.

She brought the cutter inside the large landing area—for that was exactly what it appeared to be—and settled on the flat stone.

She shut down the cutter's systems and ordered her officers to locate and disconnect the power supplies from all systems. That way no signals would go out, and it wouldn't respond to remote commands.

The ramp lowered. A minute later, the consoles went dark. They were safe.

She smiled at Castille as she came into the back. "I didn't think we'd pull it off. Congratulations. Your plan was brilliant."

He grinned back at her. "I wish I could say that I hadn't had my own doubts, but I'd be lying. What is this place?"

Veronica shrugged. "The only way to know for sure is to go take a look. Our guests will be out for a few more hours."

To say the interior of the landing area was gloomy would be something of an understatement. The reflected sunlight cast some illumination inside the hollowed-out landing area, but not nearly enough to see much detail.

She searched the compartments inside the cutter until she found a stash of handheld lights. Once everyone had taken one for themselves, she stepped out onto the landing pad.

It was obviously man-made. The stone was far too smooth to be natural. The scuff marks indicated other vessels had landed here in the past.

The rear of the landing area had a standard Imperial hatch imbedded in the wall. The mystery deepened. What the hell was this place?

* * *

"WHAT DO you mean they've escaped?" Talbot demanded.

He'd barely had time to step on board *Audacious* to brief the commodore when the marine acting as the head of the carrier's security element cornered him.

Lieutenant Yvonne Gutierrez shrank a little. "We don't know yet, Major. Their guards went to relieve the duty marines and couldn't find them. An implant search led to a compartment near the officers' mess. We're searching the ship. We'll find them."

The woman took a deep breath. "They didn't all escape. Commander Castille killed the senior staff from the orbital. Commodore Murdock was the only survivor. He broke her neck, but she was still alive.

"I called an emergency medical team, and they managed to resuscitate her. No word on if she'll make it, but someone wanted them all dead."

He resisted the impulse to curse. It wouldn't help. No matter how good it might feel. "I want to know the moment you find them. Get more marines to the flight deck too."

"Aye, sir."

He headed for the lift. This was just terrific. How in the world had they managed to turn the tables on their guards?

There'd been a risk of trouble when they'd agreed to allow them to access to the ship. Never in his wildest dreams had he envisioned them actually escaping.

He sighed. Well, there was no getting around it. He needed to explain this to the commodore.

Minutes later, he arrived to find the flag bridge in a state of almost chaos. Zia turned to him. "Do we know what happened?"

"Not precisely. It seems they overpowered all four guards without an alarm getting out."

Commodore Anderson said something not suitable for a senior officer. "I'm looking at the flight logs now. We've had a lot of cutters land and take off. With ferrying people away from the Dresden orbital, a lot of boats stop here to pick up things to take down to the surface."

One of her officers raised his head. "Ma'am, I've identified a cutter than never returned to base. It's not answering any of our calls, and I'm not getting a transponder ping."

Talbot checked the information through his implants. "It looks like the cutter came from *Persephone*."

The commodore frowned. "What the heck would they be doing here? I'll ping them."

After a few moments, her face paled. "Oh crap. They were bringing Kelsey's mother. Apparently, she'd raised hell, so they were sending her over to spend a few days in a real cell."

He stared at the planet on the main display. "They have her, then. Somewhere down there. Kelsey is going to go ballistic."

"And with every reason," Zia said. "We'll get every boat we have searching for them. We'll find them."

Talbot wished he believed that, but he didn't. They'd underestimated the prisoners. Now they'd pay the price for their arrogance.

18

Kelsey stared at Zia through the communications screen on her desk. "What do you mean they've kidnapped my mother?"

Her voice was so calm that it felt as if she were watching her reaction from the sidelines.

Zia's mouth turned downward. "It seems that our prisoners came up with a grand plan to take out one another's guards. Commander Castille and Commander Giguere arrived at a certain cross corridor at the same moment. That allowed each group to attack the other's guards.

"We didn't foresee this level of coordination. We should have had more stringent monitoring and additional guards."

Kelsey let out a long, slow breath. "There'll be plenty of time to lose my temper later. How long have they been gone?"

"Over an hour. Closer to two. All indications are that they've gone to ground on the planet. The landing zones were on the other side of the planet from *Audacious*, so we didn't see precisely where they went.

"I've diverted all available cutters to begin an in-depth search. If it were me, I'd have submerged the cutter in water just off a coast. That would eliminate the possibility that our scanners would pick them up.

All they have to do at this point is wait. Sooner or later, we're going to leave."

Kelsey felt her lips compress. "I'm not going anywhere without my mother. She might be a huge pain in my ass, but she's my *mother*. Deploy as many marines as you feel comfortable with down to the surface. I want every island scoured from one end to the other. Leave no cranny unexplored."

Zia nodded. "Already in progress. Kelsey, I'm really sorry."

The princess sighed. "The precautions sounded reasonable to me too. It's easy to forget that we're not the only people that can pull off miraculous escapes. They didn't hurt their guards, so it's unlikely they'll hurt my mother.

"We'll find them. It's just going to be a matter of searching for a needle in a haystack. Do the best you can and keep me informed."

"Aye, ma'am," Zia said. "*Audacious* out."

Kelsey buried her face in her hands. Oh God. How could one little woman cause her so much trouble?

Intellectually, she knew that her mother wasn't to blame for this particular incident. That didn't stop her from blaming her emotionally. That was unfair, but it was going to take Kelsey a long time before she saw her mother differently.

Her implants chimed with another incoming call. This time from Carl. She put him on the screen.

"You better not have bad news," she said bluntly.

He raised an eyebrow. "Why? Are you getting lots of bad news right now? Anything I should know about?"

"You first."

"Okay. We think we've got the flip tuner worked out. I have a prototype installed on a regular probe that we can test. If, of course, you think that's okay."

She sat up straighter. "That's good news. The probes we left in the other system say it's empty right now. How do we need to do this? How does this even work?"

The young scientist seemed to consider for a moment how to phrase his answer. "In a general sense, the flip tuner focuses the energy put out by the flip drive into a narrow band of frequencies.

With a regular flip point, that's not necessary. It only has one destination.

"With a multiflip point, there are alternate paths that—supposedly —a ship can transit. We have to fine-tune where the energy resonates. The frequency of the vibration is what I believe makes one path more likely than another."

Kelsey didn't pretend to know much at all about flip-point physics. "If you say so. Are we even certain that there are multiple destinations available to us?"

Carl shrugged. "Theoretically, yes. Practically? We won't know until we find one. At this point, I have no way of scanning a multiflip point to determine how many potential destinations it has or even what frequencies would work to get us there. The science is too immature. Perhaps once we've used this one, the process will become clearer."

"We'll double check with the probes on guard in the other system first. We absolutely do not want to transit something they might detect through that flip point."

"Got it," he said. "Now, what bad news is raining on your parade?"

"The senior officers from the destroyer and Commander Castille from the orbital escaped. They're somewhere on the planet. Worse, they got their hands on my mother, two marines, and a cutter pilot."

Carl winced. "Okay, that's bad news. Do you think they're in any danger?"

"Realistically? No. Of course, all that changes if my mother won't shut up. They might just shoot her to keep her quiet."

The young man laughed a little. "They may not be our Fleet, but I think they have the restraint to avoid something like that. Particularly since they're probably worried we'll find them."

"Do you have anything in your bag of tricks that might allow us to find them more easily?"

"Nothing springs to mind, but I'll give it a little bit of thought. Also, I have one other bit of good news. The researchers that we liberated are working with me to help bypass the lockouts on the manufacturing equipment. No guarantees, but they're a pretty smart bunch. We might manage to get everything working in spite of the lockout."

"If there's anything that I can do to help, just let me know," Kelsey said. "What about an AI? Did they have enough equipment on the orbital to actually build one?"

"I sent some of the engineering people from *Audacious* to look, but they didn't find anything. Well, not AI hardware like we've seen before anyway. They did find some equipment that might be connected with the AI project, but I'm not ready to talk about it until I'm sure what I have. It might prove useful, but it might just be a curiosity too."

"Understood. Great work."

The young man smiled. "Thank you. Which ship am I going out to the flip point on? *Persephone* or *Audacious*?"

As much as she wanted to stay close by, Kelsey knew that Zia could conduct the search more effectively than she could.

"I'll take you out there. I need something to distract me. I'll call the bridge and get us moving."

Once Kelsey finished talking with him, she got the ship under way and leaned back in her chair. Why did life have to be so complicated?

* * *

ANNETTE BROUGHT her fighter into a flat arc over the island Talbot had found. The scanners registered a number of ships and people, but tagged them all as friendlies. The missing cutter was nowhere in sight.

That meant it was either somewhere under the water or on another island entirely.

Frankly, "island" was the wrong word to use in describing this place. It might be smaller than a continent, but it was certainly larger than what she considered an island. If they had to search it closely, they'd be working for months.

The escaped prisoners had an entire planet to hide on. There was no way they were going to discover them unless they got lucky.

With a sigh, she brought up a plot of the general area and looked at how the squadron was deployed. Some of the fighters were covering other portions of the island, while the rest scanned as deeply into the water as they could, looking for any anomalies.

She made a wide circle around the volcano at the center of the island. It was a little too prominent to be the escaped prisoners' chosen hideout, but it paid to be thorough.

The scanners penetrated the rock deeply enough to be certain that it was natural stone. A few lava tubes were large enough to show up on the scans. No unusual metals.

Annette made one pass over the top of the volcano, looking down as she inverted her fighter. There was water down inside the caldera. Her scanners couldn't penetrate to the bottom. It was as impenetrable as the ocean.

She weighed the option of going down and immersing her fighter, but decided it wasn't worth it. It would take her hours to search the water inside that thing. Time better spent looking for the prisoners over a wider area.

* * *

RAUL WATCHED the fighter arc across the sky from his hiding place in a deep crevice near the excavated landing pad. Once it vanished, he waited for it to come back. If the pilot had spotted anything out of the ordinary, he'd come back for a second look.

Nothing.

He had to admit that he was surprised. Even with the positive face he put on for Commander Giguere, he'd secretly expected their enemies to recapture them quickly. This type of convenient escape only happened in fiction.

Once he'd convinced himself that they were still safe, he made his way up the crack until he could see down into the caldera from a small ledge. Whoever had built the concealed landing area had done so in a way that made it invisible from above. Based on the coating they'd found on the rock inside it, it was shielded against scanners.

Someone had wanted to be absolutely certain that no one knew about this hidden facility.

He made his way back down the crevice and to the landing area.

He walked past the powered-down cutter and stopped where the rest of them had gathered next to the sealed hatch.

Lieutenant Bakersfield—Commander Giguere's engineering officer—was still working on it. Personally, he was about ready to suggest something more forceful. Living out of a cutter would be uncomfortable enough, even if it had power. Without power, it would be horrible.

"Are you certain that you're going to be able to open that hatch, Commander?" he asked politely.

The man nodded. "I've already got access to the control panel, sir. I'm just trying to figure out which sequence of codes will trigger the hatch to unlock. This isn't a very difficult entry. It really wasn't meant to keep people out."

Raul raised an eyebrow. "Truly? It seems to me that locks are made specifically for keeping people out."

"Perhaps it would be better to say that this lock is only meant to keep honest people honest. Anyone could force their way in without much difficulty. We're only working this carefully in an attempt to keep the hatch intact."

Moments later, the light above the lock turned green, and they all heard the sound of bolts retracting.

The man grinned at Raul. "See? Piece of cake."

Those of them with stunners raised them as the hatch slid open. The short corridor just inside was initially dark, but the overhead lights came on as soon as Commander Giguere stepped inside.

"It still has power," she said. "That can't be good. An operating fusion plant will lead them right to us."

Raul shook his head. "I think not. While I was outside, I saw a fighter fly overhead. If it had detected either the cutter or a fusion plant, it would've come back. Whatever is down here, it's well shielded. That makes it very interesting to me. I love secrets. Especially when they belong to other people."

The woman smiled a bit. "Then let's go see what they're hiding."

19

K elsey watched Carl work at his borrowed console. The young scientist was always so focused. Once he'd settled in, it seemed as though he'd forgotten the rest of them were on the bridge.

He'd tried to explain some of the mathematics and flip physics to her, but she'd waved him off. She knew her limitations.

The probes they'd posted in the Rebel Empire system showed no enemy traffic. Of course, that could change at a moment's notice. She'd taken the precaution of positioning a probe on the other side of the multiflip point and two more watching that system's regular flip points.

The distant probes would send their information back to them at light speed, so it was always possible that someone would arrive in the system while they were conducting the test. That was a risk, but one they'd have to take.

This would be the perfect time to use one of Carl's FTL coms, but she still worried that a passing Rebel Empire ship would detect something. The temptation was strong, but she resisted the impulse.

She turned toward Carl. "It looks as though the system is clear. Proceed with the test."

"Yes, ma'am."

Carl manipulated his controls, and the probe she was watching through her implants vanished. It had successfully flipped, but they wouldn't know for another minute if it went to the system they knew about or somewhere completely new.

The timer counted down, and the probe reappeared on their scanners. It began streaming data immediately.

Kelsey didn't even need to wait for Carl to speak to know that his frequency tuner had worked. The system the probe had arrived in wasn't the one they'd fled through. This one was occupied.

"The probe appears to have gone to a different system," he said after a moment. "I'm detecting radio transmissions. Lots of them."

"So I see. Congratulations. What can you tell me about this new system?"

He turned in his seat to face her. "Even at a glance, it's easy to tell that it's heavily occupied. I'm detecting hundreds of grav drives moving around. There are also signals coming from multiple areas of the system as well.

"Based on this information, I believe this new system is more heavily occupied than any Rebel Empire system we've seen to date. Ma'am, I think this might be a core world."

"It's far too early to make that kind of assessment," she said. "We'll continue examining the data and allow the facts to lead us where they do. Make sure to shunt all this to operations. I want our intelligence staff combing through what you've picked up.

"A minute's worth of data isn't enough to make any kind of assessment. Was there anything close enough to the multiflip point to detect the probe?"

"No. The multiflip point is far enough off the beaten path to prevent anyone from detecting a ship flipping in. The probe is completely safe."

"It's a little early to send a ship, but that's good information to have. Get the probe back on station and have it monitor for an hour. That should give us a better baseline of how many ships are in the system, whose they are, and which system it is."

He nodded. "The system is definitely occupied by humans. The unencrypted traffic is in Standard. I may be able to identify it based on the visible stars.

"That's not something that the Old Empire needed to do, but I've made progress updating their flip charts to consider the most prominent stellar masses in our section of the explored galaxy. At the very least, I should be able to roughly place which sector the system lies in."

"Do that," she said. "Now that you've proved your theory is correct, can you tell if this is the only other possible destination?"

"Not without trying a number of additional test flips. The theory I'm working under says that energy inside a specific range should lead to a single destination. We need to determine how wide a window of energy is required for a specific branch.

"Theoretically, there could be as many as a dozen more. I suspect there will be fewer. The fact that its gravitational energy signature is so much weaker on this side indicates that it has more branches from this side than in the Rebel Empire system. Say five on this side, three on the other.

"Those are just numbers I've thrown out for comparison. I won't be able to make an educated guess of how many branches there are until I have an adequate baseline. That means we need to find more multiflip points to examine."

"I'm certain that we'll find more as we proceed, but we might not have the time to examine them as thoroughly as you'd like," Kelsey said. "Do the best you can in figuring this one out while we don't have someone breathing down our necks.

"You said you had other probes prepared. Just how long do you think it will take you to figure out how many branches this multiflip point has?"

"I'll be able to define the window of frequencies that leads to this new system inside half an hour. We might discover other destinations in the process. Once I have that information, it should only take three or four hours to probe all the potential windows.

"It's possible that some energy ranges won't actually take the probe anywhere. They might be dead zones of some kind. The theory indicates that's possible too. Also, based on the size of the window, it should allow me to determine whether or not a ship is capable of flipping to the target system."

Kelsey frowned. "I thought that once we had the ability to tune our flip drives, we would be able to pass through to any of the destinations."

He made an ambivalent gesture. "That assumes we'll be able to successfully incorporate these tuners into our flip drives. I'm extremely hesitant to recommend modifications to our existing hardware. It's just too dangerous.

"It looks as if the ghosts tried to build a tuner into the liner's flip drive. It burned out. There are significant limits to how much we can affect the frequency ranges on existing drives. The ship's overall mass plays a role too.

"Eventually, we'll be able to build new flip drives that have built-in tuners. Then we should be able to access all the possible branches in these multiflip points. Until then, our options might be limited."

She felt herself sighing. He was right. They absolutely couldn't take a chance of stranding one of their ships.

So, they'd be restricted to exploring systems that the carrier could transit to—if any. Thankfully, they didn't have to take the Dresden orbital any farther. Once they finished transferring the prisoners down to the surface, they could move it into the outer system.

"Are you going to be able to guess at the tonnage a particular destination will allow?" she asked. "Or if a ship's drive is even capable of reaching that system?"

He nodded. "*Persephone* has a very robust flip drive. While I can't say it's tunable, we can focus the output a little more tightly. That should allow her to make the flip into most of the systems on the other side of the multiflip point.

"I'm pretty sure the same is not true of *Audacious*. The more multiflip points I examine—and the more we transit—the better my future guess will be. I'll also need to attempt designing an external frequency tuner for *Audacious*. If I can, that might open up some possible destinations the carrier can reach."

"The ghosts probably had large ships. Maybe not in the same class as *Audacious*, but that means it's possible. Back to work and find us a way home. We don't transit unless you find something interesting."

With the search for the escaped prisoners showing no signs of immediate success, Kelsey knew they had time to examine this multiflip point in detail. Frankly, she was looking forward to learning more about the new system. It would distract her from worrying.

* * *

"They're not on this island," Talbot told Annette. "I'd hoped it would be that easy, but we'll have to expand the search."

The two of them sat in the temporary building the marines had erected on the island. The fighter pilot rubbed her face. "This is going to give me ulcers. How in the world did this happen? We had them locked down on a ship full of our people. Not only did they knock out their guards, they waltzed right down to the flight deck and stole a cutter. Who does that?"

He felt his lips quirk into a wry smile. "I seem to remember my wife pulling off a few stunts like this. We underestimated them.

"Look on the positive side. They didn't kill any of our people, so her mother is probably safe. As an added bonus, they have to listen to her bitch about everything. You can insert the obligatory mother-in-law joke here."

She gave him a quelling stare. "I wouldn't let your wife hear you say that. Logically, I know you're probably right, but that doesn't help.

"We have to do something. We can't just leave her here. Lord knows what she could tell them. Probably nothing militarily significant, but she knows the name of our home world. The marines and the pilot definitely know too much.

"If the Rebel Empire figures out where to come looking for us, they'll exterminate us. We absolutely cannot leave without recovering every single prisoner that escaped. Heaven help us if they've spread any classified information to the people down here. If they have, I don't know what we'll do."

"We've had ships ferrying people down to all the populated

locations," he said. "The missing cutter is not anywhere near the colonists."

"They could be moving underwater," Annette said. "Their speed shouldn't be tremendous, but they could be in any number of hidden locations at the bottom of the ocean by now."

"We've dropped listening buoys all around the islands," he said. "Cutters normally don't have to worry about making noise. Their engines vibrate in a manner that will produce a detectable signal of their passage, if they come close enough to a buoy.

"With them scattered all around the occupied islands, our escapees are not going to be able to come close to the colonists. As we clear each island, we can focus more of our forces on the rest. We'll very shortly know that the landmasses are clear.

"Then it becomes a waiting game. Their supplies aren't infinite. The cutter isn't designed to keep their air clean indefinitely or carry enough food and water for an extended hide. They're going to have to find a place on the surface. One where the colonists have planted food they can eat. When they do, we'll find them."

Talbot rubbed his face. "I just hope nobody finds us before we do."

20

It took several hours to satisfy Veronica that they'd examined every square centimeter of the abandoned base. By her estimation, the hidden facility had housed roughly a thousand people. It hadn't done so in quite some time, though. A thick layer of dust coated everything.

That made it very easy to determine that no one had been inside the base in hundreds of years.

In fact, the dust was so extreme that it made exploring the facility a filthy, choking experience. Clouds of the damned stuff rose any time someone dared step on it.

They'd retreated to the cutter and scavenged some emergency breathing masks. Those at least allowed them to both breathe and see.

Once they'd finished exploring the base, she sent her officers off to the edge of the lake to clean up. That required loosening some of the uniform constraints. It wasn't as though they'd brought any luggage. They only had the clothes on their backs.

Each of them washed their uniform and hung it from the cutter to dry. That left them sitting around in their underwear. Not exactly something Command would be pleased about.

Too bad.

Commander Castille bit into a survival bar. "I expected more from this place. You know, a secret lair filled with sharks wearing lasers. That sort of thing."

She chuckled. "Well, the joke's on us, then. This damned place is uninhabitable. If there's anything hidden, it's under a pile of dust."

"Why do you think they built it?"

She shrugged. "My guess is that the people running from the revolution built it. They wanted to avoid paying for their crimes. They shielded the fusion plant and this landing area damned well."

"They left a number of computers. Have we tried accessing them yet?"

"I tried to get into a few, but they're all locked," she said. "That isn't to say my people can't gain access. They're just going to need time to work on them."

Castille smiled sardonically. "We seem to have an abundance of time. Until we can be certain that our erstwhile captors have departed, we're stuck here. Judging from the amount of dirt inside that place, preparing quarters for our use is going to be a time-consuming, thankless job."

Veronica had to agree. She hated housecleaning on the best of days. This took it to a whole new level.

"While we couldn't gain access to the computers, that doesn't mean we didn't find any information," she said. "We picked up a number of tablets the builders left behind. We plugged them in. Once they've recharged, we'll see if there's anything worth recovering."

She gestured toward their still-unconscious prisoners. "What about them?"

Castille considered the four. "The marines won't talk. The pilot probably won't, either. The woman is a possibility, though."

"She's going to wake up soon. Do you think she'll have useful information?"

He shrugged. "I have personnel files from the station in my implant storage, and she's not anywhere in them. She doesn't look anything like a freighter crewman, so I doubt very much they picked her up off one of the in-system craft.

"Based on her clothing, she's someone of substance. Since she doesn't have implants, I might venture someone from a powerful mercantile family. We don't have many people on Dresden that fit into that category, and they'd all have implants. Her identity is a mystery."

One look at the woman's fingernails confirmed she hadn't worked a day in her life. No, she was wealthy. Most likely powerful too. At least until their captors got their hands on her.

Perhaps they'd captured her on the way to Dresden. It wasn't as though they had any insight into the roster of captives these people had. It was almost certain that they hadn't intended for Veronica to see this woman at all.

It was going to be interesting watching Commander Castille interrogate her. While wearing nothing but his underclothing.

She gestured toward the ceiling. "How long do you think they'll continue looking for us?"

"A long time," he said with a grunt. "We know things about them that they probably wouldn't like our superiors hearing.

"We don't know any of the important parts, yet. Where they're from being the biggest question. Somehow, I don't believe that they come from the system the crazy computer had pinned down.

"Not only are they too powerful, but they seem too knowledgeable. If they'd had access to even a portion of this technology, that mad computer would never have been able to hold them."

About that time, one of the marines twitched. The stunner effects were wearing off.

Castille stood and gestured toward the ramp. "Everyone out. Take the military prisoners with you. Stash them in a compartment on the base. I want to control what the woman sees when she wakes up. A bunch of mostly naked people will give her the wrong impression of what's going on."

Veronica raised an eyebrow as she stood. "And what kind of impression are you going to give in your underwear?"

He grinned. "A good one, from all accounts. However, I'm going to dress before she wakes up, even if it's still damp. If she's used to being in control, she's going to resist. Most of those types think Fleet officers are jumped-up proles. I can't afford to feed into the mind-set."

She walked down the ramp with him. He probably did cut a wide swath through the ladies. He wasn't her type, though. Not even close.

After he'd dressed and gone back inside the cutter, she stared out over the water. No matter what Castille believed, she strongly suspected the contents of the tablets—and even the computers themselves—would horrify the security officer, as they would her, if for different reasons.

Based on the long-abandoned state of this facility, if they could find any information at all, she'd be willing to trust that it was accurate.

She wondered what she would do if their captors had been truthful with her. What if the AIs truly were the monsters those people said? What if her entire life had been a lie?

At this point, did it really matter? She'd served the Empire for decades. Was she going to stop now?

Would Castille even let them stop? Would he want to? Security officers were intensely dedicated to the Empire. He'd keep fighting, even if the truth was ugly.

That raised an interesting question. Did he already know the answers to the questions she'd been asking herself? Did he willingly serve things like Levy thought the AIs were?

She sighed. No matter how this played out, their lives were changing. She could feel it in her bones.

* * *

RAUL SAT near where the prisoner lay on one of the acceleration couches. He'd left her hands bound in front of her, so she'd be fairly comfortable. He might have to change that if she proved uncooperative.

The woman's eyelids flickered momentarily and then flew open. She raised her hands to her head and groaned.

He sympathized. Stunners left the most obnoxious headaches.

"My apologies for the rough manner in which you've been treated," he said.

She glared at him. "What the hell is going on here? Who the hell are you?"

"My name is Raul Castille. I'm afraid that you're still a prisoner, but you've traded up for a better class of captor."

The woman rubbed her temples with her fingertips. "That remains to be seen."

He spread his hands with a smile. "Now that you're awake, why don't we get to know one another? While it's true that I have you at a disadvantage, our situation is not all one-sided. For example, I don't know who you are. Perhaps you could enlighten me."

"How could you possibly *not* know who I am? Were you born in a cave?"

He blinked, nonplussed. "Apparently so. I take it that you believe yourself to be someone important. You're going to have to give me a few pointers if you expect me to grovel appropriately."

The woman managed to draw herself up haughtily. "I am Justine Bandar."

"You're related to Kelsey Bandar? Why did she have you in custody?"

The woman stared at him as though he were an imbecile. "I'm Justine Bandar, ex-wife to the Terran emperor, mother to the crown princess. One of the most powerful nobles in the Empire."

She sounded so arrogant that he had no difficulty believing that she was telling the truth. Except for the fact that he wasn't ready to buy into this story that there was another Empire.

"Ah. I see the problem. I'm not from the Empire. At least, not *your* Empire."

Her eyes narrowed. "Seriously? I thought my daughter was making that up."

Raul opened his mouth to say something, but closed it again. He wasn't quite certain how to respond. He'd expected defiance or fear, not whatever this was.

"Well," he said after a moment. "This is going to be a refreshing change of pace for me. Why was your daughter holding you prisoner? Did you break some law?"

"If I'm not going to give my daughter the satisfaction of cooperating with this absurd charade, what makes you think I'm going to behave any differently toward you? I did nothing wrong."

Yes, this was going to be significantly different from his normal interrogation technique. The woman wasn't going to be much of a physical threat, so perhaps he should lead with the carrot.

He rose to his feet and stepped toward her. "Now that you're awake and I have a better idea of who I'm dealing with, I think it's safe enough to unlock those restraints."

She wasted no time in extending her hands toward him.

Once he removed the cuffs, she rubbed her wrists. "At least this is a step in the right direction. That doesn't make up for you giving me this beastly headache.

"My daughter has kept me locked in a dreary little room since she caught me. I was never one to pay much attention to the news. I honestly have no idea who you are."

Raul had worked almost exclusively with Fleet personnel for the last decade. His experience in dealing with civilians—particularly those belonging to the higher orders—was strictly limited. That's what this woman was, though she probably used different words to describe her social class.

"It sounds as though your daughter did you a great injustice," he said, making certain to have a compassionate tone.

"You have no idea. This is all so much more complicated than it needed to be."

"It turns out that I have time to listen, and I'm told that I have a sympathetic ear."

Justine Bandar considered him for a moment. "Perhaps the two of us do have the potential to exchange information. I'll tell you my story, if you tell me yours. And I want some water and a pain pill."

He had absolutely no idea what they were going to discuss, but if it gave him insight into the enemy, it was more than worth the time to be chatty. It only took him a moment to get her some water and a pain pill.

Raul handed them to her and leaned back in his chair. "You have my word that I will share information as freely as you do. Why don't you begin?"

This was going to be fascinating.

21

It only took Carl about fifteen minutes to identify the occupied system. The maps they had of the old Terran Empire called it Archibald.

Kelsey thought that was one hell of a name. Archibald was one of the original core worlds. *Persephone*'s database listed it as once having a population above ten billion.

Of course, that was before the Fall. Based on the space traffic they'd observed and the sheer number of communications they'd intercepted, that was probably still accurate.

It's population undoubtedly dwarfed Avalon's. She'd seen the recordings of Imperial City in the old days. Cities like that probably covered Archibald.

While the historical data available to her was interesting, Kelsey sat on pins and needles waiting for the probe to return with more information. It arrived on schedule without any issues and began streaming what it had captured into their systems.

It was going to take time to make sense of all the details. All she wanted from the initial readings was a feel for how dangerous this place was going to be for them.

Carl looked up from his console. "Based on the communications the probe intercepted, I can confirm that this is Archibald."

Kelsey stood and walked over to him. "That's nice, but it doesn't really get us where we need to go."

"I agree," he said. "Several of the other probes we've sent out have found other flip branches that are potentially more useful. Both are empty systems that aren't on any Imperial map that I've discovered."

"Any sign of the ghosts?"

"Nothing yet. That doesn't mean they didn't use those systems, though. They had to go somewhere. Also, I need to check the multiflip point from the other side."

Kelsey cocked her head. "You mean the two sides might access different systems?"

The young scientist nodded. "Almost certainly. Just because it links to the system we're in with one branch doesn't mean that all of its available branches will go to the same locations as this side. We're going to have to do a thorough check to be sure."

Kelsey supposed that made sense. Exploring these new multiflip points was going to be incredibly complex. If she understood correctly, it was theoretically possible to flip from one side to the other, pick another branch flip to a new system, perhaps many times. All without traveling across any of the systems they visited.

That allowed a traveler to visit a ridiculous number of systems in an extremely short period of time, but only after they had mapped out the frequencies required to transition to those systems.

The ghosts might be only hours away, though perhaps any number of unmapped flips stood between them.

"Are those two systems the only other possible branches from this multiflip point?" Kelsey finally asked.

"Probably not. I still need to figure out the frequency boundaries and probe each zone to be certain."

Carl bent down. "In fact, one of the probes just visited a fourth system. Hm. I'm picking up a few radio signals. There's definitely somebody there, but they aren't spread throughout the system. All the transmissions appear to be coming from the same area of space."

"Send the probe back to get us more information. That might be where the ghosts went."

Another hour passed. Kelsey spent some of the nervous energy building inside her by getting food for everyone on the bridge. They'd just finished eating when the probe returned.

"I don't think this is a ghost system," Carl said slowly.

"Why not?" Kelsey asked.

He wordlessly threw an image onto the screen.

Kelsey wasn't certain if this was a news program or some other kind of entertainment, but the person centered in the video was definitely not human. Very close, but with some startling differences.

The being was tall and slender with pale turquoise skin. Based on the being's prominently displayed assets, the speaker was female.

The similarities between these beings and humans were incredible. She had two eyes, a nose, and a mouth in the same locations as a human woman. As were her breasts.

Her eyes seemed larger, though not by much. Her nose was slender and short. Her mouth wider. Unless Kelsey was mistaken, her teeth seemed a tad pointed too.

Kelsey thought she looked exotic, but beautiful. "Well, I didn't expect to find aliens. Can you explain why they look so much like us?"

The young scientist shrugged. "I have no idea. The only other aliens we've encountered were radically different."

The race of beings that had built Omega station in the Nova system and traveled to a different dimension had been aquatic.

Their study of the Omega race was still in its infancy. What she knew for certain was that anything was possible when it came to alien life. The Omega race was nothing like humanity in physical shape.

Kelsey frowned. "You tapped into their video pretty easily. Shouldn't figuring out their transmission protocols have taken you a while?"

"You'd think so. Here's another mystery for you. They're using standard Imperial frequencies and encoding."

She blinked. "Excuse me? These are aliens. How is that even possible?"

"I haven't got the faintest idea. What I can tell you is that they're only located on one planet in the system. It's in the habitable zone, though far outside the range this probe can pick up. They may not be as advanced as this makes them seem."

Kelsey rubbed her forehead. "We don't have time to investigate all these mysteries. We need to find the ghosts, not aliens that somehow got their hands on Imperial technology."

"What makes you think the two aren't connected?" Angela asked from her console. "Perhaps the ghosts traded with the natives. If they were advanced enough to make use of Imperial technology, they might have provided something useful in return."

"Isn't there some kind of rule that forbids interfering with aliens? Some kind of prime directive?"

"You've been watching too many of those old prespaceflight entertainment vids. The Old Empire never met an alien species. Why would they have a rule against uplifting them?

"Even if they did, these ghosts were desperate. I think they'd be willing to break that particular rule if it gave them an advantage they needed to survive."

Kelsey shook her head. "Dispatch three stealthed probes into the system to gather more information. In fact, send probes into all the empty systems as well. Start mapping them. We'll leave the one probe at the Archibald multiflip point to continue gathering data.

"Carl, I need to know how many potential branches this side of the multiflip point has. I want probes in every single one of them within the next hour. You can spend time after that doing your experiments to narrow down the frequency bands, but I need to know what we're dealing with.

"Until we find out more information, we'll designate this system as Pandora, so we have a name to call it. Besides, the alien's skin color makes me think of that old movie where they used the name."

"On it," Carl said.

Kelsey returned to her seat and gestured for Angela to join her. "This is spinning out of control. The number of systems we can potentially access is going to keep growing exponentially."

"That's a lot better than having no potential destinations," the tall marine said reasonably. "At least we might find another system that leads us back to Pentagar or Harrison's World. Potentially even home."

"If we're lucky. If not, we'll need to find the ghosts. They went somewhere. It would be very useful to make friendly contact with them."

The marine clapped Kelsey on the shoulder. "You're still new at this. Just be glad no one is shooting at you."

Kelsey supposed that was true. Things could always be worse.

Of course, things could always get better too. Maybe Talbot would find the escapees quickly. She might not like her mother very much right now, but she wanted her safe. Fast.

* * *

Once her uniform dried, Veronica began examining the tablets they'd been charging inside the abandoned facility. Most of the contents seemed innocuous. Their owners had used them for everyday tasks, and there were no files worthy of further study.

That was until she found a journal. That proved both fascinating and horrifying.

The fascination stemmed from the fact that the man who wrote it —Commander Frank Beaumont—had obviously been keeping a record of his daily activities and thoughts for years. The entries spanned five decades.

The earliest entries gave her a flavor of what it was like growing up on an agricultural world far from the center of the Empire. It documented how his family raised food for more populous systems.

Frank's father hadn't been pleased when he'd joined Fleet. That didn't seem to bother Frank all that much. The two of them seemed to have issues.

Veronica only skimmed the entries, but it quickly became clear that this man hadn't lived under anything like the old dictatorship as she knew it.

Then came the revolution. That's where things became horrifying.

Once fighting broke out, he documented everything. She no longer nursed any doubts that Captain Levy had told her the unvarnished truth. The AIs had lied. The horrors she read made her physically ill.

She forced herself to continue reading until his ship—the battlecruiser *Infamous*—escaped an ambush while escorting a number of civilian ships filled with refugees near Dresden.

He documented how the AI-controlled ships had mercilessly vaporized the defenseless civilian vessels where they could. That alone told her the truth. It was monstrous.

The commodore commanding the protective task force had rallied and counterattacked. She'd defeated the attackers, but reinforcements attacked the pickets she'd left at Dresden. That forced her into hiding.

Their task force didn't have supplies to stay in the outer system forever, but it was too dangerous to travel farther. They repaired what they could and waited.

His account didn't specify how he'd gotten to this system. Perhaps he didn't know.

She set the tablet down on the dirty console and rubbed her eyes. She could continue reading, but his story had already answered the most important questions she'd had. She knew who'd built the base and why they'd concealed it so well.

How could this be happening? How could everything she knew be a lie?

And what the hell could she do about it?

Castille wouldn't accept this. She knew it. He'd either declare it to be some kind of trick or find a reason to disregard the story. What he'd probably done to Commodore Murdock made it clear the lengths he was willing to go for the Empire.

Thankfully, she didn't have to make a decision about how to proceed right now. He was still busy questioning the female prisoner. Whatever they were discussing must've been fascinating. He'd been in the cutter for hours.

The two marines and the cutter pilot had woken shortly after the woman. Her people had them in an old conference room. She'd resisted the urge to question them. Maybe that had been the wrong call.

She went in search of cleaning supplies. Once she had enough basic equipment, she had Graham take it all to the conference room.

Armand stood outside the hatch with a stunner strapped to his waist.

"I'm going in to talk to them," she said without any preamble. "Alone."

"I don't think that's a good idea, ma'am. There are three of them and only one of you. Even with a stunner, they could take you."

She smiled. "That's why you'll need to be down at the other end of the corridor, so you can shoot them as they come out."

Veronica held up her hand when he started to object again. "I've made my decision, Commander. By all means, keep Graham here with you. If I call for help, you can come in. Carefully."

"At least allow us to make sure they don't jump you," Graham said. "You know, push them back into a corner."

"Fine. Just try not to shoot anybody. I want to talk to them."

At Armand's nod, Graham set the supplies on the deck and opened the hatch. The three prisoners sat around the filthy conference table.

When they started to rise, Veronica stepped into the compartment, her stunner raised. "Up against the bulkhead, gentleman. I'd rather not have to stun you again."

The two marines looked to the cutter pilot for guidance. When he raised his hands slightly and stepped over to the bulkhead, they grudgingly followed.

Veronica glanced at her men. "Bring the cleaning supplies inside and put them on the table. Wait outside. If I call for assistance, come in shooting. Stun everyone, including me."

Once Graham had placed the box of cleaning supplies on the table, Veronica closed the hatch.

She smiled at the three men. "I realize we've gotten off to a terrible start, but I think we have a lot to discuss. I'm Commander Veronica Giguere, in case you hadn't guessed."

"We're not going to tell you anything," the pilot said with a stony face.

"Oh, I think you will. First, I'm going to tell you a story. Then you can explain to me what it means."

The men glanced at one another. "I have no idea what you're talking about," the pilot said after a long moment.

Veronica pointed to the box. "This place is a mess, and you're going to be here a while. Take the supplies and start cleaning the other end of the compartment. While you do, I'll pass on a story that I just read. I think you'll find it fascinating. It's about a man who fought the AIs."

She moved a chair to the corner and sat. "Let me introduce you to Frank Beaumont. He grew up on a farm. Maybe it's just me, but that sounds like a dirty, smelly place. Anyone here know about that?"

When they shook their heads, she launched into his story.

22

Annette decided that riding out a flip on *Persephone*'s hull was even worse than when she'd hidden in her fighter while they invaded the Dresden system.

The Raider ship's lower mass provided almost no protection. Even with her implants, it took her almost a minute to regain full control of her stomach.

Still, she understood why they had to go through like this. *Audacious* was too large to go through the multiflip point, so that meant they'd had to strap the fighters onto *Persephone*'s hull.

If they were going to make a habit of this, Annette was going to get Carl Owlet to design some magnetic clamps the pilots could release from inside the cockpit. In fact, that wasn't a bad idea at all.

It took a few minutes for the crewmen in vacuum suits to release her fighter. She used her grav drive on its lowest setting to edge away from the ship. They released the other five fighters over the next fifteen minutes.

That definitely wouldn't work if they needed to do this again.

Once her scouting group had formed around her, they headed deeper into the Pandora system. Fighters were hard to detect—even when traveling quickly—so they could accelerate faster than a larger ship.

According to the plan, *Persephone* would monitor the system via her probes while Annette scouted the planet where the signals originated. If there were any trouble, the princess would come hauling butt and give them some cover.

The probe that they'd originally sent to the alien world had provided an interesting mix of information. The majority of the planet wasn't industrialized. The night-side view showed very little in the way of alien-made lighting, even inside what were obviously major cities. Electricity was uncommon, it seemed.

Yet there were those troubling transmissions.

She took control of the probes that *Persephone* had just launched and sent them ahead. They'd arrive in planetary orbit several hours before her. She could task them to look at anything they determined to be interesting once she arrived.

Annette brought up a map of the planet over her implants. She started studying the rough layout of the major cities and trying to determine what political entities they might fit into. If these people were as underdeveloped as they appeared, the odds of them having a single planetary government were nonexistent.

A closer examination of some of the urban centers brought something unusual to her attention. They'd laid one of the larger cities out in a very unusual pattern. It wasn't near a river, either. She couldn't imagine why they'd put so many people there.

It wasn't prudent to send a signal to the probe from this far away. The risk of detection was too high. She'd have to send one of her probes to take a closer look when they got there.

Frankly, she had no idea what she'd find.

* * *

As MUCH AS he wanted to focus on the search for the escaped prisoners, Talbot had other problems that desperately required his attention. They had to relocate the prisoners from the orbital to the planet's surface. That meant the construction of the shelters was on a very tight schedule.

Unfortunately, the crews he'd brought to the surface were slowing things down. He needed to get them moving again if he was going to meet Kelsey's deadline.

He took a pinnace from the search area to the island they'd selected for the primary construction. The landmass was about as far away from the original villages as possible. He didn't want the female population here causing a war with the all-male original settlers.

As he'd expected, no one was working when he landed.

Talbot settled his light armor, checked his stunner, and motioned for his escort to follow him down the ramp. He didn't need a lot of backup, but he wanted to make a point.

It seemed as though the construction personnel had elected one of themselves as their leader. The tall, heavily muscled man had a bird of some kind tattooed on his arm. He showed Talbot a smug expression as the marine walked toward him, but said nothing.

Talbot stopped about two meters away. "Are we really going to do this?"

The other man smiled, showing a lot of teeth. "I'm not sure what you mean."

"Oh, don't be coy. You think you're going to stand there telling me that you and your people aren't going to do the work. I'll complain that you're delaying everything. Then you tell me what you want before you get back to work.

"That isn't going to happen. All you're doing is putting yourselves into a hard spot."

The man's grin widened, and he spread his hands. "If I'm wrong, tell me what's going to happen. The way I see it, you Fleet bastards don't have a lot of choice. No buildings? People are going to freeze."

"That's about what I expected you to say. Here's where things go south for you. We're going to keep bringing people down no matter what you do. If you want to screw your own people, go right ahead. Anything that happens from that point forward is on you."

The man looked uncertain but didn't say anything.

Talbot turned on his heel and headed back into the pinnace.

Either these idiots would get back to work, or they'd have to deal with the crisis they'd created.

The weather wasn't terrible. Chilly was a more appropriate description than cold, so no one was in serious physical danger. He'd provide more than enough cold-weather gear to keep them alive no matter what the idiots did.

That didn't mean they'd be happy, though. Not his problem. He needed to get back to the search.

* * *

RAUL SPOKE with Justine Bandar far longer than he'd intended. The woman was fascinating. Just as arrogant as anyone he'd met from the higher orders but delightfully easy to converse with.

And very informative. She'd shared what he considered classified information with wild abandon. All he had to do was get her complaining about either her daughter, her ex-husband's bastard, or the situation she'd found herself in.

It was easy to manufacture the compassion required to get her rolling. Once she started talking, there didn't seem to be any governor on what she'd discuss. By the time they'd been together just a few hours, he had a good overview of this supposed New Terran Empire.

Thankfully, even with all the ships that Veronica had seen, it didn't appear that these people were as great a threat as he'd feared. They only occupied a small area of space, and their population was sparse. Their basic technology level was also far inferior to the Empire.

Best of all, he had the name of their capital: Avalon. He had no doubt that he'd be able to locate them on a map. Once the Empire knew where to send their warships, they'd end this problem in very short order.

He walked down the cutter's ramp, leaving the woman under guard behind him. He'd already made the decision to house her separately from the other prisoners. He didn't want them convincing her to shut her exceptionally pretty mouth.

It took about twenty minutes to locate Veronica. She was working in one of the compartments inside the old base. She seemed to be cleaning what had obviously been personal quarters, so perhaps she was arranging a less dusty place to stay. Smart.

He rapped on the hatch to get her attention. When she'd turned her head, saw who he was, and set her rag down on the table, he stepped inside.

"My apologies for interrupting," he said. "I've completed questioning the woman. Her story is very interesting."

Veronica nodded. "I'm sure it is. We've discovered a few things too. One of the tablets had a journal. It covered about fifty years from start to finish, so we're far from being able to say that we've read every word, but it has raised some disturbing questions."

Raul picked up the rag and cleaned off a handy chair. He settled comfortably and crossed one leg over the other. "Surely you're not going to tell me that it implicates the lords as being homicidal maniacs bent on human domination."

She stepped over and closed the hatch. "That's exactly what I'm telling you. The story was from five hundred years ago, written during the events in question. The account paints a very different picture of the old Empire too.

"I need to be frank. The old emperor doesn't sound at all like the despot they taught us about in school. In fact, I'm convinced the people that captured us are more correct than we are about the AIs."

He kept his expression pleasant, but his mind was racing. Their circumstances were dire. He couldn't afford to have this kind of disruption in the middle of an already chancy escape.

"I'll need to read the relevant journal entries myself, but let's assume that you've interpreted them correctly just for the sake of the discussion. So what? The past is done. We can't change it.

"We have to live in the world as it exists. The lords are our masters. Did they do terrible things to gain that mastery? Perhaps. Nevertheless, they are the ones we serve."

Her eyes narrowed. "I'm a Fleet officer. I know where my loyalties lie, but have you been playing some kind of game all this time? Do you security people already know all of this? I just want to know."

Raul laughed, though there wasn't much humor in the situation.

"Oh no. I'm hearing this for the first time. If anyone in the Empire knows, I'm not aware of it. Perhaps I don't have the clearance.

"I do know this, though. It changes nothing. These people want to destroy our way of life. Worse yet, even if they offer a better society—and I'm willing to provisionally entertain the possibility—they don't have the military force needed to overthrow the AIs. Not even with everything that they've captured at Dresden."

Veronica sat in another of the chairs. "Tell me what you know."

"The woman's name is Justine Bandar. She's the mother of the woman who greeted us on the carrier. The ex-empress of the supposed New Terran Empire. She's given us everything we need to stop these people. We just have to find a way to get the word back to our superiors."

He considered her for a long moment. "I sympathize, Veronica. I truly do. There are many things wrong with the Empire. Things I wish worked differently. Perhaps in time we can change them.

"If our former captors told us the truth as they saw it, the AIs can obviously learn. Things have improved since they overthrew the old dictatorship. If that's even the right word."

When she didn't add anything, he continued. "Obviously, terrible things were done, if their stories are accurate. But do you truly believe these people can create change for the better? Or would it just be for the worse? If the AIs are as bad they told us, then they will react very strongly to this threat.

"And not just toward the New Terran Empire. Do you really want to have them repress our people too? That's a real possibility."

He leaned back in his chair and watched her. She obviously had mixed feelings. The question was, would she end up supporting him and the Empire, or go in the direction he suspected her heart tugged her?

He'd have to watch her closely. He'd regret it if he had to act against her as he had Commodore Murdock and the rest, but he knew his duty. Hopefully she was smart enough to know hers.

23

"I have some more information," Carl said.

Kelsey looked over from the main screen where she'd been examining some of the images the aliens were transmitting. "Give it to me."

The young scientist stood and walked over. "We're still working on the language, but I can tell you that there are less than a dozen transmission sites.

"They're not transmitting continuously, either. Sometimes signals last for a couple of hours, but other times only for a few minutes. I don't think they're news programs or even entertainment."

"What are they?"

"I think this is message traffic. Back on Terra before they had the ability to transmit radio signals, everything had to go through something called telegraph lines with physical wires.

"If you needed to get information to someone a long distance away, you'd deliver a message to a transmission station, and they'd send it on. It might need to go through several retransmissions to reach the final destination, but the recipient eventually got it.

"I believe we're seeing something very much like that. The delivery style and the fact that the transmissions only take place intermittently indicate they're only communicating when there's something to say."

Kelsey considered that. "Once Annette gets on station, she should be able to help clarify the situation."

"Agreed," he said. "None of the transmissions have had a human being in it. That may mean there are no humans on this planet."

She certainly hoped that wasn't the case. It would be a lot easier if they could find a representative of these elusive ghosts to negotiate with. If they chanced across one of their ships in space, there was the very likely possibility that they'd shoot first and never bother asking questions.

"I understand that I'm asking you to guess, but do you think it's worth our time and effort to contact these people?"

Carl considered her question for a moment. "Honestly? No. I'd say these people are preindustrial. Perhaps even feudal. Of course, they're aliens. It might not be that simple.

"Would they make good friends? Possibly, but we're not out here to make friends. We have to get the information we have back to the Empire. That has to be our first priority."

That's about what she'd thought, but she'd wanted to hear someone else say it.

"How long until Annette is on station?" she asked.

"Less than an hour now."

"Keep going through those transmissions. I'd love it if you could figure out some type of translation program."

He gave her a skeptical look. "That's not likely. The language isn't even close to Standard. I'll need better understanding of common words and concepts to develop a translation program. These transmissions have people talking but no context. The video shots are just of the people speaking.

"The individual we call Omega was different. He'd interacted with humans before and had a lot of computing power to throw at improving his translation code. Just being able to speak to these folks is going to prove impossible in the short run, I suspect."

Omega hadn't just known humans before. He'd known Carl. Several of him, in fact. True, they'd come from alternate realities, but that had to give the alien some insight when it came to interacting with this one particular human.

The station that Omega was part of had been a gateway to other universes. He'd become part of the ring they'd discovered in the Nova system so that he could facilitate the evacuation of his species to avoid extinction at the hands of their errant star.

Something about the nova—not just in their universe, but also in numerous others—had somehow linked many of the stations in ways that she didn't understand. They'd become one on the inside. Omega was the same in all of those universes. A living bridge between them.

The idea of other realities boggled her mind. Yet one more thing she didn't have time to distract herself with.

"I know you're probably right, but how often do we meet an alien species?" she finally asked. "Even counting Omega, this is only the second time. And no offense to him, but he's only a single being trapped on a station in an extremely inhospitable system.

"Pandora is a planet full of people. Think of how much we could learn from them. Not technologically obviously, but this is important. Perhaps it's not our most pressing issue, but I don't want to let this opportunity slip past."

"I get that," Carl said. "We still have five days before Talbot finishes removing the prisoners from the Dresden orbital. If you don't mind, I'll start using my probes on this side of the multiflip point and see if there's any overlap in destinations. I honestly don't expect to find much, but we should look."

"That's a good idea," she agreed. "I think we can assume the Pandorans won't see us all the way out here. Let's poke around the multiflip point and map out the places it leads. It's conceivable that one of the links will provide us with something useful."

She sent him back to his console just as Angela came out of the lift. The tall marine had gone to get sandwiches for the bridge crew. Something they all appreciated.

Her executive officer handed her a small pile of them. "Here you go."

Kelsey accepted the plate gratefully. "Thank God. I'm starving."

When she'd taken the edge off her hunger, she focused her

attention on Angela. "I've decided that we're going to flip back to the system with the orbital for a bit. I think it's time to send you to *Audacious* for the next implant procedure."

Her tall friend scowled. "Seriously? We just brought my boyfriend on board, and you're sending me off?"

Kelsey laughed. "You're not going to be getting frisky for a bit. You might pull something important off him."

The marine snorted. "Don't tell him that, or I'll never get any. Kelsey, we're in an alien star system hunting for potentially hostile ships. I hardly think this is the time to remove your executive officer from the equation."

"I think it's pretty safe to say that we're not going to run into anyone in this system. While it does have at least two regular flip points, there's no sign that the ghosts visit on any regular schedule, and this is obviously not one of their home systems.

"If you want to become a full-blown Marine Raider, you've got to keep going with the procedures. This next one is for your legs. Once Doctor Zoboroski finishes, you can come back. As my executive officer, you can do your job sitting down."

That didn't seem to make the marine any happier. "If I have to move somewhere, I'm going to fall on my face. I saw you after your procedure. It's going to take me days to figure out how to walk again, isn't it?"

"Probably," Kelsey agreed. "That still doesn't change anything. It's not going to be as bad as you think, Angela. I had to recover from everything all at once and had no one to guide me through the process. You do.

"By the time we're ready to leave this system, you'll have recovered to the point where they can do the left half of your torso. You're almost there. Don't keep looking for excuses to put it off."

Angela scowled. "Yes, ma'am. I don't have to like it, though."

Kelsey smiled a little. "I think you'll like it just fine once you're done. Imagine what a badass you'll be. You'll be able to tie me into a pretzel when we spar."

The marine smiled. "You sure know how to make a girl feel better."

* * *

ANNETTE EDGED CAREFULLY into orbit around the planet Princess Kelsey had dubbed Pandora. The probes hadn't discovered any artificial satellites, but she needed to be cautious.

After half an hour, her fighters had circled the globe several times and determined there was nothing outside the atmosphere. That certainly confirmed the Pandorans were primitive, relatively speaking.

She passed the information to *Persephone*. Nobody down below was going to detect the larger ship, so they could come in and get a better idea of what they were dealing with.

While Annette waited for the ship, she set her people to doing a visual inspection of the planet. She wanted to have a high-resolution map by the time the princess arrived.

Annette focused her attention on the strangely shaped city she'd observed through the probes. As it was in daylight now, she was able to see what made it look so odd.

It wasn't a city at all. It was a debris field.

The strange layout of the lights she'd seen at night was because they'd set up a number of small encampments around what was obviously the wreckage of a crashed ship.

A quick check confirmed that it wasn't broadcasting a distress beacon. It had been there a while and must not have had an operational fusion plant.

They'd need to send drones into the atmosphere to see just what was happening, but it certainly appeared as though a lot of people were combing through the wreckage, based upon the number of buildings.

Annette didn't see any intact sections, so she couldn't identify the ship's class. It was obviously a big one. Significantly larger than *Persephone*, for sure.

The Marine Raider ship was the only Old Empire ship they'd found that was even *capable* of landing on a planet. Anything that produced this much debris shouldn't have been in the atmosphere in the first place.

She started estimating the amount of wreckage. The ship below was at least a heavy cruiser. Perhaps even a battlecruiser.

Based on how contained the wreckage was, someone had managed to keep it together most of the way down. Otherwise, the wreckage would be scattered across many square kilometers.

Annette zoomed the resolution on the probe as far as she could. It felt like she was sitting about ten kilometers up.

The locals were definitely scavenging. A number of large tents surrounded the wreck, and Annette could see people carrying objects into them. A larger ring of permanent structures surrounded them.

Since people didn't build cities in a week, this had been going on for a long time. Years, certainly. Probably decades.

Annette finally broke off her examination when *Persephone* pulled into orbit hours later. She signaled the Marine Raider ship, and Princess Kelsey answered.

Using her implants to communicate made it seem as though she were standing in front of the other woman.

"What have you got for me?" the princess asked.

She laid out everything she'd found.

"That's a big ship," Annette said when she was done. "I have difficulty believing they intended to take her down to the surface. Whoever landed her was one hell of a pilot."

The noblewoman looked skeptical. "Landing? No one walked away from that."

"That's one of the things you learn as a pilot, Highness. Sometimes you don't walk away. That doesn't negate the skill that got them close.

"The locals seem to be scavenging equipment. Based on the number of buildings and the nature of the wreckage, I suspect it's been down there for decades."

Princess Kelsey looked at the view screen in front of her. "The computer is doing some estimations based on the amount of wreckage. It's tentatively identifying it as a battlecruiser. I can't begin to imagine how long it would take a primitive group to strip something that size.

"They certainly didn't figure out how to use the communications gear in a decade or two. Not unless somebody survived to show them how it was done."

Annette couldn't imagine anyone had directly survived the crash, but she supposed it was possible. Miracles did occasionally happen.

"I suspect any survivors abandoned ship via escape pods before the crash," she said. "That would get a lot of people clear in a hurry. Someone obviously stayed on board that ship right up until the very end, though."

The princess nodded. "We're not picking up any distress beacons, so whatever happened took place a long time ago. The pods aren't good for more than a few months of power, but the ship would still be transmitting if any of the fusion plants survived."

"No chance of that," Annette said. "They probably killed most of them before they entered the atmosphere. A crash like this would've blown them for sure."

"Head back home," the princess ordered. "It's going to take a while for the probes to give us a more comprehensive picture. You might as well be comfortable while they do it."

"Aye, ma'am. We're on our way."

Annette sent a signal to her people, and they all turned toward *Persephone*. It would be good to get out of the cockpit, take a hot shower, and get something to eat. By the time she felt human again, they'd have a better idea of what kind of situation they were dealing with.

24

Veronica was just finishing her unappetizing ration bar when Graham rapped his knuckle on the open hatch to her new quarters. She held up a finger while she finished chewing the last bit and swallowed it. She followed that up with a long drink of cold, fresh water.

"What have you got for me, Graham? If it's better food, you have my complete attention."

The young engineering officer laughed. "If only we were so lucky. No, I'm afraid we're stuck with these nasty ration bars for the time being. You have to wonder, why can't anyone make survival rations that actually taste good?"

"It's one of the great mysteries of the universe," she allowed. "I take it you have something interesting for me."

"You could say that. I've gotten into their main computer."

She straightened. "Are you serious? That's great!"

"I won't bore you with all the technical details, but suffice it to say, someone wasn't as conscientious as they should've been with password security. Once I gained access, I managed to compromise the system administrator's login. Sloppy. They should be ashamed."

Veronica laughed. "I'm not going to complain about someone

else's failure when it suits our needs. Have you found anything interesting?"

He shook his head. "I literally just finished cracking the system administrator's account. I figured you'd want to know right away."

She stood. "You're damned right. Let's go see if we can find something interesting."

They'd been in the abandoned facility for five days now. She'd stayed on the cutter the first night. That convinced her to clean up some of the abandoned quarters. She still wasn't satisfied with the level of cleanliness.

Still, it could've been worse. Candace Wells—her helm officer— was splitting her time between her quarters and Justine Bandar's. The haughty woman was running her ragged, and Veronica knew the quiet officer was ready to strangle the harpy.

Graham led her deeper into the base. They'd restored one of the lifts to service. It beat using the stairs.

The computer center was at the lowest level. Whoever had built the base had decided it was best to put it right next to the fusion plant. Probably so they'd be certain of destroying it, if they decided the facility had to go.

It turned out her young engineering officer had done a much better job of cleaning out his workspace than she had her quarters. The room was spotless.

She looked around in amazement. "How the hell did you find enough time to clean this place and break into the computer?"

He frowned at her. "I used the cleaning bots."

Veronica put her hands on her hips and gave him a flat stare. "You have the cleaning bots working, and you didn't tell me? I've been busting my ass to get my room in half-decent shape."

"I thought I'd told Commander Fuller. Maybe I only dreamed I did. You should probably take some of them back to your room."

"Graham, you're exasperating. Get your head out of the computer innards and think of other people."

"Sorry, ma'am. I'll try to do better."

He gestured toward the computer console. "I've taken the liberty of adding all of us to the system. You have complete access to everything. The only thing that I've restricted is the computer security protocols. For safety sake, I decided to disable them. We wouldn't want to wipe the system by accident."

She sat at the console. "No, we wouldn't."

Veronica used her implants to access the computer. It readily opened for examination. She initiated a search for classified files.

That brought back a lot of hits. The computer was packed with classified information, at least as far as the people who'd built it were concerned.

The first thing she did was to search for a listing of ships associated with the task force. She found it in the logs created by a Commodore Sanjay. A side query indicated that she was the commanding officer of the task force that had escaped and built this base.

It seems that she'd escaped the revolution with quite a few ships. Three battlecruisers, six heavy cruisers, nine light cruisers, and fourteen destroyers. Quite a strike force.

They'd been escorting a motley mix of civilian vessels packed with refugees. There was a long listing of the ships, but there was no rhyme or reason to them. They'd probably grabbed every bit of shipping that could hold people when they ran. All told, they'd shepherded almost a hundred civilian vessels.

None of which they'd left in this system. Except for an old cruise liner that they'd been doing some type of experimentation with.

She frowned. It took her several minutes to locate the file with information about the modifications done to the cruise liner. It proved unexpectedly enlightening.

Sanjay's task force and the civilians under her protection had escaped the Empire through an unknown kind of flip point. One that turned out to be very difficult to detect.

One of the scanner officers had found the anomaly in the system nearest Dresden. They'd risked sending a probe through and found this system. The one containing the planet she was standing on.

They'd named it Icebox. Apparently, they'd arrived in deep winter.

She'd have to figure out what they'd done here at a later point.

Right now, she was just concerned with why they'd modified the cruise liner.

The answer made her laugh. It turned out the anomaly was a one-way ticket. Once they'd arrived, they'd been unable to leave. The system hadn't contained any regular flip points, either.

After quite a bit of research, they'd modified the flip drive on the cruise liner to attempt a transit back to the system they'd fled. It had failed to transit and burned out the flip drive.

Well, that explained why they'd left the ship in orbit. Where had they gone? Had they finally figured out how to use the anomaly? Had they built this place only to return home and die in some unknown battle?

She spooled to the end of Commodore Sanjay's log. That entry was more than two decades after they'd arrived at Icebox. It followed the previous entry by six years.

The commodore had left a brief note that she was leaving a repository of classified files on the computer at this base—which they'd apparently abandoned at some point—and was putting it into hibernation before they left the system.

Veronica searched the commodore's files and found the most recent dispatches. She'd expected to find that they'd perfected a device to modify their flip drives. What she found was far more unexpected.

Apparently, they'd never managed to go back through the anomaly. Instead, they'd settled this planet and built a city down on the coast below the volcano. Shortly before Commodore Sanjay made her final entry, they'd discovered a flip point in this system. One in a location they hadn't expected.

She blinked and stared at Graham. "I think I found us a way out."

"Seriously?" he asked. "That's great."

Veronica smiled wryly. "We'll see. It turns out there's another flip point in this system. One our captors probably don't know about."

He scratched his head and gave her a quizzical look. "Why not?"

"Because it's not positioned where they'd expect to find it. That gives us an opportunity."

* * *

Raul was washing his face when Veronica caught up with him. She started to say something but stopped and took a closer look at his face.

"What happened to you?" she asked.

He smiled ruefully. "Believe it or not, I was attacked by one of the prisoners."

She swore. "I knew this was going to happen. It was one of the marines, wasn't it?"

"Justine Bandar. It turns out she's not pleased with the quarters we've provided for her."

Veronica blinked. "Seriously? She hauled off and popped you?"

"Thankfully for my ego, no. However, she has a stellar throwing arm."

To his chagrin, Veronica started laughing. He didn't blame her. It was ludicrous.

Once she'd laughed herself out, he drew himself up with all the dignity he could muster. "If we're finished—and by we, I mean you—what brings you by?"

She smoothed her expression, but he could still see the humor dancing in her eyes. "I just wanted to let you know that Graham managed to access the base computer. Obviously, we're going to have a lot to go over, but I found something I think you need to know about."

He stiffened, his bruised face forgotten. "You have my full attention."

"I found the log belonging to the task force commander who built this base. A Commodore Sanjay. It turns out she and her ships were here for several decades before they left again. That's because they couldn't go back through the anomaly that led them here, and there were no other flip points in this system."

He raised an eyebrow. "So, her people figured out how to go back through the anomaly? Why did it take so long?"

"They never figured out how to go back through the anomaly," Veronica said. "It proved to be a one-way trip. They did, however, discover a flip point that they'd missed in their initial examination of the system."

"Another anomaly? What do we know about them?"

"A regular flip point, actually. They missed it because it's positioned far beyond the orbit of the outermost planet."

He digested that information for a moment. He didn't serve as a ship's officer, so he wasn't familiar with the normal layout of flip points. "And that's unusual?"

"Unheard of. Regular flip points sit between the habitable zone and about the middle of the outer system. The one we're talking about here is significantly farther out. Even a ship going out to the outermost planet—for which there is no conceivable reason—wouldn't have detected it."

"I'll bite. How did they manage to find it?"

She shrugged. "I didn't stop to look. I figured the fact that it existed at all was all that mattered. That said, it doesn't really improve our prospects. We don't happen to have any handy flip-capable ships."

That deflated him a little. "True. It doesn't sound as though our captors are going to find it, either. If they can't go back through the anomaly, I'm not sure what we're going to do. We can hold out for another few months, if we cut our rations, but these people need to leave if we're to have any chance of returning to the Empire."

Veronica pursed her lips. "Maybe. Maybe not. While we were on board the carrier, I overheard several of the officers talking about their operations. They're a bit nervous about the prisoners on the planet getting ahold of the Dresden orbital.

"They planned on using their cutters to shuttle everyone down to the planet's surface. Once the orbital is empty, they intend to move it into the outer system. That means the recovery ship is going to be going about two-thirds of the way toward where we want to be.

"I suppose we should at least consider stealing the freighter they have with them, but it doesn't have a reason to leave orbit. They'd get suspicious fast, even if we could man the ship. The recovery ship is made for a small crew. A freighter isn't."

He felt his eyes narrowing. "Very true about the freighter. The recovery ship does present an opportunity. All we need to do is find a way to take advantage of it."

Veronica nodded. "We need to get back into orbit without them detecting us, sneak aboard the recovery ship, overpower the crew, and waltz right out under their noses. Sounds like a piece of cake."

"Don't be so negative," he said with a smile. "We've already proven very resourceful. We'll need to brainstorm potential plans. Do we have any idea how long before they plan to move the orbital?"

She shrugged. "Not really. I figure it'll take at least a week to get the people off the orbital. Then they need to strip the research and manufacturing equipment you told me about. Ten days, give or take."

"Then we have a little time. Pass my congratulations back to your engineer. Well done. This gives us a fighting chance. If we can escape and get this information back to the Empire, we'll solve the problem of the ghosts and the New Terran Empire."

25

Talbot exited the marine pinnace and entered the Dresden orbital. His was far from the only boat in the large bay. Just about every cutter and pinnace in the task force that wasn't involved in searching for the escapees was transporting people to the surface.

In fact, that's why he was here. He needed them to up the pace if they were going to clear the orbital on schedule.

Major Gabe Collins was waiting for him in the landing bay. Gabe was the commanding officer of *Audacious*'s marine detachment, just like Talbot commanded the marines assigned to *Invincible*.

Admiral Mertz had moved every marine in the task force to *Audacious* for the raid on Dresden and put Talbot in command of the assembled brigade-strength force. That made all this his responsibility until they made it back home.

That meant there was no room to spare in marine country, but he had more than enough trained fighters to take care of any problems. Too bad he didn't have the pinnaces to move them around.

"Things must be bad if you're waiting for me," Talbot said. "Why don't we just go to the conference room and hash this out?"

Collins nodded. "It just felt rude not to be here for your arrival, Talbot. I didn't want you to feel snubbed."

Talbot laughed. "It's good to see you still have a sense of humor. Let's see if I can fix that."

They didn't have to travel far to find a conference room. There was one right off the landing bay. Once inside, they sat at the large table.

Collins grimaced. "We're running about half a day behind. It seems that some of the civilians are getting froggy. They've realized they're being moved and are trying to slow walk us."

"Slow walk?"

"They're not resisting, but they're going very, very slowly. I'm not sure how we can speed them up without physically grabbing them and hustling them onto the cutters. I've considered stunning a few to allow the others to learn by example."

"As satisfying as that might be, I don't think we need to antagonize these people any more than we have to," Talbot said. "Kelsey was very clear that we're to leave them with as positive an opinion of us as possible."

Collins smiled. "I'm not precisely sure how that's supposed to work, considering we're stranding them on a strange planet."

"That is a challenge," Talbot acknowledged. "We can only do the best we can. Does the resistance seem widespread? I thought the prisoners were isolated from one another."

"It took us a while to figure out how they were getting messages back and forth. We used the cafeteria staff for food preparation and then had marines escort them to deliver it. We started watching them more closely, but it was already too late. The damage was done."

Talbot considered that for a moment. "That makes sense. You're telling me that it's going to be roughly twelve hours more than your original target?"

"Things might go more smoothly once we've moved more people, but that sounds about right. On the plus side, with fewer people on the orbital, we have less potential for prison breaks."

That had worried Talbot in the beginning. With over ten thousand prisoners, they'd have been unable to contain a general riot without someone getting hurt.

"And that's the way I'd like to keep it," he said. "I'm authorizing the delay, but try to keep it to a minimum. Kelsey is busy exploring the alien system she discovered, so she may not be back by the deadline anyway."

Collins raised an eyebrow. "I'm surprised you're not raising a stink."

Talbot laughed. "I'm starting to learn that I have very little control over what my wife does. If I want to stay sane, I need to focus on things I can actually control. Major Ellis is keeping an eye on her, so I'll just have to cross my fingers and hope for the best.

"What about the manufacturing equipment? How far along are we on getting it moved over to *Audacious*?"

The other officer smiled. "We're running ahead of schedule on that. We've finished cleaning out the secure labs and shipping everything over. The manufacturing equipment is larger, but we're probably about two-thirds of the way done.

"We could finish it in a day, but I have people going through the cargo manifests and storage areas to make certain we don't miss anything important."

"Don't rush it. It's important we get things right. Are you finding anything interesting in the cargo bays?"

"Actually, yes. Dresden is a major industrial center where they build a lot of Fleet equipment. We can use most of it.

"There's also a lot of raw material for use by the manufacturing machines on the orbital. Lots of rare elements used in the implants and AIs. Even though we don't have the ability to use the equipment right now, it's going to be a boost once we start."

Carl Owlet still hadn't managed to break into the computers controlling the manufacturing machines. To be fair, he hadn't had a lot of time. He'd had to explore the multiflip point and its potential destinations.

Kelsey had brought him back from the alien system when she dropped Angela off for her next implant procedure. The marine had finished and gone back, but Carl had already mapped both sides of the multiflip point, so there was no longer a need to have him in the Pandora system.

His young friend hadn't been pleased that he wasn't with Angela anymore. Ah, young love.

In any case, this side of the multiflip point led to five different systems. One of them was a core world of the Rebel Empire: Archibald. Three were unoccupied and unexplored. The last one was an alien-occupied system Kelsey was currently exploring.

The multiflip point from the alien side led to four systems: the one with the unwilling colonists, Archibald, and two different unoccupied systems. So there was some overlap, but not much.

From what Talbot had heard, *Persephone* could use the multiflip point, but *Audacious* was too large. The recovery ship was an unknown, but it certainly couldn't flip with the Dresden orbital. That made it far too massive.

His young friend had been working hard with the scientists they'd freed from the research station. Talbot still wasn't certain they should be allowing them to work on such critical systems, but Carl had vouched for them.

"If you can finish clearing out the equipment and supplies by the time you've moved the last of the prisoners down to the planet, I'll be satisfied," Talbot said. "If it takes longer, it takes longer. Have you at least broken all the manufacturing equipment down?"

"Most of it is crated," Collins said. "We just have to dedicate the cutter space to move it over to *Audacious*."

"Good. I'm not going to feel completely comfortable until you're done."

A rap at the hatch drew his attention. His pilot stood there.

"Sorry to disturb you, Major. I got a message from *Audacious*. They'd like us to stop by before you head back down to the surface."

"Any idea why?"

The man shrugged. "No idea, sir. It came directly from Commodore Anderson."

"Then we'll drop in and see what she has for us."

He rose to his feet. "Keep up the good work, Gabe. What you're doing here is very important. It's going to make a universe of difference when we get back home."

* * *

KELSEY FELT as though she were about to go insane. Almost a week had passed, and there was still no sign of her mother. It took all her willpower to put her worry into a mental box and focus on the tasks she had to accomplish.

The alien society helped distract her, but if Talbot didn't find her mother soon, she'd go nuts.

They'd put the time they'd spent orbiting the alien world to good use. Angela had deployed a number of probes above the most interesting sites, and they'd dispatched marine pinnaces at night to release drones.

Still no luck in deciphering the alien language, but that would come in time. They were recording every transmission they detected. If they couldn't figure it out now, Marcus could have a go at it when they returned to the New Terran Empire.

Angela was adjusting to her upgraded legs. She only fell over occasionally at this point, and she'd only bounced off the ceiling once.

Kelsey was secretly jealous. The marine had adjusted to the physical changes brought on by the Marine Raider implants a lot better than she had.

"Kelsey, I think I found something," Angela said.

She rose and walked over to Angela's console. The marine had a video display running, and Kelsey immediately grasped the importance of what she was seeing.

The scene was a smaller town. Most of those were agricultural in nature, either hosting many farms in the surrounding area or supporting ranching of native beasts. Often both.

The buildings were made of wood, the roads were unpaved, and the people seemed simple in their lifestyle. That probably included the human male she saw walking in the center of the image.

The man was dressed like the aliens, and he seemed unconcerned at being in their midst. He was in his early twenties. His brown hair and blue eyes stood out in sharp contrast to the aliens around him.

Over the week that they'd been observing the Pandorans, Kelsey had discovered they had a range of skin tones. All of them were blue to some degree, but it seemed that the shades darkened as they aged.

The aliens didn't seem overly disturbed by the man's presence. That wasn't to say they weren't curious or standoffish. They made way to allow him through, and many stared at him as he passed by, but no one seemed overly afraid.

Humans, it seemed, were a known quantity.

"Is he alone, or are there more?" Kelsey asked.

"He's the only one I've seen so far. We can keep track of him now, though. He might lead us to others."

The marine turned in her seat. "Have you decided whether or not we're going to make contact?"

Kelsey nodded. "We don't really have a choice. We need to know what happened here and what they can tell us about the ghosts. His familiarity with the local population leads me to suspect these folks haven't been in contact with the ghosts in some time."

"Maybe. What's your plan?"

"Continue monitoring him for now. Make certain you bring in extra drone coverage so he doesn't slip out the back of some building. We need to know where he goes and who he talks to. If there are other humans in this town, he'll eventually lead us to them.

"If not, he'll leave at some point. Once he's on the road, we should be able to arrange a discreet meeting. One without too much danger for anyone involved."

The natives' method of transportation was as primitive as the rest of their society. The poor walked, those with more means rode beasts similar to horses, and the very wealthy rode in enclosed carriages. None of the latter made their way out to little places like this, though.

Angela gave her a stern look. "You're going to let someone else make contact."

Kelsey smiled. "Don't be ridiculous."

The marine sighed. "I suppose that shouldn't surprise me. Well, let me rain on your parade a little. You're not going down there without a proper escort. If things go sour, we're going to pull you out. That's not open to negotiation."

"Not that I'm negotiating, but I don't expect to run into any trouble I can't handle. These folks aren't exactly the most advanced people in the universe. While we've seen some gunpowder weapons, almost everything they use is muscle powered. I don't think I'm going to run into anything that I can't deal with."

Angela rubbed her face. "Don't confuse primitive with harmless. One of those crossbow bolts can leave you just as dead as a plasma grenade. They also have numbers. If we get them stirred up, they can overwhelm us. Remember that Custer guy you told me about? Don't make this your Little Big Horn."

"Thanks for *that* perspective," Kelsey said dryly. "This doesn't have to be some kind of conflict, Angela. All I'm going to do is talk to the man. If I've worked things right, it'll be in private. Everything will be fine."

Angela didn't seem convinced. "I'm sending Annette down to scout the best landing places ahead of time. I'd go myself, if I could. Be careful, Kelsey."

26

Annette took her fighter down to the surface while it was still dark below. The planet's relatively large moon had set about an hour ago, and the area was so deep into the sleep cycle that very few people could even potentially spot her.

Not that she intended to get close enough to the town for the residents to become aware of her. That wasn't her mission.

Instead, she took her fighter along the road leading from the town at a very low speed. While she wasn't setting up a real ambush, arranging for Princess Kelsey to meet with a traveler wasn't too far off.

The more she examined the rut-filled track, she became convinced "road" wasn't the appropriate word. This was just a big trail. No wonder the rich and their carriages avoided the town.

She imagined it cost a good deal more in time, effort, and money to clear and lay a solid roadway capable of supporting coaches in relative comfort. Just clearing the trees and removing the stumps would be backbreaking.

The path she was following wasn't nearly so refined. It looked as though the people that had cleared it had cut any offending trees off as close to the ground as possible, but the stumps still protruded five to ten centimeters off the ground.

That would cause a serious jolt on some rich guy's butt, she imagined.

In less than an hour, she'd located half a dozen potential spots for a quiet meeting. Time to check them out on foot to be sure they were suitable. She'd start with the most promising.

Annette landed in an isolated clearing relatively near the road and killed the lights inside her cockpit. She sat in the dark for a few minutes while her eyes adjusted.

Once she was certain her eyes had adjusted as much as they were going to, she raised the canopy. The scents of the forest washed over her.

The smell wasn't terrible, but it was unusual. Annette had grown up in a city. Traipsing around the wilderness was not something she'd ever done before. She'd best go slow and watch her step.

There was a wide variety of noises coming from the darkened woods. Small creatures moving about, insects doing whatever bugs did, and other unidentifiable sounds.

It was spooky. She quickly decided that retiring to some place out in the wilds was not for her.

Annette pulled a pair of marine goggles from the compartment beside her knee and put them on. They rendered the outside world a pale green, but the darkness vanished. These high-tech devices took what little ambient light existed and amplified it.

She climbed down the side of her fighter and stepped onto the ground. Fallen leaves crunched under her feet.

The noises coming from the forest stopped. The animals must've heard her. It took a few minutes before they resumed whatever they were doing.

It took her half an hour to make it to the road. The area wasn't anywhere close to the town, really, but it sat between the small community and a larger town up the trail.

The road leading away from the town in the other direction was much more isolated. It was—amazingly—in even worse condition than the one she stood near. Even wagons wouldn't be going that way. It only supported people on foot or riding the local beasts of burden.

If the human they'd spotted took that route out of town, she'd have plenty of time to scout out other potential meeting locations.

Annette found an area adjacent to the road where travelers camped. She could see where they'd cut the vegetation away and dug fire pits. The efforts seemed relatively recent.

She calculated the distance from the town and decided this might be where a traveler on foot camped overnight. If the man were traveling alone, or in a small band of people, this place would be perfect.

They could set a marine pinnace down in the clearing she'd used and quickly move to observe any people resting here.

That didn't mean there wasn't going to be excitement when Kelsey introduced herself. That wasn't Annette's problem, though. She just needed to make sure the area was as secure and isolated as possible.

She'd been standing still for a bit, so she noticed when the local wildlife shut up. The silence made her crouch. She hadn't spooked them this time. Was there something else out there?

A strange sound came from across the road. She edged over far enough to take a look. What she saw surprised her.

A dozen of the natives had slipped into the area on the far side of the road. Based on how easily they moved in the dark, these aliens had better night vision than they'd expected, so she'd best be careful.

Each of them had one of the short-bladed swords they seemed to favor strapped around their waists. They also had the native equivalent of crossbows for ranged attacks. Their clothing seemed fashioned to blend in to the foliage.

Each of the Pandorans began shaping the foliage into something that would conceal them from view. They were setting up an actual ambush.

Suddenly paranoid about her own safety, Annette looked into the woods behind her. To her chagrin, she heard movement between her and the clearing where her fighter sat.

It was too bad Carl Owlet hadn't gotten the improved implant coms into circulation before this mission. If she had one, she'd have been able to communicate with her fighter from several kilometers away.

No use crying over spilt beer.

Annette edged deeper into the woods and a little up the closest hill. She moved slowly and deliberately, watching where she placed her feet. She couldn't risk making any noise.

She found a position where the foliage concealed her. She'd chosen to wear a black flight suit, so there wasn't much danger they'd spot her in the dark. That didn't mean that she was safe, though.

Annette had no idea who these people were or what they intended to do, but they'd probably hear her if she tried to sneak past them.

She had no choice but to settle in and hope that she could slip out of the area as soon as the ambushers settled in. That was going to take a while.

It probably meant that she'd miss her next scheduled report to *Persephone*. That should bring a little attention her way. All she had to do was keep her head down, and she'd be fine.

* * *

VERONICA SWATTED AT AN UNIDENTIFIABLE BUG. She had no idea what it was, but it was huge. They filled the air in the forest that she and Castille were walking through.

"Are you sure this is the best idea?" she asked as she dodged a root that threatened to send her tumbling. Again.

The security officer glanced over his shoulder at her. "Of course I am. How else are we going to find a way to get back up to orbit? The moment we turn on the systems in that cutter, they have the potential to track us."

"Just hold up a minute." She stopped so that she could focus her attention on him without breaking a leg. He obliged her by lowering the machete he was using to forge their path through the thick vegetation.

"Graham can go over every circuit in that cutter," she said. "If there's some type of remote control mechanism, he can disable it. Sneaking onto their landing field seems a little... rash."

Castille smiled. "That's why they'll never expect it. Relax. This is just a scouting mission. I just want to see how they've laid things out in case we come back to retrieve something."

"Like what?"

"A transponder," he said. "Just getting into orbit won't do us much good if they realize our cutter isn't sending a response to their automated traffic control. That'll make them suspicious. We're going to have to slip onto one of their cutters and steal a transponder so we become a known quantity."

She considered that. Grudgingly, she admitted his logic made sense. That didn't make this crazy trip feel any safer.

"If they spot us, it's over," she cautioned him. "Once they realize we're here, they'll bury this island in search parties. They'll find the base."

"Then we need to make certain no one sees us."

He returned to the task of hacking his way through the vegetation, and she fell in behind him.

It took them hours to get near the abandoned town. Once they did, they had to make their way through the foliage without the machete. She'd be covered in scratches by the time they were done.

The slow pace meant it was almost dark by the time they arrived in the overgrown streets of the town.

There were still a few people doing something on the far side of the town, but they were easy to spot by their lights. They apparently didn't want to trip over anything. Smart.

Castille led them deeper into the empty town. They'd discussed going around and approaching the landing area from the forest, but he'd decided against it. The crew that maintained the landing area was too active, and the risk of them hearing the Fleet officers tromping through the wilderness was too high.

Veronica stopped when they arrived at a large building covered in white stone. It was of higher quality than the buildings around it. If she were judging their location correctly, they were also standing at the center of the town.

"That looks important," Castille said. "I wonder what they used it for. A government center of some kind?" He spoke softly so that his voice didn't carry.

She shrugged in the darkness. "Probably. I'm not seeing any lights moving around inside, so why don't we use it while we wait for the rest of these people to go to bed?"

He considered that for a moment and nodded. "Good idea. Let's go in carefully, though. If there is someone inside, I'd rather not announce our presence."

They made their way up the steps to the large doors. Someone had wedged them open. Probably the same people that had swept the debris off the steps.

The interior of the building was lost in gloom. Neither of them dared use a light as they edged inside.

Castille held out a hand to stop her.

Veronica froze, listening closely to see what had alerted him to danger. She didn't hear anything.

"I'm going to use my light on low," he said. "I don't want to trip over something in the dark."

Her heart raced as the light came on. Even at its dimmest setting, it momentarily blinded her. She stood there blinking until her eyes adjusted and she could begin to see what was around them.

The large room that they stood in seemed to be a lobby of some kind. Maybe this was a hotel.

Off to one side, the remains of what had probably once been comfortable chairs sat crumbling on the smooth stone floor. Ahead of them was a long desk, very much like what one would find in a grand hotel.

It took her a few moments to recognize the words on the wall behind the desk. They caused her to suck in a deep breath. Fleet headquarters.

"Well, I suppose we know where they set up shop now," Castille said wryly. "I wonder if they ever expected people like us to find this place."

That seemed like an inane question. Whoever those people had been, they'd probably felt the same way about their Fleet as she felt about hers. Or, perhaps more appropriately, as she had.

The revelation about the AIs had shaken her to her core. The bedrock of her existence now felt like sand under her feet.

There were plenty of things about Fleet that Veronica disliked. The backstabbing between officers vying for the plum positions, the social strata between the officers and the crew, and some of the odious missions they occasionally had to carry out.

Now she wondered if that kind of thing was intentional. Had the AIs set up a series of competing interests inside Fleet to make certain it was never a threat to their rule?

She'd probably never know. Hell, just knowing the truth about the revolt made her death or disappearance much more likely if they made it home.

One more thing she couldn't change.

"If we're going to stay here, we should probably move to one of the upper floors," she said after a moment. "We don't want someone to wander in and find us."

"We'll take the stairs," Castille said. "The second floor should be sufficient for our needs. We'll pick an interior room and take turns getting a few hours of sleep. That should refresh us from our journey."

Some kind soul had wedged the door to the stairs open, so they didn't have to risk making noises that might carry in the night air. They made their way up to the second floor and found a suitable room toward the center.

It had obviously been an office at some point. The plain metal desk that sat inside looked forlorn and abandoned.

Veronica closed the door slowly. It made a low squeaking noise that set her teeth on edge. Thank God, no one was around to hear it.

She opened her pack and pulled out the tape she'd brought along. She tore off a thin strip and covered the gaps. Now they could turn the light up without risking someone seeing anything in the gloom.

Yeah, this office had definitely seen better days. The remains of shelves had crumbled on the outer edges of the room, dumping their contents to the floor. She hoped nothing poisonous was nesting inside the mess.

Castille looked around curiously before pulling a roll of padding out of his pack. He laid it out in the clearest area.

"Take the first break," he said. "I'll keep watch for a few hours and then wake you."

Veronica lay down and tried to relax. Thinking about the people who'd once worked here made that hard. She dreaded going to sleep because she was afraid that she'd dream of the horrors they'd endured.

She might as well just close her eyes and pretend. She didn't want to talk with the security officer right now.

Part of her had begun hoping that the enemy found them. That thought might be traitorous, but she wasn't sure it was the worst option. She needed to know more if she was going to do what was best for her people.

Whatever that was.

Somewhere in the midst of worrying about her problems, she fell into a dreamless sleep.

27

It turned out the reason Commodore Anderson had called Talbot back to *Audacious* was because Commodore Murdock had managed to pull through the emergency surgery to repair her damaged spine.

Perhaps repair wasn't the best description. Commander Castille had done an excellent job. The doctor had privately confided to Talbot that he'd expected the woman to die in spite of everything he could do.

Murdock's long-term prognosis was poor. Even with the advanced medical technology of the Old Empire at their fingertips, nerve repairs were tricky. Particularly the spine.

The odds were high that Murdock would never walk again. She might also never regain the use of her arms. Paraplegics were rare in modern society, but she'd be one of the unlucky few.

Commodore Anderson had instructed Talbot to remain on board the carrier so he could speak with the prisoner when she woke up. Oddly, Murdock had called for him before her surgery.

Not by name. She'd called him "that marine officer" when she demanded to speak to someone during one of her waking moments.

Talbot had eaten dinner and gone to sleep in the quarters he and

Kelsey shared when they were aboard the carrier. He'd set the alarm to get him up early.

That proved wise. He'd only just finished breakfast when Zoboroski called him down to the medical center.

Talbot rapped his knuckles on the hatch leading to Zoboroski's office a few minutes later. "Morning, Zac. How's she doing?"

The doctor grimaced. "About as poorly as I expected. She's lost the use of her arms too. They best thing I can say is that I've saved her life."

He shook his head a little. "I'm not certain she's going to thank you for that."

"Living up to my oath to do no harm is sometimes complicated," the doctor admitted. "The odds are very, very high that she's going to be confined to a bed for the rest of her life."

Talbot grunted. "I assume the fact you've called me means she's awake."

Zoboroski nodded. "She's demanded to speak with you again."

"Why me?"

"You're going to have to ask her that."

Talbot sighed. "Then I suppose I'd best get this over with. I assume you've already told her the bad news."

"As if I'd make you do that. I talked with her right before I called you. She knows how unlikely even a partial recovery is going to be."

"Then I'd best go see what she wants."

Zoboroski rose from behind his desk and led Talbot down the corridor. He stopped short of the compartment where Talbot suspected Murdock was waiting for him.

"I'll leave the two of you alone to discuss whatever it is she wants to talk about," Zoboroski said. "The only instructions I'm going to give you are not to push her into a rage. One of the two of you is going to have to be the adult. I'm afraid that's you."

"Has anyone ever told you what a spoilsport you are?"

"It's part of my medical training." Zoboroski clapped him on the shoulder. "Good luck."

Talbot took a deep breath and walked into the compartment.

Commodore Emilia Murdock looked completely different from

what Talbot remembered. The supercilious woman had rubbed him the wrong way from the moment he'd met her, but she'd never looked so helpless. So frail. Not even when he'd cornered her in the interrogation room.

Frankly, she looked decades older lying in that bed with her hands neatly arranged on the covers. It was creepy knowing that she was unable to move them from where they lay.

"It's about damned time," the woman said in a hoarse voice. "You'd think my rank would earn me at least a little courtesy."

He pulled up the visitor's chair and sat. "My apologies, Commodore. I wasn't on board when you called. I'm sure someone said this, but we're very sorry for what happened to you."

The woman snorted bitterly. "You're the one that put me under his control. You could've locked me into a cell somewhere else. It would've sucked, but at least I'd be able to move."

"We could have," Talbot said. "We didn't have any reason to expect Castille would attack you. Why did he?"

"He said he had to kill me so that I wouldn't talk."

"You were going to talk? Frankly, I hadn't pegged you as feeling cooperative."

When she didn't say anything, he continued. "He obviously had an escape plan worked out. A successful one, I might add. Why didn't he just take you with him?"

"I don't know," the woman said tiredly. "He didn't even give me the option. One minute I was sitting in my room reading a book and the next he was on top of me with his arm around my neck.

"Bastard had the gall to apologize for what he was about to do. Then he jerked my head back, and it was all over. If I never hear a sound like that again, it'll be too soon."

The best timeline they could put together said that Castille had struck right before he'd left the quarters to go to lunch. As a courtesy, they hadn't had the computer monitoring the prisoners' quarters. That turned out to have been a mistake.

Castille had gone into each person's room and killed them one by one. He'd used some kind of blunt object to crush the mens' skulls, and then he'd strangled the civilian computer specialist. Finally, he'd snapped his commanding officer's neck before coolly leaving the suite as if nothing had happened.

Yeah, Castille was one coldhearted bastard.

"I regret to inform you that you were not the only one he attacked," Talbot said softly. "Commander Castille murdered Commanders Irons, Gomez, and Jeanette Martin before he attacked you."

Murdock closed her eyes. "God. This is a nightmare."

Talbot chose to say nothing. There was nothing he *could* say.

After a minute, Murdock opened her eyes. "I want to make a deal. I'll give you what you want in exchange for asylum and the best medical care you can give me. I understand the odds of me recovering are slim, but I want to live."

Talbot felt his eyebrows rise. "We agree, of course, but we were already going to give you the best care we could. I'm not sure you can give us what we really want, though. I understand that the critical computers on board the orbital require multiple codes in order to access their contents."

Commodore Murdock gave him a nasty smile. "Commander Castille made an error. He tried to kill everyone that had those codes, but he missed someone. It takes two of us to access the system. He left two of us alive."

"Two?" Talbot asked. "Who else did he miss? I thought that Commander Renner hadn't yet received her authorization codes."

"She hadn't. Castille's codes would've expired as soon as she assumed his duties. Besides, she's security. She would never have cooperated with you. She's probably just as bad as he is.

"No. I'm thinking of someone else. You see, we have a number of researchers aboard the orbital. They're prisoners too, so they'd probably be willing to cooperate with you, if you sweet-talk them.

"The woman in charge of them has a code, though she doesn't know it. It's an emergency measure in case some type of accident kills off most of the command staff. It's the same code she uses to manage the research systems."

Talbot smiled. "Well then, I think we have a deal."

"Good," the woman grunted. "I want that bastard to know I stuck a knife in his back after he tried to kill me."

* * *

KELSEY ARRIVED on the bridge less than five minutes after the duty officer woke her. "What's happening?"

The man rose from the command console and allowed her to take her seat.

"Captain Vitter is overdue. I tried calling her, but I haven't received a response. I rerouted some of the drones to cover the area around her. There are a number of Pandorans setting up what certainly looks like an ambush. I found her on a hill nearby. She's pinned down but undiscovered.

"Also, it seems the man you wanted to meet must've eluded the drones we had watching the town. He's traveling alone on the road and moving slowly, but I think he'll reach the ambush point at about dawn. Assuming, of course, that the camping area is his true destination."

Kelsey quickly checked the information he'd gathered. It certainly did appear as though someone had set up a very slick ambush, and the fact the man had felt he needed to sneak out of town was very interesting.

Whom had he offended? His discreet departure and the large number of people sent to kill or capture him meant there was more going on than met the eye.

"Gather the marines," she said. "I'm heading down to the surface shortly. How much danger is there that the ambushers will find her?"

The man shrugged. "I don't know. She's still close to their area of operations, and they have forces between her and her fighter."

She reviewed what the drones were seeing in real-time. There were several dozen aliens concealed in the woods around the camping area. From the way they were moving around, they could see just fine.

While a few of them were taking up positions watching the road, most were building concealment around the camping area. None of them was particularly close to where Annette was hiding, so Kelsey didn't have to come rushing in guns blazing.

The tricky part of this was going to be extracting the pilot without alerting the aliens to her presence.

She called Angela while she considered her options.

"What's wrong?" the marine demanded after only a moment.

"Aren't you supposed to be asleep?" Kelsey asked. "It's the middle of the night."

"Marines learn to sleep with one eye open. You're up, so there must be trouble. Fill me in while I get dressed."

Kelsey briefed her on the situation. She concluded with an overhead map of the area around Annette with little red dots representing the potentially hostile aliens.

"I'm not quite certain how we're going to extract Annette," Kelsey concluded. "This is something you're better suited to figure out."

The doors to the lift slid open, and Angela strode onto the bridge. The com link between them terminated.

"That was quick," Kelsey said. "I think you've pretty well adjusted to your new legs."

Angela sat at her console and brought up several displays. "It's amazing how motivated one gets when a crisis occurs. From what I can see, Annette is safe for the moment. We'll want to get her out before dawn, though.

"The more interesting challenge is our human friend. He's going to walk into an ambush if you don't go tell him. He doesn't seem like the trusting type, so I'm not sure how open he's going to be to you just popping out of the dark."

"That's actually the easier of our two problems. I'm going to have the marines drop me off on the road in front of him. He'll see me when he comes to that stretch. Humans are curious creatures. He'll look around for a trap, but he's going to talk."

Angela gave her a doubtful look. "You're going to meet him all by yourself? Don't you think that's a little risky?"

"I'll be armed. If he gets froggy, I'll stun him. With drones all around us, I'll know where he is at every moment. With my enhanced vision, I'll see him more clearly than he can see me."

Kelsey smiled coolly. "And let's not forget that I'm a Marine Raider. If he wants to fight, I'll be moving a lot faster than him, and I'm one hell of a lot stronger. This isn't nearly as dangerous as it seems at first glance."

Her executive officer nodded reluctantly. "Are you going to have that conversation at the same time we're rescuing Annette?"

"If you can come up with a good plan, yes."

The marine smiled. "That's actually an easy one. The forest canopy is solid, so the aliens won't be able to see the sky very well. We'll take one of the pinnaces over her position and lower a line. It looks as if there's an opening in the trees a few dozen meters from her position. That'll work just fine."

Kelsey had to admit that was a neat solution. "Perfect. Once they get her out of the area, they can join the marines guarding me.

"Just in case the man proves more resourceful than I anticipate, the pinnaces can swoop in and drop marines on top of him in thirty seconds. They'll be in unpowered armor, so I don't think he'll be much of a threat."

That seemed to suit Angela better. "I like it."

"Good. Let me know if the situation down there changes."

Kelsey stepped into the lift and headed down to the tiny part of the ship set aside for marine country.

Finally. A little action.

While she hoped this didn't turn violent, she'd felt as though she'd been boxing at shadows for the last week. She couldn't do anything to resolve the problems besetting them. She'd felt helpless.

That changed now.

28

According to Raul's implants, they had four hours before the sun began lightening the sky. As expected, there wasn't very much happening at the landing field.

That wasn't to say that everything was quiet. A number of people were up and performing various tasks as he and Veronica slipped from the edge of town and into the jungle bordering the area.

Half a dozen people clustered around one of the cutters, performing some kind of maintenance. Everything around them was well lit. That meant they'd be unable to see anything in the darkness beyond the reach of the light.

Three cutters sat in the landing zone, two buttoned up tight. They had small shelters set up nearby. Probably for crew.

Raul stopped behind a stack of crates to observe the workers. Veronica crouched beside him.

He examined the crates with a frown. "What do you think they have inside these?" he asked quietly.

The destroyer commander examined the crates as well as she could but ended up shrugging. "There's no telling. There certainly doesn't seem to be any reason for shipping things down here. Perhaps it's stuff they recovered from inside the town."

"I suppose it doesn't really matter," he said. "Tell me, how difficult would it be to gain access to one of the unoccupied cutters?"

"They can be opened from the outside, but you have to have the right code or be able to bypass the lockout. Graham can do it. Not while people are working on another cutter right next to him, though."

Raul found it hard to argue with that kind of logic. No matter how they played this, they were running a serious risk. They'd have to sneak into the landing area, break into a cutter, and swap out the transponder without anyone realizing they'd ever been there.

The only way his plan had a chance of success was if the enemy never realized they'd made contact with him and his people. If they had to stun any of the workers, that would send up a huge red flag, and searchers would flood the island.

If anyone realized they'd tampered with one of the cutters, they'd be on the lookout for strange vessels. Only through complete obscurity could they waltz right past the enemy warships and steal the Dresden orbital back from them.

"Let's slip around and take a closer look at the sealed cutters," Veronica said. "I know Graham is going to ask me some questions, so I'd prefer to have decent answers for him."

"What kind of questions?" Raul asked.

"The first one is whether or not those cutters are locked. It's entirely possible they just closed them up without a code."

Veronica eyed the workers in their bubble of light and headed over toward the parked cutters. She walked slowly but seemingly made no effort to hide herself.

His heart in his throat, Raul walked after her. Amazingly, they made it to the parked cutters without any issue. No one had seen them.

He stood watching the workers while Veronica stepped up beside the forward landing gear. She climbed one of the struts and meddled with something inside the opening the strut normally occupied.

She climbed back down and stepped over to him. "The maintenance hatch is unsecure. They didn't bother arming the security system, either. I'm going in for a look. Keep an eye out in case anyone comes by."

Veronica scampered nimbly up into the cutter.

The night was so quiet that he could almost hear what the workers were saying to one another. He pondered the risks and then moved away from the cutter until he could hear them clearly.

Once he was close enough, he knelt on the ground and listened.

For the most part, all they were doing was bantering back and forth. Trash talk, basically. He was about to give up on hearing anything interesting when one of the women asked a question.

"Any word on when we're going to wrap up work at this site?"

An unseen companion inside the open cutter responded. "We're supposed to be ready to pull up stakes in forty-eight hours. Word is, that's the earliest we can leave the system. If they finished relocating all the prisoners by then."

"You think they'll really move all those people in two days?"

"Who the hell knows? Once they do, we can get the hell out here. If they can find the empress."

Raul watched the woman shake her head. Based on her expression, the woman didn't think very much of Justine.

"Ex-empress," the woman stressed. "And don't forget that she snuck on board our ship. She's a criminal."

The man inside laughed. "People like her always get away with crap that would land us in prison. She's not a criminal. She's a noble. Get used to it."

The sentiment amused Raul. Apparently, some things were similar in both empires. The rich and the powerful rarely had to face the consequences of their actions.

He was still chuckling to himself when he heard a soft whine somewhere above him.

Shocked, he looked up. A bright star was moving rapidly in the heavens above and growing brighter.

Holy crap. There was a cutter coming in for landing.

Based on the layout of the field, there was a very good chance it was going to land right on top of him.

* * *

ANNETTE FELT PRETTY good about her chances. The aliens seemed to
have settled into their various positions. Maybe she'd be able to slip
away unnoticed after all.

Her flight suit wasn't the most insulated uniform she'd ever worn,
so she was thankful that she'd thrown a jacket on when she'd climbed
out of her fighter. It made sitting still in the cooler air tolerable.

Things went well until she heard the aliens between her and her
fighter begin moving toward the ambush location. Now they'd pass
close by her position.

Annette had pegged them as reinforcements for the people out by
the road. If they ran into trouble taking down their prey, no doubt the
reserve provided enough force to make sure everything worked out in
the end.

She wasn't certain what had signaled them to move forward. None
of the aliens overlooking the road had gone to meet them, yet the
backup forces were moving forward to join their friends.

Since they were going to pass very close to her location, she made
herself even smaller and got closer to the ground. She had a flechette
pistol and a stunner, but she'd prefer not having to reveal herself.

That seemed good enough until she heard someone coming up
the hill toward her.

Annette moved to the other side of a large tree. Conscious of
every sound she made, she held her breath.

Someone came into the clearing where she'd been a moment
before. She could see him stealthily moving between branches in the
foliage.

She willed the man to keep moving down the hill, but he stopped.
The pause was only momentary. He moved forward and started down
the hill on the other side of the tree she crouched behind.

Or so she thought until someone grabbed her by the back of her
jacket and yanked her off balance.

She pulled her stunner as she fell, but the alien man knocked it
from her hand before slamming her to the ground and jabbing the
pointy end of a knife to her throat.

Annette lay there, frozen in shock and sudden fear. The man sat on her torso, pinning one hand with his knee while he held the other one down with his free hand.

"Well, I seem to have found a little bird," he said softly. "Don't chirp, or I'll be forced to hurt you."

Astonishingly, he spoke Standard as well as she did.

She'd fallen hard, and the night-vision goggles had come loose during their struggle. They lay somewhere off in the darkness. With them gone, she couldn't clearly see him, but she thought he was the same man who'd been in the clearing.

The two of them stared at one another for what felt like an eternity. She forced herself to relax. There was no way that she was moving him. Surrender was the only option.

"I don't suppose I could convince you to let me up," she said softly. "It's a little hard to breathe down here."

He shook his head with a small smile. "I think not. There's too much risk you'd give me away."

She pondered that for a moment. Give him away to whom?

"You're not with the people down there, are you?" she asked.

"And neither, it appears, are you. This is indeed an intriguing surprise. If you aren't with the Kalorian soldiers, then who are you with?"

"I don't suppose I could plead ignorance?"

He chuckled softly. "You humans. You always think you're so funny. Tell me how you knew Jacob was coming this way tonight."

Her mind raced as she tried to think of what to say. In the end, she decided to be honest.

"Actually, we were hoping to meet Jacob away from prying ears."

"We? Are my men going to find other humans lurking in the woods? I really don't understand what game you think you're playing. People are going to die before the sun comes up. Why are you hiding here in the forest?"

She opened her mouth to respond, but he pressed the knife into her throat a little. "On second thought, I don't think I have time to hear your response right now. Don't struggle. That will only make this hurt worse."

He dropped the knife beside her head and reached into his jacket.

She tried to throw him off but failed. He had her pinned and obviously knew how to fight.

He pulled an object from his belt. Annette only had a moment to recognize the stunner before her world went dark.

29

Talbot left the medical center and went straight to Carl's lab.

As he'd expected, the place was a hive of activity. They were still retrieving equipment from the Dresden orbital, and crewmen were maneuvering much of it into areas inside the massive compartment.

Carl was at the center of the activity, directing where to secure everything. Standing at his side was the former director of research on the Dresden orbital, Doctor Jacqueline Parker.

The dark-skinned woman was still an enigma to Talbot. He couldn't begin to imagine the life she'd lived. Not from her chaotic memories of Erorsi and the savage Pale Ones as a child, to having the Rebel Empire plant explosives in her head.

Carl spotted Talbot when he was almost to them. He raised his hand in greeting. "I thought you were down on the surface looking for Kelsey's mother."

"I was. Hello again, Doctor Parker. Commodore Anderson called me back up to talk to someone."

The young scientist gave him an appraising look. "Must have been important."

"You could say that. Am I remembering rightly that you set up a copy of the manufacturing computers for testing?"

Carl's eyes narrowed. "I did, not that it's helped very much. Why?"

"Because that means we can check something without risking the real cores. I just left Commodore Murdock. She says that she's willing to assist us. Not only that, she told me where we might be able to get the second code required for access."

Parker's jaw dropped. "Are you kidding me? You got that horrible old woman to cooperate with you?"

"Did you hear about the escape, Doctor Parker?" Talbot asked.

Her expression became guarded. "I heard a little bit. The security bastard and some other Fleet officers managed to get off the ship."

"But you didn't hear what happened to Commodore Murdock and the other senior officers from the Dresden orbital?"

She frowned. "No. Why?"

"Because Commander Castille killed everyone except Commodore Murdock. He still managed to paralyze her from the neck down."

The shock on Parker's face was profound. "Oh my God. I might not have liked working for them, but most of those people were relatively decent. Castille and Murdock were the ones I couldn't stand."

"It's a horrible thing," Talbot agreed. "The only bit of good to come out of the situation is that Commodore Murdock gave me her code. Now all we need is the second code to test it."

"If all of them are dead, who has the code?"

He pointed at her. "You do."

The woman started laughing. "That's the most ridiculous thing I've ever heard. Major Talbot, they used explosives in my skull to compel me to work for them. And rest assured, when I finally became a liability, they'd have taken me somewhere and set it off. Those people wouldn't trust me with something like that."

"It makes a crazy kind of sense," he disagreed. "No one would ever expect you to have it. Murdock said you had the code in case no one else was available. It's the same one you use to access your computers as the lead researcher."

Parker didn't look convinced. "If you say so."

Carl gestured toward the side of the lab. "We can verify it easily enough. Let's step over to the manufacturing computers and give it a try."

The three of them walked over to a console and Carl sat. "As I said, the cores are encrypted but I was able to make copies. The originals are safely stored elsewhere. If something goes wrong, these will wipe themselves, but we'll still be able to try again."

The young scientist focused his attention on Parker. "How does this work? Talbot gives a code and then you do?"

Parker nodded. "Try to access the core. It should prompt you for the first code. Major Talbot can enter it at that point. If that code is accepted, it will prompt for a second one. That's where I apparently come in."

Carl stared at the console for a moment and then looked at Talbot. "Ready for you."

Talbot used his implants to access the computer. When he felt its presence, he sent the code that Commodore Murdock had shared with him. The computer immediately indicated the code had been accepted and prompted for the next code.

"It's ready for you, Doctor Parker," Talbot said.

She focused on the computer for a moment before a shocked expression spread across her face. "I'll be damned. It accepted the code!"

Carl frowned in concentration for a moment and then grinned. "We're in! The core is unlocked!"

Talbot stood there and watched for a moment as the young scientist explored the access he had gained to the computer. After several minutes, he tapped Carl on the shoulder to remind him that he was still standing there.

The young scientist's eyes focused on him. "Sorry. I got distracted."

"Did that completely unlock it? I'm going to go report to

Commodore Anderson in just a minute, and I'm certain she'll want to know."

Carl smiled widely. "As far as I can tell, your codes gave me complete access. Be sure to send them to me so I can use them again, if need be.

"I've already initiated the copying of the data to a clean computer core. We should be able to access all the information we need to manufacture Marine Raider implants and AI computer hardware. Everything seems to be there."

Talbot hadn't realized he'd been tense until he felt himself relax. "That's great news. I wasn't sure what we were going to do if we couldn't get that information."

His friend shrugged. "We'd have figured something out. We always do."

"The man I have on the orbital said he'd have the last of the hardware to you sometime today. Does that match up with what you're seeing?"

"It does. If anything, he's running ahead of schedule. By my estimation, we should have the last of the manufacturing and research equipment aboard in about six hours. It may take another half a day to move all the supplies that I've flagged as necessary for the manufacturing process, though."

"Excellent," Talbot said. "That's one thing off my plate. As soon as we can get the Dresden orbital cleared, we can move it to the outer system. Then I can focus my attention on finding the escapees and rescuing Kelsey's mother. Good work."

His young friend grinned. "It seems like you did all the hard work."

Talbot waved at Parker and headed for the corridor. He'd stop in to brief Commodore Anderson and then get back down to the planet. The clock was ticking.

* * *

VERONICA JUMPED a little when Castille climbed into the cutter and pushed the hatch closed.

"What's wrong?" she demanded.

"There's another cutter coming in," he said. "I barely got under cover before it turned its landing lights on."

"That tears it," she said. "We need to get out of here, and I don't think we can afford to try sneaking back in again."

He frowned. "What do you mean? We have to come back for the transponder."

"No, we don't. I'm taking it right now."

"That's going to tip them off," he hissed. "We're not ready to make our play yet. I overheard the workers outside saying it was going to be another day or two before they finished getting the prisoners off the orbital."

"Are you going to count on the enemy being punctual? We don't have time to waste coming back here tomorrow night. By then, the schedule will definitely be too tight. We need to be in orbit at that point.

"They're never going to realize there's a problem so long as we keep this cutter from taking off. They'd have no reason to test the transponder if the cutter is grounded for maintenance."

Raul raised an eyebrow. "Is it grounded for maintenance?"

"Give me fifteen minutes, and they won't be flying this thing for a few days. It'll take them that long just to diagnose where the trouble is."

She wasn't an engineering officer, but Veronica knew her way around small craft. She'd started her career as a cutter pilot. That meant she had more than enough experience to know what would disable one. Particularly in a way that was infuriatingly hard to find.

Veronica went into the engine compartment and started digging through the guts of the grav drive controls. The flight-deck officer on her first assignment out of the academy had disabled a cutter by doing exactly what she was doing now.

It had taken her three days to trace the fault. Three infuriating, agonizing days of him staring over her shoulder and belittling her skills while she sweated.

Years later, she'd decided the man had been an evil genius. That one incident had driven her to learn more about cutters than she'd ever dreamed possible. Not that she'd ever forgiven him for putting her through hell. The sadist didn't deserve the credit for any nonexistent good motives.

The thing she liked best about this particular trick was that it disabled access to the avionics compartment along with the grav drive. Even if they tried to ping the transponder, they wouldn't get any reading on it.

Once she had the console open, she unplugged several connections and removed a component. One of the toolboxes attached to the bulkhead provided an instrument that let her send a surge of power that overloaded it.

Frying it only took a moment. She then painstakingly reassembled the console. When the pilots began their preflight, the engines would indicate they had a fault. The maintenance people would dig into them, but they'd be fine.

Only by tracing every bit of diagnostic circuitry would they locate the faulty component. Even with multiple people tearing the system apart, they wouldn't find it for at least two days. Her ego tried to egg her on to three, but that might be pushing it.

When she'd reassembled the console, she dug into the avionics compartment and removed the transponder. If anyone actually looked inside, they'd see the gaping hole where it normally sat.

She didn't expect that, though. Why look at something when you had your implants to tell you its condition? Veronica had met plenty of officers that never bothered physically checking anything. She was willing to bet the maintenance crews and pilots down here would behave the same.

Once she'd put the tool back in the toolbox, she bagged the transponder to keep it from being damaged and returned to the flight deck.

"I've got it," she said. "Let's see if it's safe for us to depart. I'll let you go down to the ground while I secure everything."

Castille still didn't look convinced, but at least he'd stopped arguing.

She unsealed the emergency hatch and lowered her head cautiously until she could see the area around them.

The new cutter had opened its ramp, and a number of people were moving the crates she and Castille had hidden behind on to it. Not only were they focused on their task, but the lighting also made it impossible to see anyone outside their general area.

Moving as quietly as possible, she lowered herself onto the landing gear and edged to the side so Castille could pass her. Once he'd made it to the ground, she sealed the hatch and followed him down.

Now all they had to do was get out of the area without anyone seeing them.

So, of course, someone stepped out of the shelter they were passing. A man in a lieutenant's uniform stared at them from just a few meters away.

"What's going on?" he asked sleepily.

30

The marines dropped Kelsey off on the road about a kilometer in front of where the human was presently walking. In the low light conditions, he'd have to be virtually on top of her before he noted her presence.

She found a convenient place in plain sight and started waiting.

With her enhanced vision, she had no trouble seeing him as he came around the closest bend. He was wearing a dark cloak with its hood up—probably to ward off the chill—but she could still clearly see his face.

He was actually walking beside the road. That made sense. It would be hard to see the ruts in the dim light cast by the stars.

Honestly, she wondered why he was traveling in the dark of night. All it would take was one pothole and he'd break a leg.

To her amazement, he slowed while he was still fairly distant. From the way he was looking around, he'd sensed something.

Kelsey wasn't moving. She had no idea how he could've detected her presence. Yet, something had obviously raised his guard.

Well, she might as well get this over with.

Keeping her pace slow, she began walking down the center of the road toward him. She kept an eye on the ruts to avoid ruining her entrance.

The man quickly focused his attention on her. He seemed as though he might be ready to flee but stopped himself. Perhaps he realized there was only one of her.

"I come in peace," she said as she came to a halt about thirty meters from him. "I mean you no harm."

"Says the person accosting a weary traveler in the middle of the night in the back end of nowhere," he said dryly.

Kelsey couldn't see his hands under the cloak, but she assumed he was holding some type of weapon. Based on the tech level, it was probably the hilt of a sword, but she wasn't going to take unnecessary chances. It was possible he had access to Imperial technology.

"I realize how this looks, but I wanted to warn you there's an ambush set for you ahead."

His head came up sharply. "Really? And out of the goodness of your heart, you've decided to come tell me about it? I can barely see you. How did you know who I was?"

"I'm about to make a light."

No need to be hasty. She didn't want to goad him into intemperate action.

She turned on a camp light that she'd brought with her. It wasn't a tight beam. More of a distributed light source that would allow people to see inside a tent. It didn't illuminate him much, but it would show her quite clearly.

"My name is Kelsey Bandar and, as you can see, I'm quite alone."

The man hesitated a moment and then walked forward until he was only ten meters away. In the light, she could see his expression clearly. He looked shocked.

"I thought myself familiar with all of the humans living in this area. How could I possibly not know you?"

Kelsey smiled. "I'm not from around here."

He eyed her uniform. "No. I'd say not. I'll wager you're not even part of Clan Dauntless."

She raised an eyebrow. "Clan Dauntless? No. I'm not part of any clan. I'm not from this world at all."

The man stared at her for a long moment before shaking his head. "We always knew this day might come, but I never believed it. Not deep down. Why have you come for me?"

"I'm just looking for information. I was completely serious about the ambush too. You probably shouldn't keep traveling along this road. It's not safe."

"No. I imagine not."

Kelsey's enhanced hearing heard a soft click that her combat reflexes identified as likely a safety flipping off. She threw herself to the side, and flechettes tore through the space where she'd been standing moments before.

She landed hard in the deep grass to the side of the road, already drawing her stunner and opening fire.

The man was quick. He ducked low and rolled to the side, still firing at her.

Kelsey heard the pinnace's drives kick into maximum thrust in the darkness above her. Marines in unpowered armor would be on them in seconds.

"Stunners only!" she sent over the combat link. "Don't hurt him!"

For a moment, she thought the man was going to get away into the forest, but she managed to line up a shot at the very last moment. The stunner bolt took him in the back just as he passed into the trees.

Kelsey stood slowly, wary of additional small arms fire. If she'd only clipped him, he might still be awake enough to shoot her.

The pinnace touched down right in front of her, and marines came boiling out. Half a dozen of them raced to the woods while the rest secured the area.

Two of them came back with the man slung limply between them. The corporal accompanying them handed her a Fleet flechette pistol.

Kelsey examined it for a moment before she stared at the unconscious man. "Well, well. Aren't you full of surprises? I think you and I are going to have a very interesting conversation in a few hours."

She gestured toward the pinnace. "Load him up. As soon as they recover Annette, we're getting out of here."

The corporal grimaced. "There's some trouble. Some of the

aliens just attacked the other aliens. Captain Vitter isn't responding to communication attempts from the other pinnace. They're not picking up her implants at all."

"Crap," she said. "Everyone in. We're going in hard and fast. Again, stun only, if possible."

By the time they were loaded into the pinnace, she was already strapping on a set of unpowered armor. Everyone might think she was dangerously impulsive, but it was only when she had no other choice.

They arrived over the ambush site about the same time the second pinnace landed near Annette's fighter.

As soon as the ramp came down, the marines charged out. Kelsey could hear metal-on-metal impacts in the dark woods, as well as people screaming and shouting. There was a battle taking place.

The first people Kelsey saw were two aliens swinging swords at one another. One of them quickly achieved the upper hand and stabbed the other through the torso. The second alien fell with a grunt.

She shot the victor with her stunner, and to her amazement, he shook it off. A second shot took him down, though.

"Be advised that the aliens have some resistance to stunners," she said over the combat link. "Shoot twice and be sure. Don't leave anyone awake behind you. They might stab you in the back."

With the pinnaces and drones scanning the forest, they took out the fighters inside half an hour. A number of the aliens were dead or grievously injured.

Kelsey ordered the dead and injured loaded onto one of the pinnaces. The prisoners went on the other. She sent both small craft back into orbit to *Persephone*. They'd come back for her in less than an hour.

The only thing they didn't find was Annette Vitter. The pilot was gone.

* * *

RAUL STEPPED in front of Veronica and smiled at the lieutenant.

"They asked if you could give them a hand loading the crates," he said with a smile.

The man gave him a slightly confused look before nodding. "Sure. I was about to go do that anyway. Thanks."

The skin between Raul's shoulder blades itched as he kept walking. All it would take was for the man to ask the wrong person who they were and they'd sound the alarm.

But no cry came. The odds were good that the man had assumed they were legitimate. By the time anyone figured differently, he and Veronica would be long gone. Hopefully, they wouldn't realize their mistake at all.

"I thought we were toast there," Veronica said softly as they made their way into the ruined town. "That guy had us dead to rights."

"One thing I've learned in security is that people are inclined to believe what they see. Behave as if you belong, and you can get in almost anywhere.

"For example, the secure area on the Dresden orbital. One of the enemy officers waltzed right in and attended a classified briefing. No one realized they'd made a mistake and escorted the wrong person inside."

Veronica looked impressed. "Somebody had some serious balls."

He nodded. "Yes, she did. Let's hope we don't run into her again before we make our exit."

By the time they'd made their way across the ruined town and back into the forest, it was almost dawn.

They waited until there was enough light to continue on their way. They were especially careful when they climbed the slopes of the volcano, so it was almost noon by the time they'd safely arrived at the abandoned base.

He couldn't believe they'd gotten away with it. That almost made him laugh. Compared to the crime they were contemplating, this was petty theft.

The destroyer's engineer had gotten the water system in the base back online, so he showered while the attached unit cleaned his uniform. He still had to make do with survival rations but perhaps not for much longer.

Once he was clean and full, he went in search of Veronica. He found her on the stolen cutter with her engineering officer. It looked as though they were installing the stolen transponder.

"Refresh my brain how this works," he said to them. "Does this transmit our identity at all times or only when specifically queried?"

"Only when someone sends a signal requesting our identity," the engineering lieutenant said.

"It's standard procedure in our version of Fleet to query a vessel when we first detect it," Veronica said. "The ship then tags the identity of the vessel and assumes it is legitimate if the transponder is good. There's no reason to continually request an identity."

"So as long as they haven't realized we've stolen the transponder, they shouldn't give us another glance?"

"Probably not, though if they're expecting the cutter to come back to the carrier and then we head for the recovery ship, that may raise some alarms."

"Well, we can't very well go on board the carrier," Raul said reasonably. "Otherwise, we might just as well have surrendered down below and saved ourselves the trouble."

The destroyer commander smiled. "True enough. Even if they ask us where we're going, a decent lie might get us through. Like you said, people are inclined to believe stories that make sense."

"And what story might we have for bypassing the carrier and heading for the recovery ship?"

"Damned if I know," she said. "I'm going to be thinking about that before we take off. When do you plan on going?"

He considered the time. "We need to leave as soon as it gets dark again. We don't want the people below seeing us lift off from the volcano, but we have to get out of here."

"What about our prisoners?"

There was something odd in her tone. He wondered if she suspected he'd executed the Dresden senior staff.

If she did, she had to realize why he'd done it. He couldn't allow the enemy to have access to the manufacturing equipment. The ability to produce Marine Raider implants or re-create the lords would be a disaster.

Yet he didn't expect her to accept that without some misgivings. She was a Fleet officer, not a security officer. Summary executions to protect the Empire were outside her normal duties.

"We'll take them with us," he said in his best reassuring voice. "The intelligence they can provide is worth the risk."

"Having someone guard them while we hijack the recovery ship is going to be awkward. We don't have enough bodies as it is."

He smiled widely. "As much as it pains me, I suppose we'll have to stun them again. Justine will be most put out with me."

Raul imagined the noblewoman would be quite angry. Yet, he had to confess it would give him great pleasure to take her down. Her shrill voice was getting on his very last nerve.

"Everyone needs to get as much rest as they can," he said. "Get a good meal, take a nap, whatever it takes to relax. Once we start moving, things are going to be tense and stay that way for quite some time.

"With any luck, we'll be out of the system before they realize we've left the planet. By the time they grasp that there's another flip point, we might even be several systems away. Once they lose us, we'll be able to make our way back home eventually."

Then the war would begin in earnest. With his help, the Empire would crush the last remnants of the old dictatorship and the ghosts.

The lords were quite generous to those who pleased them. He could only imagine the rewards he'd earn for his part in this. He could retire a wealthy man. One raised to the higher orders by their decree.

Oh, yes. The days ahead were going to be very nice indeed.

31

Annette woke slowly. She remembered almost immediately that she'd been stunned, but her groan ruined any chance of pretending she was still out.

She opened her eyes and tried to ignore the stabbing headache. She was still outdoors, but the landscape had changed. Instead of being in a small clearing in the forest, she was on a mostly open hillside covered with large rocks.

Some were big enough to block the wind, and a large overhang of stone provided a break for a cheery little fire. The flames bathed her with warmth.

An alien—presumably the same one she'd been fighting—sat nearby. His hands were busy with a small knife and piece of wood, possibly carving something, but his eyes never left her.

"I see that you're awake," he said levelly. "Good. We have some talking to do, you and I."

He'd bound her hands in front of her and tied her ankles together. Her captor was taking no chances.

"What makes you think I'm going to cooperate with you in that conversation?" she asked as she sat up slowly.

"I could make some grand statement about how I have you

completely in my control, but I'm not certain that's the best course of action," he admitted. "You seem to be a woman of action. One in possession of unusual and unique equipment."

The alien gestured to his right where she saw her weapons. Since he'd had a stunner of his own, he probably knew what the flechette pistol was too.

Her night-vision goggles were missing. He must've overlooked them in the dark when he'd kidnapped her. Pity. She'd loved those things.

"There are a finite number of these weapons in existence," the alien continued, his tone almost lecturing. "While it is not unheard of for one to turn up in an unusual location or in the possession of someone who should never have had it in the first place, it is never functional.

"You see, it takes power to charge the magazines. Yet, I must assume you know that. Both these weapons are fully charged. I confess to a great curiosity in how you managed that."

He smiled, his expression almost human. "Perhaps we should begin by introducing ourselves. My name is—as you might expect—not a comfortable one in the human tongue. You may refer to me as Derek. That is similar enough to be useful in interspecies communication."

"Annette," she said. "My people are going to find me. When they do, I suggest you surrender peacefully or risk getting seriously injured."

The alien's smile widened. "I *do* like your confidence, but we've traveled quite some distance. The likelihood of your friends finding us is very small.

"While I am a civilized man, it would behoove you to remember that my people do not take well to threats or intimidation. Even if only implied."

Annette laughed. "I have no idea what you're talking about. Frankly, you're the first person of your species that I've ever met. Based on what I knew, I never expected you to be able to speak Standard as well as you do."

He frowned slightly. "I find that aspect of your story... unlikely.

Humans might be standoffish, but none of them live in such isolation that they wouldn't have ever met one of my kind."

"That's where the problem comes in. I'm not part of the population on this world."

The alien considered her for a long moment. His smile slowly faded until his face was expressionless.

"That is a serious and frightening statement."

She raised an eyebrow. "Serious? Yes. Frightening? It doesn't have to be."

When he didn't respond, Annette continued. "It's obvious that I've stumbled into something that I didn't expect. Frankly, that isn't too surprising considering how very little we know of your people. All we were trying to do was have a quiet word with the human traveling on the road."

"Allow me to make certain that I understand you correctly," the alien said slowly. "You are claiming that other humans have now found us?"

"That's right, and my compatriots won't stop looking for me."

"And *that* is why you frighten me. If what you say is true, it might best serve my interests to shoot you in the head right now and walk away."

That shocked her. "Why in the world would you kill me out of hand just because I'm not from this planet?"

"Because humans are dangerous, unpredictable, and dogmatic on the very best of days. Without access to the technology that was once theirs, your kind is relatively safe. If more of your kind has arrived, war is at hand."

Her mind raced as she tried to figure out what the hell he was talking about. Why would the ghosts be such dangerous people?

"Do I appear unpredictable and dogmatic? I'll agree that I'm dangerous, just on general principles, though."

The alien's smile returned. "I like you. That isn't to say that I might not have to kill you before the night is through. I suggest you tell me enough of your story to convince me that you should live."

"Since I have absolutely no idea why being human would be inordinately dangerous, I'm not certain what I can say to reassure you.

Perhaps if you told me why you feared my people so much, I could explain why that's not true."

He considered her for a long moment. "Very well, I'll play your game for a little while. If you want to pretend that you don't know your history on this world, I will explain it in greater detail.

"Rest assured, however, that I do not actually believe you come from somewhere else. I'm uncertain what game you're really playing, but it's not going to work out in the way you hope."

The alien took a deep breath and launched into a short story. "This story begins just over six human decades ago. That's when Clan Dauntless arrived on my world. We knew nothing of your people or the war you wage with one another before a great burning streak filled the sky.

"*Dauntless* itself came down with a great clap like thunder heard across the kingdoms. None knew if the gods had decided to smite us or if some other great calamity was at hand. Then our people began finding humans."

He reached over to his side and grabbed a small pack. He opened it and pulled out what looked like beef jerky. He used his knife to cut part of it off the chunk and handed it to Annette.

She held it in both hands and tore a strip off. It tasted good.

"These humans came from escape pods, or so we eventually learned. Your clan chief ordered *Dauntless* abandoned when it came crashing down. A wise decision, as none survived the crash. All who remained on board perished.

"Over the next several months, my people gathered the surviving humans in our territory. We did not speak Standard, of course. Some humans chose to fight. They died. Others surrendered. They lived.

"That turned out to be natural selection. Survival of the fittest. Those who could not set aside their warlike natures culled themselves from your gene pool. Only those who could be reasonable remained."

He smiled a bit coolly. "Which isn't to say that humans are not wily and capable of fighting. No. Only now the unthinkingly violent are gone."

The alien extended his hand toward her. "You do not seem to be the type who is prone to lashing out at anything or anyone that opposes you. That disinclines me to believe your story, because if you are not of Clan Dauntless, then you are either from a different clan or from the great enemy. Both of those possibilities seem unlikely to me."

"That's an interesting story," she admitted, "but there are a few holes in it. You see, it turns out that there are other humans in the galaxy. Some that are neither associated with the humans on this world or their enemies.

"Which brings me back to why I came in the first place. We're trying to find the associates of the people who crashed that large ship. I'll assume that the battlecruiser in question was *Dauntless*. I'm not certain how clans come into this, but I'm hoping that becomes clear in time.

"My name is Annette Vitter. I am a Fleet Captain belonging to the Terran Empire. Not the Empire these people would have been fighting. My people also escaped the great civil war that we call the Fall. We're only just now beginning to struggle against the AIs."

She smiled widely. "If you don't mind taking a little trip, I can prove my story. And, my commanding officer would no doubt make it worth your while to listen to what she has to say."

The alien leaned forward. "It sounds mad to me," he said softly. "One of my closest friends belongs to Clan Dauntless. It was him that you tracked along the road.

"Which, allow me to assure you, would not have turned out the way you hope. He is one of the smartest men I have ever met. Confronting him would not have turned out the way you'd planned."

He sat silent for a long minute. "I find myself uncertain what I should believe. If you want me to go back toward where the ambush happened, that isn't going to happen. I left my men to eliminate our enemies. They will rejoin us here tomorrow. That will be soon enough to find out the truth of what you're saying."

The alien added some wood to the fire. "I suggest you get some sleep while you can. Once they arrive, we'll be traveling quickly and not back the direction we came from."

* * *

Talbot stared at the cutter. "Is it normal for a grav drive to just fail like that? I thought these things were pretty robust."

The marine crew chief shrugged. "Me too, Major. We still haven't tracked down what's wrong, but I suspect we'll be able to fix it relatively easily when we do. I've never seen anything like this, frankly. It has to be some bizarre combination of factors we've never seen before. The drive is probably fine."

The marine officer had barely made it back to the island before the crew of the cutter reported the problem. Luckily, this wasn't a critical mission. One of the other cutters would be able to take care of business until they got this one fixed.

"I suppose asking you how long it's going to take to fix this would be an exercise in futility," Talbot said. "Do the best you can and let me know as soon as it's functional again."

The crew chief nodded. "Will do, sir. Any word when we'll be done down here? The insects are starting to bug the hell out of me."

Talbot laughed. "Insects. Bug. Nice. I'll bet you've been waiting all day to use it on me."

The marine-enlisted man shrugged. "I was bored."

"They shuttled the last of the prisoners down about an hour ago. I figure they'll have moved the last of the cargo in about four or five hours. Then we can focus on searching this blasted planet."

The other man considered him for a moment. "I'm not sure we're going to find the escapees, sir. Now that they've managed to evade discovery for this long, the odds of them just turning up have to be falling dramatically."

"You'd think so, but that's not really true," Talbot said. "They've got a limited amount of oxygen on board. They can't just hide at the bottom of the ocean forever.

"At this point, we're pretty certain they're not on any of the landmasses along the equator. We've got cutters and pinnaces searching the frozen north and south, but they're even less likely to be able to hide there for a long period of time."

"Why's that, sir?"

Talbot gave him a chilly smile. "They've got survival gear but nothing that will allow them to live in the frozen tundra for very long.

No. They might manage to continue hiding for another two or three weeks, but they're going to have to come out and get some food or air. When they do, we'll get them."

The other man excused himself to head back inside the cutter and get back to work.

Talbot stared off into the forest. It was maddening. Patience was going to win the day, but he wanted to do something now.

Well, he should just focus on doing his damned job. Sooner or later, the rebel officers were going to make a mistake. When they did, he'd have them.

The key was going to be getting ready ahead of time. Opportunities were fleeting. When the other guy made the wrong choice, you had to be ready to capitalize on it. He'd be ready.

32

Kelsey watched her human prisoner as he began to shrug off the effects of the stunner. She'd relocated him to the cabin her mother had used when she'd been on board *Persephone*. It would provide a more relaxed setting in which to question him.

Now that he was unarmed, he was no longer a threat to her. She suspected he was a very resourceful man. Not only had he carried a flechette pistol and a stunner, but he'd also had a worn marine knife.

She'd thought the metal immune to scratching, but the blade he'd possessed had obviously seen hard use. The surface of the blade had actual nicks. Maybe he'd carved his way through a bulkhead, as she'd once hypothesized such a blade would allow her to do.

The young man blinked and sat up. His transition from unconsciousness to wary wakefulness was immediate. He took her in and then scanned the rest of the compartment.

"It seems my confidence in myself was ill-placed," he said. "You're much quicker than you look."

"That sounds about as insulting as saying I'm smarter than I look."

The man grunted softly in apparent agreement. "No insult

intended. Or perhaps I should say no further insult intended. Would this be the appropriate time to say I regret trying to kill you?"

"I think that's a great place to start," Kelsey said. "Why did you feel the need to attack me?"

"Shouldn't you be concerned that I'll do so again? I rather expected to wake up in chains."

Kelsey had a stunner at her waist, but it was the concealable one. She undoubtedly looked unarmed.

"I'm not nearly as defenseless as I appear. If you feel the need to get up and take a swing, please, be my guest."

The man smiled wanly. "Perhaps they treat guests differently where you're from. It's generally considered poor form to attack one's host."

"Yet it would be very instructive for you," she said. "I'm not going to call a guard in. I'm not going to pull some hidden weapon and disable you. If you want to determine that I'm telling you the truth, let's settle this right now. I am not the defenseless woman I appear to be."

Kelsey stood and advanced to stand in front of the couch where he sat. "Here I am, right within your grasp. You tried to kill me. Don't tell me that you'd shy away from hitting me."

He remained seated. "Under the circumstances under which we met, I felt justified. That justification does not hold true now."

She sighed. "You just had to ruin my dramatic moment, didn't you? Well, I feel justified in making my point."

"If striking me atones for some of my actions, then feel free," he said calmly.

"Thank you."

She grabbed him by the front of his shirt, hauled him to his feet, and raised him as close to the ceiling as she could. His feet dangled just above the floor.

He stared down at her smiling face, his mouth agape. The moment drew on, and she held him there effortlessly with one arm.

"I feel confident in expressing that you have my full attention," he said in a quiet voice.

Kelsey set him back onto his feet and pushed him back onto the couch. When she was certain he'd stay seated, she walked back to her chair and sat.

"When I say that I'm not from around here, that means I am not from your planet."

"I fully accept that, at this point," the man said. "No one can possibly be that strong. Not without technology beyond anything in the legends. Even my father's stories from *Dauntless* don't mention anything like that."

"As I said last night, my name is Kelsey Bandar. I don't know who you are or who your people are. At this moment, we are on board my ship in orbit. We've been observing your planet for several days and noted the crashed vessel on the surface.

"The aliens have obviously been extracting technology from it for quite some time. The fact that you had a stunner and flechette pistol indicate that you have not lost the technological acumen of your people.

"The thing is, I know nothing about where you came from. My computer indicates that's probably a crashed battlecruiser on the surface. I assume your people escaped the rebel forces during the civil war inside the Terran Empire.

"So did my people. We're just now beginning to fight what has sprung up in its place. I've heard rumors from prisoners about something they called the ghosts. Ships that attack from nowhere and then vanish again. If I had to make a guess, your ship was one of those. Am I close?"

He stared at her silently for a long moment. "My father would be very angry if I assisted you in any way. That being the case, I feel almost obligated to do so.

"My name is Jacob Howell. I've heard my people called ghosts before. We don't call ourselves that, of course. So I think it does no harm to tell you that we are indeed the people you believe us to be.

"That said, I don't believe you're going to find very many people willing to trust your story. My people are significantly easier to deal with than the other clans, I suspect, but none of them will willingly assist you in any way."

That's not what Kelsey wanted to hear. Especially not when she still had a missing officer to find.

"That situation can be dealt with in time. I have a more pressing matter to discuss with you. Someone set up an ambush for you. A number of aliens were lying in wait at a campground. I'm not certain what precipitated it, but they began fighting amongst themselves.

"Somewhere in the melee, one of my officers has vanished. Undoubtedly, some of the people involved in the fighting got away. They've taken her with them. You're going to help me get her back."

He raised an eyebrow. "If she's as strong as you, then I cannot imagine how that occurred."

"Don't play games with me. I'm a civilized woman, but I'm not going to let someone blather inanely at me when one of my people is in danger. If you ever expect to get back to where you came from, then you'd best start making me happy. What was going on down there and where might those survivors have gone?"

They stared at one another silently for several long moments before he spoke again. "If, as I suspect, your officer is in the custody of one of my friends, I'm not going to tell you a thing."

Perfect, she thought sourly. Any other time she'd be pleased to find somebody with integrity. Now it was just a big pain in the ass.

"We're continuing to search the area. We'll find whoever has my officer. If anyone has harmed her in any way, I'm going to hurt them. Do us all a favor and start talking."

"No."

This was going to be as tiresome as she'd expected. Well, it wasn't as if she had anything else to do while the drones scoured the area around the ambush looking for Annette and the people holding her.

* * *

VERONICA STEPPED into the cutter just after dark. Castille had already moved the prisoners inside. The men were sullen, but the ex-empress was incandescent. Castille had bound and gagged her.

"It certainly seems that you have a happy camper on your hands," Veronica said cheerfully.

The security officer grinned. "You could say that. You'd be wrong, but you could still say it. What's our plan going to be?"

She headed for the cockpit, trusting that he would follow. She began strapping herself in and waited for Graham to get the power back on. The engineering officer had gone over the cutter with a fine-tooth comb. He'd declared himself certain there was nothing that would give them away or allow the enemy to control them remotely.

Veronica turned in her seat while she waited. "As soon as it's fully dark, we'll come out of the volcano along the open side and put the mountain between us and the landing field. We'll go out to sea and then head for orbit at a leisurely rate.

"Once we get high enough to determine the distribution of the ships in orbit, we'll start for the orbital. If we have any luck at all, no one will even question our presence. They'll assume that the people on the ground got the damaged cutter functioning again.

"If no one pays any attention to us, we can adjust our course and go straight to the recovery ship. If they direct us to land at the orbital, we're going to have to do that.

"If that happens, you're going to have to come up with a plan to get us from the landing bay to somewhere else that will get us onto the recovery ship."

Castille sat at the flight engineer's console. "Let's hope that doesn't happen. It would make our lives so much simpler if we could go straight to the recovery ship."

He sighed. "Which almost guarantees they're going to direct us to land at the orbital, doesn't it?"

Veronica still thought that wasn't the worst outcome. The enemy might order them to land on the carrier. They'd be completely screwed if that happened. Best to plan on something that at least allowed the mission to go forward.

"If they send us to the orbital, what are you going to do about the prisoners?" she asked. "We can't parade them around in front of anyone."

Castille frowned thoughtfully. "Perhaps we should preemptively stun them. There are some crates inside the base I can pack them inside. If we have to move, we could unload the crate and carry it deeper into the orbital.

"I'll have to improvise if somebody asks us what we're doing, but if that happens, we're going to be in trouble anyway."

At that moment, the consoles came to life. Veronica began performing a quick preflight to make sure that all the systems were showing green. The last thing they needed was to have something go out on the flight. Having to declare an emergency would be embarrassing.

All systems looked operational, so she returned her attention to Castille.

"If you're going to get a crate, you should get it loaded now. By my calculations, we have about twenty-five more minutes before we can leave, but I'd rather not waste a single moment. We really have no idea what their schedule of operations is."

He nodded and stood. "Yes, arriving on station an hour after they depart would be awkward."

Once he'd left the cockpit, Veronica devoted her time to a more in-depth preflight. She ran a more detailed diagnostic of every major system while she waited for Castille to pack the prisoners away.

Even through the closed hatch, she heard the female prisoner screeching something and then the blast of the stunner. It made her smile. That woman *really* got on her nerves.

Candace joined her in the cockpit, taking the copilot seat. "I finished going over the exterior of the cutter, ma'am. Everything looks good."

"What's the status on the rest of the crew?"

"They're aboard and secure. We just sealed up the ramp. Commander Castille should have the prisoners in the crate in about five minutes."

Almost to the second, Castille stepped into the cockpit and resumed his seat at the flight engineer's console.

"We're ready to go, Commander," he said as he strapped himself in.

Veronica took a deep breath. This was a high-risk gamble. If they won, the payoff was huge. If they lost, they'd be in the carrier's brig.

She brought the cutter to a hover and eased out over the water inside the volcano. She wasn't going to miss that old base. Even a cell would be preferable.

Veronica could see some lights down by the abandoned town as she came over the volcano's collapsed side but knew that they would not be able to locate her visually. The risk was they'd be scanning, but she wasn't detecting anything.

Deftly, she eased the cutter around the volcano until the massive slabs of rock blocked any possibility of detection. At that point, she was able to open it up and head out over the water.

At about the twenty-kilometer mark, she began a gentle rise toward space. There was always a risk that someone was going to note their passage and wonder where they were coming from.

Considering how intensely they had to be searching for the missing cutter, that was a very real possibility.

She felt herself tensing as they exited the atmosphere. Her passive scanners had located the Dresden orbital. It was just coming around the curve of the planet.

That was a relief. It hadn't yet departed.

The huge carrier followed along behind it, partially shielded by the orbital's bulk. That really didn't mean anything, but it made her feel better than having to pass directly by the massive warship.

There were two cutters rising from different areas of the planet's surface ahead of her. She'd know very quickly if the carrier's flight control was directing each one.

Her heart jumped into her throat when the com system came to life. The carrier was signaling her directly.

"Gamma three two six this is *Audacious* flight control. I don't have you on my schedule. Where are you going, and what are you carrying?"

This was it. Either the enemy would believe the lies she was going to tell them or all hell was about to break loose.

33

Annette slept poorly, tossing and turning on the rocky ground. So far as she could tell, her captor hadn't slept at all. Perhaps that was normal for the aliens. She had no idea.

In any case, he was still sitting where he'd been when she'd gone to sleep.

Her understanding of alien expressions might be flawed, but he looked worried to her. Since he'd said he expected his compatriots to arrive by dawn, the fact they were still alone was probably the cause.

She sat up, stretched, and stared at him pointedly. "I have to take care of business, if you know what I mean. Are you going to be reasonable or are we going to have a problem?"

He shook his head and handed her a small pouch with some kind of primitive wipes.

"There's no need for difficulty," he said. "You can go over behind that large rock and take care of it. Just rest assured that I'll see you if you attempt to escape. I'm much more agile in this environment than you are. If I have to chase you down, you're going to regret it."

"I'm not going to run. Be right back."

Annette went around behind the large rock and took care of business as well as she could. The wipes were adequate.

She didn't like the idea of littering, but she certainly wasn't going to carry them around with her once she was done. She found a nice rock to bury them under. She pocketed a stone that might make a handy weapon.

Once she'd finished, she headed back around to the fire. There hadn't been anything cooking, but she hoped breakfast was on the agenda. She was starving.

He gestured toward a handy rock. "Sit. I think we have much to discuss."

"If we're going to talk, then I want something to eat. It's been a long time since lunch."

The alien grunted. "In case you've forgotten, you may call me Derek. I have some travel rations, but you may not find them very agreeable. My compatriots should have been along with our supplies by now. They are overdue."

Annette allowed herself to smile as he pulled a leather pouch from his backpack. "I'm not surprised to hear it. My friends are probably very annoyed with them right now. They'll get our location from somebody fairly quickly, so feel free to take your time."

The alien's expression turned decidedly sour. It was astonishing how familiar many of his characteristics were.

There had to be something wrong with that. Aliens were supposed to be… alien.

She took the hunk of what looked like cheese that he handed her and nibbled at the corner. It was extremely hard but not too bad in flavor. He followed that up with what looked like some kind of bread. It was like chewing rock.

"I'm not ready to believe you've captured my men," Derek said bluntly as he ate his own share of the meal. "My men are most capable. They've been with me for years. I seriously doubt anyone could capture or kill them all."

Annette smiled coolly. "You have no idea. When I said that I believe they're expanding the search and will find us, what I really mean is I'm astonished that they haven't already done so.

"As I told you, we have significantly more technology available to us than you're used to. Those weapons you have don't even begin to cover it."

"I've heard the same stories. We can all talk a good game about what humans used to be able to accomplish. That hasn't been true since before I was born. Give up this fantasy you're trying to sell me. Just tell me the truth."

"I can prove my story. All we have to do is go to where I parked my ship."

Derek gave her a bark of laughter. "As if I would take you back to where you might rejoin with your companions. The goal is to escape."

"Your goal, maybe. Mine is more complex. I'm trying to get information. I have no objection to going along with you. I have complete confidence that things are going to turn out in my favor before too long."

"I've never met anyone like you. Most humans are clannish, unsurprisingly. They stick to themselves and don't mingle with our folk. My friend Jacob is an exception to that rule, however.

"He and I grew up together at my father's court. I feel confident in saying I understand humans better than virtually any of my people. Jacob tells me that I've mastered your expressions and many of your attitudes, but I still can't claim to completely understand you."

He considered her more closely. "Even with that understanding, you baffle me. I could have killed you last night. Yet here you sit, coolly and calmly bantering with me. That's the kind of behavior I would expect from a warrior."

Annette tilted her head. "Of course it is. I *am* a warrior."

Derek shook his head. "Humans don't have female warriors. Not one. That isn't how your society works. Even if you were not from here, as you claim."

"Seriously? I thought humans were far past that kind of sexism. I'm just as much a warrior as you are. If you hadn't surprised me last night, I could've taken you."

"You might carry weapons, but that does not make you a warrior," he disagreed. "And before you ask, no. I have no desire to prove it to you."

She finished her meal, such as it was. "Then what is your plan? Do you have any water? That stuff made me thirsty."

He handed her a pouch made of animal skin that sloshed with liquid inside.

Annette stared at it and then gave him a flat look. "You carry water inside of animal skins? That's disgusting."

Derek laughed. "Don't be so prissy, warrior. What do you carry water in?"

"Sterile flasks." Putting aside her revulsion, she forced herself to drink. The water had kind of a metallic taste to it. She took the minimum she needed to slake her thirst and handed the pouch back to the man with a shudder.

"So if we're not going back to look for your men, where are we going?" she asked.

"We'll wait here for a few more hours. If no one comes, I'll take you back to the city."

She felt herself frowning. "If you mean that little spot up the road, I don't think I'd call it a city."

"Nor would I. No. I'm speaking of the capital."

"You say that as if it's supposed to mean something to me. Is that some type of political affiliation?"

"You take this game too far. I am of course referring to the Kingdom of Raden." He gestured in the direction from which the sun was rising. "It will take us about a week to get there."

Annette brought up an overlay map from her implants. There was a rather large city in that general direction, but she doubted they'd be making it there in a week on foot. The forest was far too thick for that.

"Is that some kind of joke?" she asked. "If it's the place I think you mean, we can't possibly go that far through this kind of terrain in so short a period of time."

He laughed. "And you call yourself a warrior. We'll make it there in a week, Annette Vitter. You may not enjoy the process, though."

She really hoped it didn't come to that. If they actually managed to elude the searchers that were undoubtedly scouring the countryside for her, Princess Kelsey might have to leave her behind. That would truly suck.

* * *

RAUL TRIED NOT to clutch the chair he was sitting in as Veronica responded to the query. This was the moment of truth. All their plans hinged on this conversation.

"The ground crew managed to find the fault and get us going again, Control," Veronica said calmly. "We still have a little bit of cargo that they decided to put on the orbital, so we're headed there."

Control was silent so long that Raul feared they were checking her story, but they finally spoke again. "Copy that. You are cleared to proceed."

Once he was certain the communication had ended, he let out the breath he had been holding all at once. "Well done. Very well done."

She glanced back at him. "That's just one step of many we're going to have to get right for this to work. Since we know they're watching us, we're going to have to land at the orbital.

"I can get you out so you can make your way to the recovery ship, but they're going to expect this cutter to undock again before they let the orbital go. That means I'm going to have to stay with it at least long enough to complete the undocking maneuver."

He frowned. "How is that supposed to work? I'd rather not leave you behind."

"Don't be ridiculous. While we're docked, I'm going to find a vacuum suit. Once I take the cutter back out into space, I can program it to head back to the surface. I'll jump off and land somewhere on the orbital and make my way to the recovery ship. You'll just have to let me in once you've secured the ship."

"Can a cutter successfully land without anyone aboard?"

She smiled slyly. "Probably not, but that's not a negative in this particular case. They'll expend resources searching for injured and dead at the crash site. That should conceal where we've actually gone long enough to get away, I hope."

Raul wasn't at all certain about that, but he had to trust her to do her job. He nodded his agreement.

"We'll make it work. The next task is going to be getting out of the cutter without anyone asking awkward questions. Finish docking, and I'll brief your officers.

"You're doing one hell of a job, Veronica. Don't think that I'm going to forget this. When we get home, everyone is going to know how crucial you were to the success of this operation."

The woman's smile turned wry. "After I surrendered my ship and the others under my temporary command, I'm not at all certain that's going to be enough to make a difference."

"Don't undervalue what we're bringing back with us. No one could have done any better than you did at Erorsi. They ambushed you with overwhelming force, and your commanders have already paid in full for their errors. The lords will understand that."

"I wish I felt as certain as you do," she said, sighing. "Forgive me, but you really have no idea what they'll do."

"I think I know them well enough." He left her in the cockpit after gesturing for the copilot to accompany him. Once he had all the officers gathered in the rear of the cutter, he laid out his plan.

"Once Commander Giguere lands, we'll unload the crate. We're not going to leave it in the docking area. We'll take it to the security zone. We can lock the unconscious prisoners into one of the cells and make our way to the recovery ship.

"Commander Giguere is going to take the cutter back toward the surface of the planet. She's going to exit before it leaves the area around the orbital and join us at the recovery ship. Commander Bakersfield will find her a vacuum suit."

He waited for them to nod before he continued. "We don't know their schedule of departure, so we're going to need to improvise as we go along. Does anyone have any questions?"

The officers glanced at one another and shook their heads.

"Excellent. Follow my lead if anyone tries to stop us."

He strapped himself in to one of the seats and waited. It seemed to take forever for the cutter to dock, but he finally felt it landing.

The ramp began lowering as he unstrapped himself.

They'd barely started getting the large crate with the prisoners unloaded when they ran into trouble.

A lieutenant with a clipboard intercepted them. He was staring at the crate.

"Excuse me, Lieutenant. We're done here. What's that?"

Since the number of commanders on even a large ship was extremely small, he'd pilfered the rank tabs from one of the prisoners. So had Veronica. They were both junior-grade lieutenants now. A rank that had numerous holders on a ship the size of the carrier.

"Something that was inadvertently left in one of the cutters," Raul said smoothly. "They don't want to leave it down where the prisoners can get their hands on it."

"I'll need to mark down the contents," the other man said. "Have your people set it down and open it up."

Raul eyed the officer and surreptitiously looked to see how many people would see if he had to do anything drastic to the man.

Unfortunately, four marines had just come into the cargo bay and were watching them curiously.

"Lieutenant?" the man asked. "Did you hear me? I need you to open up that crate right now."

34

K elsey was extremely annoyed with Jacob Howell. Even though it was apparent he'd accepted the basic outline of her story, he'd refused to help her find Annette Vitter. She'd argued with him until she was blue in the face, but he hadn't budged.

She admired his loyalty, but this was costing her precious time and putting her officer at needless risk.

By now, the sun had risen, and Jacob's friend was probably carrying Annette even farther from the search area. The marines had scoured the forest with drones and turned up nothing. It was as though the two had vanished.

Kelsey had gotten a few hours of sleep and allowed the man to stew in his makeshift cell. To her annoyance, he probably hadn't been bored. It was obvious he was absolutely delighted to be on an operational ship.

He'd demanded to know the ship's name. Once she'd told him, he'd insisted that she was chief of Clan Persephone. Great. That did absolutely nothing useful to her way of thinking.

Angela was hard at work questioning the alien prisoners. Kelsey suspected she'd probably get something useful before the stubborn human cooperated.

When Kelsey had reviewed the latest reports from the searchers and eaten breakfast, she headed for Jacob's cabin. The marine guards let her in, and she found the man examining the inside of the kitchen cabinets.

"What is this material?" he asked. "I've seen it before, but never in this condition. The salvaged pieces were exposed to the elements for decades."

"It's a form of what we call plastic. I'm not sure of its precise makeup, and that probably doesn't matter. I couldn't make it if my life depended on it."

She sat on the edge of the couch. "This has to stop. You're needlessly putting my officer in danger. I couldn't care less about the two of you or what's going on below. By all means, continue working whatever Machiavellian scheme you're involved in without us."

He came out of the kitchen and sat down beside her. "What does that mean?"

"Devious. Convoluted. Subtle. You can pick any of those words to describe the man the word refers to. He lived on Terra before spaceflight.

"What I mean is that I'm not trying to interfere in anything that you're doing. All I wanted to do was talk with you. I'm doing that. My goals are satisfied. I'll be happy to release you once we're done without any conditions."

His look took on a slightly amused air. "That seems rather plain spoken. You've come a very long way for information that was out of date decades before I was born. Whatever information I have about the clans won't be very useful."

"Considering that I know nothing about them, I disagree. All we've ever heard them referred to as are ghosts. We suspect they are Imperial forces that escaped the civil war, but that's just a guess. Beyond that, even old information would be useful.

"We don't want to fight them. It's very likely that we're fighting the same enemy."

His expression turned sad. "Then you are in for disappointment.

The clans won't work with you, I suspect. They'll see you as just another part of the corrupt Empire.

"I suppose giving you some information won't hurt. Your guess is correct. The clans were formed by ships that escaped during the great war. They persevered in the system on the other side of the defective flip point. If I remember the old stories correctly, they called it Icebox.

"It kept them prisoner for decades until they devised an escape into other systems. In the time since, they've grown strong. Much stronger than any raiding you've heard about would have indicated."

She leaned back in the couch and gave him a curious expression. "How do you mean?"

"First, you need to understand my background and that of my clan. Clan Dauntless was one of the founding units in the Council of Clans. Our chief supported the goals of the Council to take the war back to the corrupt Empire. To bring it down and restore what had existed before.

"When the Others came, we were skeptical. We did not believe that they had the best interests of the people at their heart. Over time, the Others swayed the Council and turned them against us. That's why we fled."

Kelsey frowned. "Others?"

He opened his mouth to say something, but closed it again. Moments later, he started again. "My apologies. I've heard the story so many times that I forgot you don't have the background to know that.

"The Others are human, but not of the Empire. They represent a political entity known as The Singularity. Their leaders favor tattoos on their faces, as I recall."

"I've heard of them," Kelsey said. "Something about their leadership being genetically engineered."

Jacob raised an eyebrow. "I'm not certain I understand what that means. In any case, my father said that these people were exceptionally cunning. They spent many long years helping the Council build the kind of infrastructure needed to fight the corrupt Empire. Fleets of powerful ships.

"The leadership of Clan Dauntless never believed that they

wished us well, though. I'm told they believed The Singularity was manipulating the Council. Suborning it.

"That is what convinced the clan to flee through the Icebox system and try to find a new home elsewhere. The Council allowed us to depart, but Singularity warships trailed closely behind and attacked us.

"We had no intention of going into the Icebox system, as I understand it. It was a dead end. Superior numbers forced our hand. There was a great battle. One in which *Dauntless* emerged victorious, but was crippled.

"Our leaders took a great chance and tried to take it through the defective flip point. Something our engineers did allowed us to make our way through, but not to the system we thought existed on the other side. We found this one instead."

"Your ship must've been in very bad shape if it crashed," she said after a moment. "My missing officer believes that someone almost brought that ship down to the surface. Was that their intention?"

He shook his head. "The story is that our leaders remained aboard the ship when her engines failed during orbital insertion. They chose to crash with the ship to allow the clan time to escape. No officer above the rank of lieutenant survived.

"Unfortunately, the prisoners that the clan had collected after the battle also escaped. The Others. They now work with the repressive regime in the Empire of Kalor. I'd wager they're suborning it in much the same way they did the Council of Clans. Unless I miss my guess, it was Kalorian soldiers who made up the ambush you mentioned.

"That is why my friend and his soldiers came to assist me. We were trying to flush them out and eliminate them. They've been causing the kingdom trouble for many years. They wanted me as their prisoner."

She considered him for a long moment. "Why did they consider you so important? What are you to them that you would make a good hostage?"

Jacob grinned. "Me? I'm nothing. It's my father they would like to control. He is the chief of Clan Dauntless. The Others still hope to escape this world."

"And you don't?"

"I hadn't, not until I learned of your ship. Now the impossible seems possible."

"It's possible," Kelsey said, "but only if you start cooperating. I'm more than willing to take you back down to the surface myself, along with all of the men we captured. We'll turn you all over to your friend in exchange for my officer. All you have to do is tell me where he is."

"At this point, I'm almost willing to give it a chance," Jacob said. "I can't honestly say I know where he would go, though. There are several possible destinations. He's a very canny woodsman. The chances of you tracking him are slim."

"They wouldn't have been if you'd talked to me last night," Kelsey said acerbically. "Why didn't you just cooperate then?"

He shrugged. "I couldn't take the chance. I believe you now, but I was uncertain then. My friend's name in Standard is Derek. His father rules the Kingdom of Raden. I couldn't risk giving you the opportunity to take him hostage."

Kelsey sighed. "Just another piece of political maneuvering that I have no interest in. Come on. I think it's time to give you a tour of the ship, and then we can go talk to your friend's men."

She rose to her feet and led him toward the door. "I don't have time to play games. Events are unfolding, and our time is limited. If I have to waste days hunting for your friend, no one is going to be happy when I find him."

* * *

VERONICA HEARD the raised voices from inside the cutter and made the decision to head down the ramp to see if she could settle whatever the problem was. She found Castille arguing with a lieutenant holding a clipboard.

That was never a good thing. The general rule of thumb was to worry if you found a lieutenant with a clipboard or a map.

She sauntered down the ramp as casually as she could and walked up to the group. "Is there a problem, sir?" she asked the man with the clipboard.

"Yes. We finished tallying the remaining cargo, so I need to see the contents of the crate to add it to our list."

"Ah," she said. "I understand. I'm afraid we're not going to be able to do that, sir."

He blinked at her. "Excuse me?"

"It's classified. Why do you think we're moving it onto the orbital at the last moment? The orders for this came from the very highest level. Princess Kelsey. You can contact her for confirmation, of course."

Veronica really hoped it didn't come to that, but she doubted it would. The odds of a lieutenant disturbing somebody of that exalted social position with something like this were slim. It was still taking a chance, but what part of this escape wasn't?

"But she hasn't been in the system for a week."

That surprised her, but she kept her face bland. She hoped it didn't mean they'd discovered the distant flip point. That would complicate matters.

"That's outside my control, and it still doesn't change my orders," Veronica said. "Look, it's only one crate. We're going to secure it inside the orbital like she told us. It's not as if it will somehow cause a problem. Do you really want to raise a stink over this and deal with the consequences, sir?"

No officer in her right mind wanted to deal with angry superiors by questioning their orders. It was much simpler just to go with the flow.

"I don't recognize you people. Are you based on *Persephone*?"

"That's right."

"Figures." After a long moment, he sighed. "I suppose you're right. It's only one crate. I'll make a note that it was delivered and stored as per Princess Kelsey's orders. If there's a problem, you can explain it."

The man moved off and drew some nearby marines with him. As soon as they stopped paying attention to her, Veronica gestured for Graham to go get a vacuum suit for her.

It only took him a few moments to get one out of an emergency locker and carry it into the cutter. The lieutenant and his companions were no longer in sight, so she casually followed him in. He set it on a chair, grinned at her, and headed back out to rejoin Castille.

Once she'd sealed the cutter, Veronica put the vacuum suit on. This next part was going to be tricky, and she didn't want to waste any time.

She lifted the cutter off the deck and took it slowly out of the landing bay. After she was in vacuum, she bled the air out of the cutter and opened the ramp.

It wasn't difficult to lay in a course that took the cutter past the recovery ship. She wasn't going to be exceptionally close to it, but she had some experience in maneuvering a vacuum suit. She'd be able to get onto the hull without too much trouble.

Once she was there, she'd wait for Castille and her people to join her.

The cutter would maintain its slow speed until it was clear of the orbital and then accelerate toward the planet at a normal velocity.

The damned computers on board weren't too smart, so it was probably going to mess up during reentry. That should make a nice splashy problem for their enemies to sort out.

She carefully made her way down the ramp and braced herself against the cutter's hull as it slid past the recovery ship. Taking a deep breath, she aimed at a good landing place and launched herself into the void.

The kick off hadn't been precisely even, so she began rotating almost at once. That didn't overly concern her. She'd be able to use the suit's built-in thrusters to steady herself and then slow down before landing.

Veronica brought up the thruster controls and blanched. The suit had no reaction mass. She was stuck with the momentum she'd gained from jumping off the cutter.

The heavens spun around her as she coasted toward the recovery ship. It was hard to tell, but she thought she was going to come close. Of course, close didn't really matter if she still missed. Or if she hit hard enough to bounce off.

She cursed herself for not checking the reservoir levels. That little bit of stupidity was probably going to kill her. She'd only have one chance at this.

To her relief, her initial jump had been true. She collided roughly with the hull of the recovery ship.

That didn't mean that everything came up roses. She hit at an awkward angle, something snapped in her left forearm, and her helmet bounced off the hull.

Veronica scrambled to grab anything and caught something mounted to the hall with her right hand. The rebound almost yanked her shoulder out of its socket, but she managed to hang on.

She ended up bruised and bloodied, but secure on her destination. She was happy with the result until she saw that the corner of her faceplate was cracked.

A quick check of the interior instruments confirmed she was slowly losing air. Probably not through the crack itself or it would have blown out already. She'd probably torn her suit when she rammed the ship.

She wasn't going to have time to wait for the rest to join her. She had to find a way into the recovery ship right now, no matter the risk.

So, of course, the nearest personnel hatch was locked up tight.

35

They'd only been marching through the forest for about three hours when Annette saw her chance to turn the tables on her captor. The hills they were moving through were relatively steep, so he kept her close in front of him to prevent her from either falling or trying to get away.

Unfortunately for him, that meant he was also in range for her to take action.

The rocks on the slope were relatively stable, but there were a few that didn't seem as deeply embedded in the ground. She kept her eyes peeled for those. Up until this point, it was so she could avoid taking a nasty tumble. Now she was deliberately going to use one of them.

She just hoped her wild plan didn't end up with her tumbling down the side of the hill and breaking every bone in her body.

Annette tried not to tense when she stepped on the loose stone, but that proved impossible when it skidded out from under her feet and she flew backwards. She just hoped Derek interpreted her premature stiffening in a different manner or missed it entirely.

The reason she'd chosen this particular stone was that they'd just passed a fairly loose bit of ground. When she fell back into her captor, his feet slid out from under him as he struggled to hold her weight and maintain his footing.

She had to give him credit. He made a Herculean effort to both stay on his feet and keep her from falling down the hill. One that fell short of absolute success, but not by as much as she'd hoped.

Derek's feet stayed mostly under him as she slammed her upper body into his, right up until a rock shot out from under one of his feet and he went down hard.

Her hands were already in motion as they fell, and she came up with the pistol he had strapped to his waist.

That didn't stop her from sliding half a dozen feet down the hill and fetching up hard against a boulder. Thankfully, she'd been able to use her artificial arm to stop her fall. She didn't feel like anything was broken, but she imagined her back was covered with bruises.

Belatedly, she realized she could've used her arm as proof of her story. A cut with a knife would have revealed the machinery within. The damned thing felt so real that she'd forgotten about it.

That was usually a plus, as she had no desire to recall the horrific crash that had amputated the original. Oh well.

Derek slid to a halt about a dozen feet away. He started to reach under his jacket but stopped when he realized she had a weapon aimed at him.

"I'd really rather not have to shoot you," Annette said casually. "I'd hoped to get your stunner, but I'll use this flechette pistol if I have to. Don't make me kill you."

The alien shook his head slowly. "That was stupid of me. I allowed you to lull me into a false sense of security and then use the terrain against me. Clever. So what do we do now? Go back and search for your Kalorian allies?"

"Seriously? You didn't hear a single thing I told you?"

"I heard you. I just don't believe you."

She smiled coolly. "Then let's see if I can make you a believer. Toss your weapons over here. Where are mine?"

"I have yours stored in my pack," he said as he gingerly levered himself to his feet.

He made a show of slowly removing his stunner from a holster on the other side of his body and tossing it halfway between them. She wasn't going to fall for the bait and come into his range.

She gestured up the hill with her free hand. "Up you go. Don't try to get fancy with any rocks. I'll be watching."

Once he'd climbed far enough ahead of her, she squatted and picked up the stunner he'd tossed. She relaxed a little bit as she stuffed the flechette pistol into her jacket. She didn't really want to kill the alien.

Annette half expected him to try something before she made it back up to his level, but he only stood there watching her expectantly.

"What do we do now?" he asked.

"I prove I was telling you the truth. We head back the way we came."

He raised an eyebrow. "You could very well be leading me back to be captured by your companions."

"You're already captured. I have even less reason to lie now. I think the fact that none of your friends came away from the ambush should tell you something too. Do you think the people you were attacking were numerous enough to take you all out, even with surprise on your side?"

"No. Still, it's a more likely turn of events than the story you've been trying to sell me."

"I suppose we'll both find out what happened, won't we? I suggest you take it slow and stick to areas where no one will see us. I'd rather not be captured by the people setting up the ambush, either."

Considering the tangles and dense foliage he led her through on the way back toward the campsite, Derek was taking every precaution to avoid discovery. Annette stayed far enough back that he would not be able to surprise her.

She supposed that meant he was far enough ahead to escape, if he really wanted to. She'd already decided to let him go if he tried. Well, if the stunner didn't bring him down anyway. She wasn't going to chase after him, and she wasn't going to kill him.

They didn't run into anyone as they came back into the area near her fighter. Annette halfway expected to find it gone, but it sat in the clearing just as she'd left it.

Derek stopped short as soon as he saw the small craft. He stared at it, not moving.

After a long, long moment, he turned his head and stared at her. "I must confess that I thought you were lying. My apologies."

She stepped into the clearing and into range of the fighter with her implants. The computer inside immediately forwarded her a message.

An image of Princess Kelsey appeared. She seemed to be staring straight at Annette.

"If you're seeing this, you made it back to your fighter before we found you. We've already cleaned up the area around the campsite and are searching for you. Let us know, and we'll have a marine pinnace on your location in five minutes, if you need it. We picked up the guy on the road too."

Annette dismissed the message.

She smiled at Derek. "Apology accepted. According to a message my friends left for me, they have your friend and your men in custody. Would you like me to take you to them or trust that I'm going to see them returned?"

His eyes narrowed. "Precisely where are you holding them? Better yet, how did you get that message?"

She tapped the side of her head. "Implants. At short range, I can link with the computers in my fighter."

To prove her point, she instructed the canopies to open.

"I've never seen or heard of such a thing," Derek said quietly, watching the fighter open up with wide eyes. "I don't believe I've ever seen a piece of recovered equipment this functional, either. Except for the handheld weapons, of course. I believe I'd like to see where you're keeping my friends."

Annette gestured toward the front of the fighter. "You get in up front. Once you're inside, I'll see that you're secured and off we go."

Getting close enough to strap him in was a risk, but one she was willing to take at this point. She didn't think he'd attack her until he'd seen everything she had to show him.

He stared curiously at the cockpit as she secured his restraints. "Even after having seen what was left of *Dauntless*, I confess that I never expected to actually fly anywhere. It still seems mythical."

"Well then, you're in for a treat."

Annette sealed up the front canopy and climbed into her seat. She'd contact *Persephone* as soon as she lifted off. She wanted to get off the ground before anything else went wrong.

* * *

RAUL FELT MILDLY ridiculous stashing the unconscious prisoners into the high-security cells. The power was on, and they'd have plenty of food and water once they woke up, so it was the best call. Still, literally anyone could come in and find them.

He took the opportunity to drop into his office. Someone had ransacked it and opened his safe. The armored door was actually half melted. He certainly hoped they had fun with the encrypted chips it had contained and the false data stored on them.

Raul reached under his desk and touched a hidden button. He then made his way into the attached washroom and opened a previously hidden safe built into the tiled walls.

This was his *actual* safe. He pocketed the data chips containing his actual files and then began pulling out his weapons. The extra stunner went into his pocket, the heavy-duty flechette pistol went onto his belt, and the plasma grenade stayed in the pouch it came in.

Out of habit, he closed and locked the safe when he was done. He then went out to rejoin the destroyer's crew. He handed his spare stunner to one of them. That meant all of them were armed now.

With the weapons they'd seized from the marines and the cutter pilot, that provided a stunner for each of the officers. Veronica had chosen not to take one with her, because she wasn't going to need any firepower for her part of this operation.

He hoped none of them had to use their weapons. If they did, someone would realize something was wrong. As it was, they were running a risk that the nosy lieutenant would, if they were still aboard the orbital when he left.

The man would probably check the interior scanners to verify that no one was moving around. He'd make a call across the interior communications systems too. The people in the cells wouldn't be able to respond, and the man wouldn't see them.

He consulted a map of the orbital and made a guess at the closest airlock to where the recovery ship was attached. It took them another fifteen minutes to get there, and they quickly donned vacuum suits.

Once they were ready, he led them into the airlock and bled off the pressure. The exterior hatch slid open, and he was pleased to see that the recovery ship was virtually on top of them.

Raul didn't have much experience working in zero gravity, but he had enough to avoid making a fool of himself. He led the others onto one of the arms where it connected nearby and then onto the hull of the recovery ship.

"I see Commander Giguere ahead," Graham Bakersfield said. "She's up near one of the airlocks that we had designated as a potential entry point."

It took a moment, but Raul spotted her. She had her arm wrapped around something to hold on to. He supposed that made sense, but something looked wrong.

They didn't dare risk anything more powerful than short-range communication. They wouldn't be able to talk with her until they were less than a dozen meters away.

Bakersfield took the lead and closed the distance to his commanding officer. The man glanced down before straightening abruptly and gesturing for them to hurry.

The man dug into a satchel he'd acquired somewhere and began scanning the surface of Veronica's suit.

Something *was* wrong.

"What's the matter?" he asked as soon as he arrived beside them.

"Her suit integrity is compromised, and she's lost a lot of air. Too much. I don't think she's breathing. She used an emergency cable to secure herself. We need to get her out of that suit now."

"Get the hatch open," he ordered. "It must be locked down if she couldn't get inside. We'll have to hope we can resuscitate her once we get inside."

The engineer pulled out a hammer, braced himself, and shattered the controls. Once he had the parts of them separated, he reached inside with his gloved hands and did something. The hatch slid open.

They managed to get Veronica's body inside the airlock, and Raul hit the control to seal it. Air began rushing in.

As soon as the pressure was high enough, they got Veronica's helmet off. She still wasn't breathing. The helm and tactical officers began working on resuscitating her.

Raul hoped their efforts were successful, but he had other work to do. He gestured for the other two officers to join him and headed into the ship.

"It's possible someone noticed the airlock cycling," he said quietly. "If they did, we're going to have trouble in very short order. If they didn't, we need to secure the ship before anyone finds out we're here.

"Lieutenant Bakersfield, go to engineering. Stun anyone you find. Search carefully to be sure no one is hiding there. Lock it down so no one can come in once we begin the assault on the bridge."

He looked at the executive officer next. "Commander Fuller, I want you to hit the crew quarters. I'll take the bridge."

The three split up and went their separate ways.

Raul almost made it to the bridge before he encountered anyone. The man wore blue coveralls that were nothing like those Fleet used. He was also warier than a Fleet officer would've been.

The man barely laid eyes on Raul before he turned and sprinted toward the bridge. Raul had his stunner in hand and took him out just short of the bend in the corridor.

He raced to the bridge and found it fully manned. One of the occupants was already heading toward the hatch. He must've heard something.

Raul set the stunner to wide angle and took them all down. All told, he'd stunned seven people.

He dragged the man in from the corridor and locked the hatch behind him.

Once he'd shot each one again with a full stunner blast, he sat down at the command console and tried to make sense of what he was seeing.

It looked as though someone had been laying in a course to the outer system. Perhaps they were getting ready to depart orbit.

Five minutes later, there was a rap on the hatch. Raul rose from his seat and walked over to the intercom. "Yes?"

If it was someone he didn't know, they were about to get the surprise of their life.

"It's Fuller. I think we got everybody."

Raul opened the hatch and gestured for the officer to come in. "Find a compartment with a hatch you can lock and drag everyone into it. Search them closely. Leave them no tools or weapons. Strip them naked. That will make sure.

"By the time they wake up, I'll have the computer system secured against intrusion. Leave Graham guarding the hatch and search the ship again. We can't chance that anyone is still hiding."

He stopped the man before he could exit the bridge. "Is there any word on Commander Giguere?"

The other officer shook his head. "Not that I've heard. Even if they save her, there may be permanent damage."

Raul grimaced. He certainly hoped that wasn't the case. Veronica was an amazing officer. Her loss would be an incredible blow to the Empire.

A chime from the command console drew his attention. They had an incoming call.

He gestured for Fuller to go. "I'll take care this. When you pass the airlock, send Lieutenant Wells to join me."

Without turning on the video, he accepted the call. "Go ahead."

"We've accounted for everyone aboard the orbital," a voice said. It certainly sounded like the lieutenant Raul had been dealing with earlier. "Is there some reason you're not using video?"

"We're doing maintenance on that system," Raul said coolly.

There was a long pause before the man continued. "Copy that. No one is showing up on internal scans, so you're clear to depart."

"Roger that. We'll see you once we drop this thing off and get back."

He killed the com. Raul had no idea how to actually move the ship, so he wasn't even going to try. He'd have to wait for the helm officer to arrive. Then he'd find out whether their resuscitation efforts had proven fruitful.

36

K elsey was intensely relieved when word came that Annette was on her way back up in her fighter. The marines searching for her had hastily loaded up in the pinnaces and caught up with her just before she was ready to dock.

The shroud the engineers had cobbled together that allowed the fighters to pull next to a standard dock and open their canopies while still inside an atmosphere was something like Frankenstein's monster. It basically provided a large, inflatable seal leading into a standard dock.

There was no way to secure the fighter to the dock, so they used the short-range remote controls to relocate it to the slot on the hull reserved for it once the pilots were clear. A work party then had to secure it manually.

At some point, they'd have to come up with a better way of doing this. Thankfully, this had worked out so far.

She'd been on the bridge with Jacob Howell. As she'd expected, he couldn't tear his eyes away from the people sitting at their positions and flying the ship. The view of the planet below on the main screen had mesmerized him.

"This is both exactly as I envisioned it and entirely different," he confided as she led him into the corridor leading to the docking area.

She gave him a smile. "That can mean anything."

He shrugged. "I don't have the words. I wish my father could see this."

"Maybe some other time. Once we have your friend on board, we can start loading all of you onto one of the pinnaces. We'll take you down wherever you'd like to go. As I said earlier, I have no need to keep you prisoner.

"I'm overdue back in the other system. There are important matters there that I have to keep abreast of. Some tasks that I hope they've successfully completed. Once I check in with them, I intend to come back and have a much longer discussion with you about the clans and the Others."

He grinned. "My schedule seems to have miraculously cleared. If you have no objection, I would take it as a great personal favor if you'd allow me to accompany you. I suspect that Derek will be of a similar mind, once he's assured that his men are safely sent below."

By this point they'd arrived at the docking area. Four marines stood by, ready for any trouble.

The hatch was just opening to admit Annette and a Pandoran. Kelsey made a mental note to inquire what they referred to themselves as.

The alien and Jacob clasped forearms. "I feared I'd seen the last of you, my friend," the Pandoran said.

Jacob gestured toward Kelsey. "I met a new friend. Allow me to introduce you to the chief of Clan Persephone. Kelsey Bandar, this is my friend Derek.

"By the way, she has all of your people here. Some of them were injured attacking the ambushers, but none died. I've spoken with them all. They're in as good a condition as possible. Better than I'd expected, honestly. The medical facilities on the ship are astounding."

The alien turned toward Kelsey and bowed his head. "I appreciate the care you have shown my people. I regret capturing Annette Vitter. I didn't believe her story."

Kelsey extended her hand. She wasn't sure the alien would take it, but he did. His grip was firm, and he made no attempt to overpower her.

"As Jacob said, my name is Kelsey Bandar, and this is my ship, *Persephone*. Jacob and I have been getting to know one another."

The alien raised an eyebrow. "Indeed? The closest human pronunciation of my name is Derek. It would please me if you would call me such."

"Kelsey is not only chief of Clan Persephone," Jacob told his friend, "but she is also a senior leader in their council. Her father is high clan chief of the New Terran Empire, and she stands to inherit his position."

Derek seemed suitably impressed. He bowed again, this time more deeply and with more of a flourish.

"I'd rather not get tangled up in that right now," Kelsey said. "As I told Jacob, I'm on a rather tight schedule. I want to continue the discussion we're having, but I have to visit the system next door. I've prepared your men for transport. You're more than welcome to accompany them down."

"I've offered to go with her on this journey," Jacob said. "I think you should come with me. Think of what you could learn for your father."

Derek seemed to consider that. "Once I have seen my men to safety, if you have no objection, I would like to accompany you. I have wronged Annette Vitter by disbelieving her story. I want to learn as much as possible before I speak with my father about you."

That would certainly make getting more information about the clans possible, Kelsey mused. "We should have your people loaded for transport in about twenty minutes. You can tell the pilot where you'd like to land and go down with them. Once you get back to the ship, we'll depart."

While the circumstances were looking up, she still hoped that Talbot had good news about her mother. As long as that situation remained unresolved, she'd be on pins and needles.

* * *

TALBOT WAS STARTING to get annoyed with the mechanics working on the damaged cutter. How hard could it be? Find whatever was causing the fault and swap it out.

No matter what the technicians checked, the solution always seemed to elude them. It had taken almost two days now. If they didn't solve the problem soon, he was going to have an aneurysm.

That's when *Audacious* called down with an alert. A cutter decelerating from orbit had come in for an emergency landing.

Marines from every quarter of the planet headed for its location and began searching. They'd found the cutter in rough terrain. It looked as though the pilot had put it down hard. Talbot set out to join them.

As he examined the crash site from the air, Talbot wondered why the pilot hadn't tried for an area a few kilometers to the south. The terrain was much more conducive to a safe landing there.

In any case, it looked as though it had survived well enough that someone probably had walked away.

Mysteriously, they found the cutter empty. The ramp was still up, but no one was aboard. Maybe they'd closed it after they'd gotten clear. Yet, where had they gone?

He immediately instituted a search of the area. The survivors would turn up in short order.

Half a day later, he'd had to reevaluate that assessment. They'd gone over every centimeter of the forest around the crash site without finding survivors, bodies, or even a trace that anyone had ever lived there.

Talbot was still trying to figure out what that meant when Commodore Anderson signaled him from orbit. "What's the word, Talbot? Give me some good news."

He scowled at her image. "I'm getting a big pile of nothing down here. It's as if the cutter was empty. Who the hell was flying this thing? What the hell were they doing?"

"I'll get that information for you by the time you get up here. *Persephone* just flipped back into the system. Princess Kelsey is on her way here now. I think you should come up and brief her in person."

Talbot sighed. "Great. Now I have to give her bad news on top of everything else. I feel like I haven't accomplished a damned thing on this planet."

"Then come on up and meet her. Leave your subordinates to continue the search. We'll figure this out."

He made his way back to the cutter he'd arrived in and instructed the pilot to take them up. Their scanners were able to detect the approaching Marine Raider ship while it was still a few hours out.

Since they were headed toward one another, it only took them about an hour to rendezvous. One of the pinnaces detached so he could board.

Kelsey was waiting for him. She wasn't alone. An unknown man in odd-looking clothing stood beside her. What floored him though, was the alien biped standing nearby.

He had seen images of the aliens Kelsey had discovered, but he didn't expect to find one on *Persephone*.

His wife pulled him into a hug. "It's so good to see you. A week away is far too long."

She turned toward the human man. "Allow me to introduce Jacob Howell. Jacob, my husband, Russel Talbot. He's also a major in the Imperial Marines."

The man reached out, and Talbot raised his hand automatically. It wasn't the type of handshake he was used to—the man grasped his forearm rather than his palm—but he recovered well, he thought.

Kelsey gestured toward the alien. "This is his friend Derek. I'm given to understand that that's not the actual pronunciation of his name, but that's the accepted version for humans."

The alien repeated the same strange handshake.

Talbot had intended to launch into an update about her mother, but the strange visitors threw him off. He wasn't certain he should speak about her at all. There was no telling what Kelsey had told them or, more to the point, what she hadn't told them.

He opened his mouth to inquire what she wanted to do, but an incoming communication stopped him. It was a priority message from Commodore Anderson. He accepted it at once.

"Talbot, we have a problem," the commodore said. "We've identified the cutter pilot. Unfortunately, he's still on the island that you came from. He's waiting for them to fix his cutter."

Talbot frowned and held up a hand to stop Kelsey from interrupting. She couldn't hear the communication, so he shunted what he'd already received to her and linked her in.

"Why do you think that pilot was the one flying the downed cutter?" he asked.

"Because we have transponder confirmation. Flight control registered it coming up from the island and docking with the orbital. It was after that it returned to the surface and crashed."

Kelsey gave him an odd look. "What are we talking about? There was a cutter crash?"

His mind raced ahead, and the obvious conclusion about floored him. "Oh crap. Commodore, you need to contact the recovery ship at once. They've got stowaways on the orbital."

"We've already called them," the commodore said grimly. "They're not responding."

"Where are they at?" Kelsey asked.

"They're probably out of the system. They've been too far out for us to detect for a while."

Kelsey smiled. "They've got nowhere to run. We'll change course immediately and pursue them."

Once Talbot was satisfied that the conversation was over, he terminated the link. He waited until Kelsey had explained the situation to their visitors.

She ended her recitation of facts with a wolfish grin. "But now they've made a terrible mistake. We'll be able to find them no matter where they go."

The man named Jacob glanced at his friend. His expression seemed troubled.

"That may not be true," he said slowly. "According to the stories I've heard, the flip point leading to the Clan systems lies that way. At least it exists in the outer system."

"What?" Kelsey demanded. "I thought the Council worlds were on the other side of what you called the defective flip point."

The man shook his head. "No. So far as I know, no ship other than *Dauntless* has ever managed to use one successfully. At least to go anywhere other than here.

"My father told me that there was a previously unknown type of flip point in this system. One that existed far outside the normal orbital radius."

After a moment, the man shrugged. "I must admit I'm not certain I completely understand the concept of flip points at all, so it's possible I'm making some kind of mistake. The story might be wrong.

"The Council of Clans revealed the existence of the distant flip points to the Others, but not the defective one. They still hoped to devise a means of using it, I believe. In all likelihood, they have found more over the centuries.

"Only the fact that we destroyed the ships that pursued us and took all the prisoners allowed us to escape through the defective flip point. Otherwise, I am certain that the Others would never have rested until they tracked us down. They wouldn't want our knowledge to ever return to the clans."

Talbot stared at his wife in horror. No. This wasn't a mistake. If the prisoners had gone to the trouble of stealing a transponder—which was what he thought they'd done—and then hijacked the recovery ship to head for the outer system, they knew *exactly* where they were going.

He had no idea how they could've known. Maybe they'd found something inside the town that he'd missed. Hell, he didn't even know how they'd managed to go undetected on the island for a week. His people had searched every inch of it.

"What's on the other side of this flip point?" he asked.

The other man shrugged. "Based on the battle stories my father told me as a child, the system on the other side has a clan world. It wasn't heavily invested, as I understand it, but that could have changed in the years since then."

Kelsey overrode Talbot before he could ask what the hell that meant. "We've got to get after them right now. We can't allow them to escape this system. Take command of the marines on board this ship and get ready. We're going to have to board the recovery ship and stop them."

His wife smiled coldly. "I've been itching to do something ever since they escaped. Now I can finally drive the events. Let's wrap them up in a bow before they even realize we're coming."

37

Veronica swam slowly back to consciousness. She had a blinding headache and felt as if someone had turned her inside out.

"How are you feeling?"

She looked over and saw Brent Kowalski standing beside her. Her tactical officer's brow was furrowed with worry.

"Like crap," she said, astonished at how weak her voice was. "Though I suppose that's better than the alternative. I didn't expect to wake up at all."

He helped her sit up. "I'll confess to having my doubts too. You were in bad shape when we found you. What happened?"

She waved a hand at him. "That isn't important right now. What's our status?"

He stopped her from standing up. "You still look pretty unsteady to me, Captain. I think you should take it easy. We're not in any immediate danger, so there's no need to rush."

She wanted to argue, but he was right. A few minutes wasn't going to make any difference one way or the other. She was alive, and they'd escaped. That was all that mattered. At least she assumed they'd escaped.

"Are we still in orbit around Icebox?"

"No. The ship got orders to move out within half an hour of us taking it. We've been slowly boosting for the outer system for almost a full shift. There's no sign of pursuit, so Commander Castille believes we've gotten away."

She'd been out far longer than she'd suspected. That worried her, but she'd deal with it when she had time.

"When has anything gone that easily for us?" she asked rhetorically. "Sooner or later, they're going to figure out what we did and come after us. When we get on the other side of the flip point, we're going to have to run for it.

"The downside is going to be that we don't have any information about flip points in that next system. The odds are very good that they'll follow us before we locate an exit from the system. So, we're going to have to find an excellent hiding place to wait them out."

Veronica decided that she was feeling as good as she was going to be. With Brent's help, she slowly stood. It would have to do.

She'd been in a very rudimentary medical center. It was barely large enough for two beds and some cabinets. She hoped they never actually needed to treat someone in it.

Veronica would have liked to say she didn't need his help getting to the bridge, but that would've been a lie. She was significantly weaker than she'd ever remembered being.

Castille and Candace were flying the ship. Well, Candace was. Castille was sitting in the commander's chair looking pretty.

He rose as soon as she came in to the bridge. "Veronica! It's *so* good to see you back on your feet. We were all very worried."

She thought he actually sounded sincere. Her feelings about him had become more complicated as they discovered the truth about the revolution. She suspected he'd be willing to do anything to further the AIs' cause. Still, he sounded pleased that she hadn't died, so that was something.

"I think I'm only provisionally back on my feet. Do you mind if I take your seat?"

He stepped away from the commander's chair and gestured for her to sit. "Please do. All I'm doing is occupying space. I don't really know what I should be doing to command a vessel in space. Candace has actually been running things."

"And running them well, I'm sure," Veronica said. "She's an extremely talented and competent officer. What's our status?"

Castille sat at one of the spare consoles against the bulkhead. "We captured the ship without any incident. Commander Fuller is guarding the prisoners. They all seem exceedingly competent, so I don't trust leaving them out of our sight. Even without tools, they almost managed to escape from a sealed compartment."

She nodded, impressed. "That does sounds remarkably competent. Are they Fleet officers?"

He shook his head. "They don't appear to be. My guess is that they're civilian specialists. I'm sure their story is fascinating, but at this point, I'm only interested in keeping them locked away until we can complete our escape."

"How far are we away from the flip point?"

He shrugged and gestured toward Candace.

"As near as I can tell, we're about two hours away from the flip point," the woman said. "We're far outside the normal area where one would exist, so there's no danger the ships in orbit around Icebox will detect it.

"At this point, I don't believe they can detect us, either. We're not moving very quickly, so our grav signature is low. We actually changed course several hours ago, so even if they come looking for us, they're not going to find us in the area they'd expect."

"They'll search the outer system when we don't come back," Veronica said. "They're eventually going to find the flip point. When they do, they're going to come after us. We need to have a plan for when that happens."

"I've been thinking about that," Castille said. "As soon as we cross into the next system, we'll get as far away from the flip point as we can and hide in the outer system. We can go out into deep space and wait. We have plenty of food and water, so all we're worrying about is time."

That was about what she'd expected. All things considered, it was the best plan. "What about our original prisoners? Did you put them in with the crew from the ship?"

"I didn't want the two groups discussing things between themselves. We brought them on board, but Justine and her military associates are in a separate cabin. As you might imagine, she's frothing at the mouth over her treatment. I can totally understand why her daughter locked her up."

Veronica chuckled. "Families are complicated. If you don't mind, I think I'll rest before we flip. I think I need to be at my best."

Castille rose to his feet. "I'll see you back to a cabin. Lieutenant Kowalski can remain here to assist Candace. We'll wake you twenty minutes before we flip."

The cabin was exceptionally plain, but it looked to have a comfortable bunk. That's all she really cared about.

Once Castille had departed, she laid down and closed her eyes. They'd caught more good luck than anyone could justify. She couldn't help feeling that it would run out at the worst possible moment. Then she was asleep.

* * *

ANNETTE CURSED the escaped prisoners again. Where the hell had they gone? She'd taken her fighters out along the course they'd held when *Audacious* had lost sight of them, but they were gone. Had they already flipped out of the system?

She sure as hell hoped not. Her fighters didn't have the capability to detect a flip point, even if they weren't relying solely on passive scanners. They might fly right past it.

"I think I have something, Captain," one of her wingmen said. "Just a hint of a signal. I think it's a grav drive."

She linked her fighter to his and examined what he was seeing. That certainly did look like a grav drive signature. It was way off the projected course, so they'd have to alter their trajectory if they hoped to get a better reading.

"Everyone, follow my lead." Annette curved her fighter around and boosted her speed a little.

She was still going slowly enough that she wasn't worried about the recovery ship spotting her. To say their scanner suite was rudimentary was a profound understatement.

Five minutes later, she was certain they'd found the recovery ship and the Dresden orbital. They were making fairly good time considering the mass of the vessel and its cargo. She was close enough to detect the short-ranged scanning pulses they must be using to search for the flip point.

Annette opened a directional channel at where *Persephone* would be and sent a message detailing where they'd spotted the recovery ship, its course, and speed. Princess Kelsey would adjust her approach to match.

The Marine Raider strike ship was the very epitome of stealthy. Given enough time, they could sneak up on the recovery ship before the enemy detected them.

If, of course, they had the time to do it. If there really was a flip point out here, the recovery ship might be almost on top of it.

* * *

KELSEY FELT like a caged animal sitting in her command chair. She wanted to pace the bridge, but that wouldn't project the right image.

The damned ship was right there in front of her, but she couldn't rush the job. This had to be done exactly right or her mother would die.

Talbot laid a hand on her arm. "She's going to be okay. I'll do my absolute best to make certain of that."

She sighed and tried to relax a little. "I know you will, but I can't stop worrying. If any part of this goes wrong, we're so screwed."

"I think it's about time you headed down to get your marines suited up. We'll launch the pinnaces in fifteen minutes. You should be able to sneak up on them with all the stealth materials built into the pinnaces' hulls."

"The marines are already loaded," he said. "All I have to do is go down and get into my armor. Just keep breathing. We'll save her."

"Then you'd best be on your way. I'll let you know as soon as we're ready to launch and give you a final update on the situation."

Talbot gave her arm another squeeze before heading for the hatch.

"Not to be a wet blanket, but you know it's not going to be that easy, don't you?" Angela asked.

Kelsey sighed and slowly nodded. "Nothing ever is. Especially around us, it seems. How long until we're within range to launch the pinnaces?"

The marine checked her console. "We could launch in ten minutes, but I think we can probably slip in a little closer. That fifteen-minute time frame you mentioned is probably just about right."

"Any sign of the flip point?"

"We're not going to see it on passive scanners. We'll just have to hope that we're nowhere close to the damned thing. We can start scanning once we secure the recovery ship and make sure the prisoners are safe."

"I'm worried," Kelsey said. "Not just about this operation, but about what we're going to find on the other side of that flip point. I have to be honest, these ghosts aren't sounding like quality allies, if you know what I mean."

She'd learned a little bit more from Jacob about the history of the clans. In one respect, they were just like the New Terran Empire. They were determined to overthrow the Rebel Empire and restore civilization. They meant to crush the AIs.

The problem was that they'd known for five hundred years that they were going to have to do this. There was a hardness to them. A grim resoluteness where the ends justified the means. At least that's how it had sounded to her. She hoped she was wrong.

These people sounded fanatical. She wasn't certain that they'd see much difference between the New Terran Empire and the Rebel Empire. They intended to rule and would fight to make that happen.

With any luck, she'd stop the recovery ship before it came anywhere close to the flip point. The clans would figure out something was up here when they came to collect their crops, but that was at least eight months away.

And it wasn't as if the new prisoners really knew what had happened to them or how they'd gotten here. All Kelsey and her people needed to do was slip away undiscovered and make it home. They could come back and make contact with the clans in a more organized manner before things went to hell.

"The recovery ship is changing course," Jack Thompson said. "They might have detected something."

The course change was relatively minor, but since it was the first time the recovery ship had deviated, Kelsey was certain it meant something. If the recovery ship was close enough to the flip point to detect it with their crappy scanners, time was exceptionally short.

She checked the timer on her implants. Talbot had left the bridge twelve minutes ago. She opened a channel to him.

"You're on. It looks as if they might've detected the flip point. Launch the pinnaces. Remember, I want everyone alive. Stunners only."

"I'll do the best I can, but no promises. If one of them does something epically stupid, like threaten the prisoners, I'm going to blow them away."

She felt a slight jar as the pinnaces undocked from *Persephone*. They glided ahead of the strike ship and arrowed toward the target. By her best estimate, they'd be there in another fifteen minutes.

Kelsey prayed that was soon enough.

38

Raul was so focused on the flip point that the helm officer had to repeat herself before he grasped what he was hearing.

"Sir? I'm detecting a scanner anomaly behind us. It's almost as if there's a shadow of some kind."

He pulled up the readings on his console and cursed. "I think you're right. There's a ship back there. It's almost undetectable, but I think some of the gravitic waves coming off the flip point are screwing with their stealth."

Raul wanted to redirect the scanners to the rear and boost their power, but he didn't dare. That would give them away.

"We can only hope those are small craft," he said after a moment. "If they can't flip, we'll still get away."

"We're only about five minutes from the flip point at this speed," Wells said. "I'll call the captain."

"No. If that *is* an enemy ship coming to collect us, there's nothing she can do. We'll flip to the other system and see what we find. If a ship comes through after us, I suppose we'll have to surrender."

Of course, it wouldn't be that simple. He couldn't allow them to take him again. It was always conceivable they could break him and get the codes to access the manufacturing equipment. He couldn't allow that, no matter what.

Time flowed like molasses. He expected the shadowy ship to attack at any moment. Yet, they didn't.

"We're inside the outer boundaries of the flip point," Wells said.

"Are you certain that if we attempt to flip, we'll succeed? Let me stress that if we fail, that ship—if it is one—will certainly attack."

"As certain as I can be without trying, sir. I've given it a large margin of error since we haven't thoroughly charted it yet."

"Initiate the flip."

He held his breath and then relaxed as they flipped into the new system. They'd made it!

"Possible hostile vessel detected," the helm officer said. "It's a big one, sitting just off the flip point."

That was not what Raul wanted to hear. "Call Commander Giguere. What can you tell me about the ship?"

Wells stared at her console. "I'm not certain it's a ship now that I'm getting a better look. It might be some kind of station. Like the guard fortresses at Dresden."

Raul certainly hoped not. The recovery ship was completely unarmed. His options if they challenged him were to flee or surrender.

"We're also picking up vessels moving inside the system," Wells said. "Quite a few of them. It seems we've stumbled into an occupied area."

"One controlled by the ghosts, or so it seems," Raul said. "Have we gotten any reaction from that station?"

Wells shook her head. "Not yet. Perhaps it's unmanned or abandoned."

No one was that lucky. Raul was certain that they'd surprised the people on the station, but they'd respond shortly.

"Incoming signal from the station," the junior officer said. "A demand for our identity and surrender in the name of something called the Clan Council. What should I do, sir?"

If only there was something they could do. These were the ghosts. The jig was up.

Then a plan of action occurred to him. They might not survive doing it, but it would certainly screw things up for the New Terran Empire.

"Maximum acceleration directly toward the station," he snapped. "Prepare to jettison the arms holding the Dresden orbital on my command. And open a response channel."

When she nodded, he continued. "This is Commander Raul Castille of the New Terran Empire. We've found you now, and we're going to exterminate you."

He made a gesture to kill the channel. "Cut the Dresden orbital loose as soon as it's on a collision course with that station."

"Jettisoning arms in three… two… one… mark!" Wells said.

The ship jarred abruptly as it ejected its cargo arms. The helm officer must've begun slowing them down because the orbital was quickly receding ahead of them.

Commander Giguere came into the compartment. "What's going on? What's our status?"

Raul ignored her. "Are we still inside the flip point, Lieutenant Wells?"

"Barely, sir. The flip capacitors are still charging but should be online in less than thirty seconds."

"Take us back as soon as you can."

Raul turned to Veronica with a sad smile. "We found the ghosts. Or perhaps it would be better to say that they found us."

"The station's firing missiles," Wells said. "They're going to shred the orbital, but that's not going to save them. The debris field is going to hit them like a shotgun blast."

Veronica stared at him in horror. "What the hell have you done?"

"The best thing I could under the circumstances," he said. "Made our enemies' lives much more difficult."

"Flipping in five seconds," Wells said.

A fierce burst of light announced the destruction of the Dresden orbital. Nothing came close to the raw power of a failing fusion plant.

As Wells had said, the debris from the explosion would still slam into the station. There was no way to stop it.

He smiled coldly. He certainly hoped Princess Kelsey enjoyed the havoc he just unleashed upon her. With any luck at all, he'd ruined any chance she had of making allies of the Empire's enemies.

* * *

Kelsey was still cursing the bastards' timing when they reappeared. Talbot had been just about to board them when they'd vanished. Now they had another chance.

"Go fully active," she ordered. "Open a channel to that ship."

As soon as she was certain the transmission was going out, she began speaking. "This is Princess Kelsey Bandar. Surrender your ship at once."

That's when she noticed something was wrong with the recovery ship. Its arms were gone, and so was the Dresden orbital. Why the hell had they cut it loose?

The other ship failed to respond but began accelerating into the system.

"The pinnaces are going to latch on in about twenty seconds," Angela said.

That would put an end to that fight. The escaped prisoners were no match for marines in combat armor. They'd be able to secure the ship in very short order.

Right then, the recovery ship cut acceleration.

Angela gestured toward the screen. "Incoming transmission."

An image of the escaped destroyer commander appeared on the main monitor. The woman looked haggard.

"We surrender."

That had to gall her, Kelsey suspected. The woman had done far too much surrendering to the New Terran Empire for her to be comfortable.

"My marines will be boarding you in moments," Kelsey said sternly. "You will not resist them. Have any of the people you took hostage been harmed?"

"I'll quibble terms with you, Princess Kelsey. We don't have hostages. That implies that we we're holding them in exchange for something from you. Those people were prisoners. And no, none of them have been harmed."

Kelsey forced herself not to relax as relief flooded through her. Her mother was okay.

"Quibble as much as you like, Commander Giguere, so long as you don't resist us."

"I don't see much point in resisting. The damage is already done. We found the ghosts on the other side of this flip point. Commander Castille made certain that they're not going to be well disposed toward you."

Kelsey had no idea what that meant, but she could figure it out later. "Where is he?"

"I believe he's returned to the cabin he was using. No doubt he wants to surrender in his own way. Or maybe resist. I have no idea."

Ice flooded through Kelsey. "You need to secure him right now. When he escaped from us, he killed almost all of his fellow prisoners. If he harms any of the people on your ship, I'm going to hold *you* personally responsible."

The woman's expression became stricken. "I'll make sure he doesn't."

The screen went blank.

Angela turned toward her. "The pinnaces just locked onto the recovery ship's hull. They'll be inside very shortly. They'll stop any shenanigans."

Kelsey certainly hoped that was true. "If they ran into the clans on the other side of that flip point, there could be a hostile response coming back through that we can't deal with. From what I've been able to gather, they sound like the kind of people that shoot first and don't bother asking questions later.

"Launch an FTL probe through the flip point and signal *Audacious* to gather every one of our people. It's very possible that we're going to have a fight on our hands before too long."

"Should they come out to join us?"

"No," Kelsey said. "Have them start for the multiflip point with the freighter. If we can conceal its existence, or at least the fact that it has multiple destinations, we might be able to slip away. I'd rather not get into a shooting war with the clans."

"I thought the multiflip point was too constrained to allow *Audacious* to pass through."

"It is. Carl is going to have to jury-rig some kind of frequency modulator for the carrier's flip drive. Otherwise, the clans are going to be able to bring enough ships to overwhelm us. Thankfully, his calculations indicate the freighter should be able to make the flip. Signal Commodore Anderson to get moving.

"As soon as we have the recovery ship secure, we need to get everyone off it and get moving too. *Audacious* will be able to beat us there as it is. We can't afford to waste a single moment."

39

V eronica raced out of the bridge as soon as she cut the com channel. If Castille did anything to the prisoners, they were screwed.

She found Armand Fuller guarding the corridor where they were holding the prisoners. He raised an eyebrow as she ran up.

"We've flipped twice," he said. "Is something wrong?"

"You could say that. Where's Castille?"

Her executive officer frowned. "On the bridge, I assume. Why?"

"I don't have time to explain. Release the prisoners. We're about to be boarded, and we're surrendering. Make sure none of our people put up a fight."

She ran toward the rear of the ship without waiting for a response. He was a solid officer. He'd do what she'd ordered him to.

Where else could Castille have gone? She didn't believe for a moment that he'd gone back to his quarters. Still, she checked them all. Empty, as expected.

That really left only one place that he could've gone. Engineering.

Her blood ran cold as soon as she arrived in the engineering compartment. Graham was slumped over the console just inside the hatch. It looked as though he'd been stunned.

Moments later, she found Castille beside the fusion plant. Not the controls. The plant itself.

"What are you doing?" she asked.

He glanced at her and smiled. "What duty demands of me. I figured your engineer wouldn't understand. You know what I'm talking about, though. I can't allow them to capture me."

She wished she'd picked up a weapon. He was bigger than she was and armed. "That doesn't mean you have to kill everyone."

Castille straightened. "I'm afraid it does. Trust me. It's cleaner this way."

Veronica nodded slowly. "I suppose you're right."

She took two steps toward him, making certain to move slowly so as not to alarm him.

It didn't work. He raised the flechette pistol he'd held behind his back. "You can stop right there. You're an exceptionally resourceful woman, so I can't allow you to come any closer."

Right at that moment, the sound of metal on metal echoed throughout the hull. Someone had just docked, and they hadn't been gentle about it. The enemy was here.

"Well, I suppose we'll have guests just in time to—"

Not waiting for him to finish what he was saying, Veronica snatched up a wrench that Graham must've left sitting next to the grav drive and hurled it at Castille.

He ducked, raised the flechette pistol, and opened fire.

Veronica was already moving, throwing herself against the fusion plant. A glance where he'd been standing showed a jury-rigged bomb composed of a plasma grenade.

She yanked it free just as he shot her leg. Intense pain lanced through her as it gave way. She landed hard, and the bomb tumbled from her grasp.

The plasma grenade shed the tape holding its activator spoon down as it rolled across the compartment and stopped at Castille's feet. The pinging noise of the light metal hitting something in the engineering compartment when it flew free was ridiculously high pitched.

Castille cursed and dove for the grenade. He snatched it up and drew back to throw it toward her.

Veronica barely had time to cover her eyes before it went off in his hand.

The blast picked her up and hurled her across the engineering compartment. She slammed into the bulkhead and felt bones breaking.

Since she was still in agony, Veronica assumed the fusion plant had somehow survived the explosion. The tears in her eyes clouded her view of the engineering compartment, but it certainly looked as if the grav drives were wrecked and the flip drive was a smoking ruin.

The fusion plant wasn't undamaged, either. The overhead lights flickered and went out as it shut down. Emergency lights sprang up, but they only dimly lit the interior of the engineering compartment.

The arrival of armored marines with their weapons out was almost hilariously anticlimactic.

They fanned throughout the compartment searching for hostiles. Two of them aimed their rifles at her, so she didn't move. Someone searched her for weapons and then bound her hands behind her. That brought on an entirely new level of pain.

She looked up at the closest marine. "I need to speak with someone in charge. You're in terrible danger. Commander Castille destroyed a battle station controlled by the ghosts. They'll be coming."

He didn't look as if he believed her, but another marine arrived in engineering a few minutes later. He squatted down beside her and took his helmet off.

"Commander Giguere? My name is Major Russel Talbot, and you are my prisoner. Again. What's this I hear about ghosts?"

She filled him in on what Castille had done in as few words as possible.

He cursed and turned to the man standing beside him. "Get everyone aboard the pinnaces. We're headed back to *Persephone* in ten minutes."

* * *

Kelsey already knew they were in trouble before Talbot called her. The FTL drone had seen the disaster.

The battle station just off the flip point was completely destroyed, but there were ships inbound. Two of them from fairly close to the flip point and others from deeper in the system.

Kelsey cut Talbot off as he tried to warn her about the danger. "You can't leave the computers on board the recovery ship intact. We have to be absolutely certain that no data about us is left for the clans to capture."

"I can destroy the computer," he said, "but if there's a tablet or data chip that has something I don't know about, I can't control that."

"Can you destroy the ship by overloading the fusion plant?"

He shook his head. "It's trashed. It looks like Castille tried to blow the ship up, but Commander Giguere stopped him. The resulting explosion still disabled everything in the engineering compartment."

Kelsey turned to Angela. "We're going to have to blow the ship up ourselves."

"I don't think that's the best idea," her executive officer said. "If it's already destroyed when the enemy arrives, they're going to suspect something. They have to see it blow up when they attack, or they'll come looking for us. The closest ships are about forty-five minutes out."

"I want the scanner records," Kelsey told Talbot. "You have fifteen minutes to get that data and anything else of interest. Then I want you off that ship and on your way back over here. If we're going to fight, I don't want to have to worry about any pinnaces being undocked."

"On it." The com channel died.

"The closest two ships could be any size," Angela said. "Even if we're lucky and it's only two destroyers, we're still going to get chewed up."

"We'll bracket the ships between Annette's fighters and *Persephone*. We'll try to reason with them. If they shoot first, they can take out one of the hostiles. We'll take out the other."

Angela looked uncertain. "If we're talking about a pair of cruisers, we're in big trouble."

Ten minutes later, Talbot sent the scanner data across. The recovery ship's scanners were crap, but the reading of the battle station would still be useful.

The FTL drone was sending them data about the approaching ships. She still couldn't be certain about the classes. There was a squadron of vessels about seven hours behind the lead pair.

"Talbot is undocking," Angela said. "He'll be back aboard in five minutes. The other pinnace just finished unloading the crew from the recovery ship. Talbot has our escapees, your mother, and the people captured with her."

The oncoming ships were about twenty minutes away from the flip point. One was a destroyer, but the other was a light cruiser.

This was going to be more dangerous than she'd expected.

The other grouping of ships was still too far away for any kind of identification, but there were two dozen grav drives in operation. That meant there was going to be a higher percentage of capital ships. There was no way *Audacious* could take on that kind of firepower.

"Signal *Audacious*," Kelsey said. "Carl has to come up with something to get the ship through to Pandora."

"I'm sure he'll do his best, but that might not be good enough," Angela said. "He's a genius, but there's not a lot of time."

"He's got all those other research scientists. They have about six hours to get to the other flip point, modify their flip drive, and get the hell out of here. Tell them we'll meet them there and hope for the best."

It was one hell of a risk. If the carrier's flip drive burned out like the cruise liner, they'd be stuck in this system. If the clans got prisoners, they'd eventually drag the truth out of them. Castille had left them in one hell of a spot.

"Five minutes until transition," Angela said.

"Arm all missiles. We'll give them one chance to talk. If they start shooting, we'll take them down. If we have to fight, have Annette fire on the light cruiser. They actually have a stronger first-strike capability than us."

Persephone wasn't built to fight another ship head to head. They'd be lucky to take out the destroyer. The antiship missiles the fighters carried would be deadly at this range. Five fighters were a small group to take on a light cruiser, but that was the situation they found themselves in.

The clan ships paused long enough to make a pass through where the battle station had been located. The wreckage of the Dresden orbital had smashed it into pieces. That was sure to piss them off.

The two warships maneuvered into the flip point. Kelsey hoped they managed to avoid exchanging fire, but knew that was a long shot.

* * *

ANNETTE TENSED as the ships appeared in the flip point. *Persephone* transmitted a plea to stand down, but the warships opened fire anyway.

Their missiles completely shredded the unarmed recovery ship, but *Persephone* used electronic countermeasures to spoof the first salvo aimed at her. That wouldn't work twice at this range.

That gave Annette's people an opportunity. It put her and her wing mates in terrible danger, but she had to count on Princess Kelsey to protect them.

At this range, the antiship missiles on her fighters would tear a ship apart if they got through its defenses. She just had to hope the counter fire didn't blow her fighters to pieces.

Without saying a word, she launched both her antiship missiles at the light cruiser. Her board lit up as the other fighters did the same. Ten small sparks closed the distance between them and the larger ship at a rapid pace.

Whoever was in charge over there had been ready for trouble. Antimissile railguns immediately swatted four of the missiles. The survivors dove in, but the defensive gunners still took out another two in short order.

The ship fired a swarm of missiles toward her fighters. That was gross overkill. If even one of them detonated in their midst, it would take them all out.

"Scatter!" she shouted over the short-range com.

Her fighters flew away from each other, and the light cruiser blew up. One of their antiship missiles must've gotten through.

Annette noted that one of the missiles had picked her as its prom date. Fantastic.

She designated it for her antimissile defenses and tried to dodge as they strove to take the missile down. Explosions behind her told her that not all of her friends were going to come home at the end of the day.

As focused as she was, she still managed to note the destruction of the destroyer. *Persephone* had killed him cleanly. No matter what happened to her, the princess was going to escape.

The decoys meant to distract the missile didn't put off the one chasing her. Luckily for her, her other defenses managed to disable it while she was still outside destruction range.

Annette brought her small ship around to help her wing mates, but the fight was already over. Her fighter was the only one left.

40

Talbot knew the clock was ticking. If they were going to make it back to the multiflip point before the next wave of Clan warships arrived, he needed to finish recovering the survivors of the battle in the next half hour.

With only two marine pinnaces, that was challenging. Not only did they need to recover the people alive, they had to destroy the life pods. A bunch of empty pods would certainly make the enemy suspicious.

Thankfully—and he used that word advisedly—there hadn't been that many survivors.

Honestly, he was surprised anyone had ejected at all. There couldn't have been time to order anyone to abandon ship. Not that fast. The battle had lasted about fifteen seconds from the arrival of the Clan warships and their destruction.

The four pods he was tracking must've launched without any orders at all. No doubt the ship's captain would have been quite angry, if he'd survived.

Persephone's pinnaces had already caught up with two of the pods and were shepherding them back toward the ship. They'd use the jury-rigged docking envelopes to get the people out.

While the marines aboard the Marine Raider strike ship took the prisoners aboard from the first set, he'd led the effort to retrieve the second set of escape pods.

That task done, he docked and allowed the other pinnace to destroy the pods as they were ejected from *Persephone*.

Once aboard the ship, he made his way to where they were detaining the prisoners. There weren't many of them. The pods were designed to hold dozens of people, but the makeshift prison compartment only had a dozen men and women inside.

His guards had them covered with stunners while the ship's medical officer examined them. To his untrained eye, most of them looked a little rattled but relatively healthy.

Senior Sergeant Coulter—the most senior noncommissioned officer aboard the ship—pulled him aside.

"We've got something of a problem with the last pod, Major."

Talbot stepped into the corridor so that the prisoners couldn't hear what they were saying. "What's up?"

"The guy inside the pod is weird. I mean seriously weird. First of all, he was in there by himself. Second, he's dressed funny and has tattoos on his face."

Talbot started to say something but changed his mind. "Put him in a separate compartment. Come get me when he's secure."

As soon as Coulter had moved away, Talbot called Kelsey.

"We picked up a surprise," he said by way of greeting. "Based on the description, it sounds like we have somebody from The Singularity."

"Seriously?" Kelsey asked. "Does this person have the same kind of tattoos as the woman in Emperor Marcus's last broadcast?"

"That's what Coulter says. The prisoner is male, though. How do you want me to handle him?"

His wife said nothing for a moment. "Make sure to have him medically screened and keep him in isolation. I want to handle him with kid gloves for the moment."

"Are we going to question him once medical clears him?"

"We'll let him stew for a while. Make sure that he has whatever food he requires, but don't answer any questions. I'll deal with him once the rest of the situation is taken care of. In fact, I think I'll wait until we're out of the system entirely."

About that time, he heard the second pinnace dock. "It sounds like we've just finished up our work here. What's the plan now?"

"We join *Audacious* and the freighter at the multiflip point. I haven't been bugging him, but I hope Carl has some type of frequency-modulation unit designed for the carrier. If not, I'm not sure what we'll do."

He nodded. "Or what we'll do if the flip drive burns out when we try to use it."

"You are just a ray of sunshine. *Audacious* will beat us to the multiflip point by about an hour. By the time we get there, the second wave of ships will be less than half an hour from transit. We have an exceptionally small window to make our escape."

"Do you think we'll make it?"

Kelsey shrugged. "Damned if I know. I suppose we'll have to surrender if we can't escape. I feel very confident that we won't be treated with kid gloves if that happens."

"What about the other prisoners? Are they in good shape? Does it look like we got any officers?"

It was his turn to shrug. "I've only glanced in, but everyone I saw was in civilian clothes. I didn't see a Fleet uniform or anything like that. We're going to have to question each of the prisoners separately and see what they have to say. There's not very many of them. Only twelve."

"I wish we hadn't had to fight them," Kelsey said. "Based on everything that Jacob had told me, these aren't the kind of people we want to align ourselves with, but they didn't have to be our enemies. At least not this quickly."

"Damn Castille and his idiotic stunt. It's really screwed things up for us. We had to defend ourselves, but we pretty much assured that the clans are going to be our enemies."

"You did everything you could to try to avoid this," he said. "Sometimes you just have to accept that the situation worked out badly and do the best you can with the hand you're dealt."

"I'll get over this," she said. "Take care of your prisoners. I'm headed down to the medical center to see Commander Giguere."

* * *

VERONICA WAS FINALLY SETTLING into the tiny medical center. Thankfully, the place wasn't swamped with injured. She'd heard the ship going to battle stations and launching missiles.

Probably against ships that were pursuing her after what Castille had done.

She felt badly about that. There'd been no need. She and her people had already lost. Getting the ghosts riled up was only going to cause them all a major headache in the future.

The doctor that had treated her stepped over to her bed.

"Good news, Commander. It doesn't look as though you're going to need a trip into the regenerator. We've been able to stabilize the broken bones, and you're already on the mend.

"That's not to say that your recovery is going to be easy. I'm afraid you're not going to be walking around until your legs are in better shape. You certainly won't be doing anything athletic until after your ribs heal."

The shots he'd given her earlier had blissfully numbed the pain. "I'm done resisting, doctor. I'm just happy none of my people were killed."

He nodded. "From what I understand, Princess Kelsey found a compartment to lock them up in. They're under heavy guard—as are you—so they won't be escaping again. You've given everyone quite a bit of heartburn over the last week."

"One does what one can."

The man laughed softly. "I suppose so. I stopped by to tell you that you have a visitor."

Someone had come to ask her questions. Well, she supposed that was only natural. She'd cooperate. The time for resistance had ended.

The person who'd come to interrogate her was a surprise, though. Princess Kelsey Bandar stepped through the hatch. The short blonde woman wasn't smiling, but she wasn't snarling, either. Veronica supposed that was the best she could hope for.

"Commander Giguere, that was quite the stunt. I had an entire battalion of marines when I stole the Dresden orbital. You took it back with half a dozen people. My compliments on a brilliant plan."

"I think it's only brilliant if it succeeds," Veronica said dryly. "Harebrained might be more appropriate for what happened. For what it's worth, I'm very sorry that your mother was caught up in this. That was not part of our plans. Just her bad luck."

"I'd guessed that from the timing," the other woman said. "You had no way of knowing she was arriving as you were trying to sneak out of *Audacious*. I don't blame you for that. In your shoes, I'd have done the same thing.

"That doesn't mean that I'm happy with it, however. You and your people have proven yourselves to be entirely too resourceful. For the time being, I'm keeping you all securely under lock and key."

Veronica chuckled. "I don't think I'll complain. We've already abused your hospitality once. I'm not certain when your doctor is going to let me out of this place, though."

"When he does, you'll join your compatriots. Let's spend a moment talking about how you were injured. I'm given to understand that you got into a fight with Commander Castille in the engineering compartment on the recovery ship. One that resulted in his death, as well as your injuries.

"I get that you were fighting for your life and the lives of your people, but I'm grateful that your actions spared my mother and the other prisoners under your care. When the time comes, you can rest assured that I will take that into account."

The short woman put her hands on her hips and stared at Veronica. "I wish we'd been able to convince you of our honesty. You would've made one hell of an ally."

Veronica laughed a little until the sudden pain in her ribs stopped her. "Surprisingly, I was mostly convinced that you were telling the truth. Then the facility we found down on the planet proved it."

Princess Kelsey frowned. "What facility? The town? Is that where you were hiding? I thought we'd searched it completely."

Veronica explained about the hidden facility inside the volcano. Then she detailed everything they'd found inside it, including the journal and all the classified files.

"I transferred everything to a data chip," Veronica concluded. "It was in my pocket when you captured me. It's not encrypted. I hope it proves as educational for you as it was for me.

"All I can say at this point is that I know the AIs lied to us. I didn't know that before, but now I'm certain of it. They're enslaving us just like you said. I'm not certain how I can convince you of my sincerity, but I'll try."

Princess Kelsey nodded. "We'll have plenty of time to discuss that once you're feeling better. Focus on your healing while we see if we can get ourselves out of the mess that Commander Castille got us into."

The noblewoman left without another word.

Veronica lay back in her bed and considered the events that had gotten her here. It had been one hell of a journey, both physically and intellectually. She felt adrift. Everything she'd worked so hard to achieve was gone.

Even once her body had healed, she had no idea what she'd do now. Even if she could, she'd never go home. She had no doubt the AIs would find out what she'd learned. They couldn't allow that kind of information to spread into the Empire.

Worse, she knew she could no longer deny the truth. Her people were slaves. Even a gilded cage was still a cage. She had a lot of thinking to do, but she had to do something about that.

41

Kelsey stopped outside the compartment where her mother was waiting. Part of her really didn't want to have this conversation, but they had to settle this business. Their relationship wasn't healthy. That had to change.

As much as it galled her, her mother wasn't going to be the one making alterations. Trying to change other people was a recipe for going crazy. If they were going to settle this, Kelsey would have to do the settling.

She pressed the admittance chime and waited. A few moments later, the hatch slid open.

Her mother stood on the other side. She'd obviously used the time to clean up from her imprisonment.

Kelsey smiled a little. "I'm glad to see that you're—"

Justine Bandar yanked her daughter into a tight hug. "Enough. I can't stand what's come between us. I don't know that I can ever change what I've done or who I am, but I love you with all of my heart, and I'm sorry I've hurt you."

That was more than enough to get Kelsey to crying. The two of them stood there, arms around one another. Finally, her mother stepped back.

"I've got some tissues beside the couch," her mother said as she wiped at her own damp eyes. "Come in and let's talk."

Kelsey sat down beside her mother and did what she could to dry her eyes. It wouldn't last, she knew. This was going to be that kind of conversation.

She took her mother's hands in hers. "I've been so worried about you. Ever since they took you, I thought I'd never see you again. I don't want what I said to be the tombstone of our relationship. Yes, I'm hurt, but that doesn't matter. We'll find a way around this."

"It *does* matter," Justine said. "You're absolutely right that I've been selfish. I always have been. I've just gotten worse at hiding it.

"I can't change the past. I cheated on your father, and I certainly should've told you that Karl wasn't your father. I just never expected to be called on it."

Kelsey shook her head. "He might not have been the man who sired me, but he is assuredly my father. And, as much as you cannot stand the idea of it, Jared is my brother."

Justine sighed. "I think that's going to be the hardest thing for me. I've hated that boy since the moment I heard about him."

"Why?"

"It doesn't make any sense," her mother said with a shrug. "It's all emotion. I've never bothered to consider why I can't stand the outcome of my ex-husband's infidelity when you and your brother came from mine.

"I'll find a way. Somehow. Just as I'm going to have to accept the fact you're married to a commoner who isn't afraid to tell me unpleasant truths."

Kelsey raised an eyebrow. "You've met Talbot?"

Her mother shuddered. "The good major came to visit me before I was kidnapped. I can't see what you like about the man. He's probably covered with hair."

Indeed, he was. Thankfully, that was something that technology could deal with.

"He's very good at everything he does. You'll need to upgrade the rank if you talk down to him again, though. We're going to be stuck with a large number of marines for the foreseeable future, and we have too many majors.

"I want Talbot in overall command of all the marines, so I'm promoting him to lieutenant colonel. That's appropriate for a brigade-level assignment. I'll get around to telling him eventually."

The corner of her mother's mouth quirked upward. "It's good to see that nepotism runs in the family. That seems oddly appropriate.

"Again, I have to accept that it doesn't matter what I think about him. He's your husband. If I want to improve my relationship with you, a good first step would be accepting that he's part of the package. I can't promise that I can change, but I'll try. I really will."

Her mother took a tissue and dried her eyes again. "I understand you captured the people that took me prisoner. I thought you were making all that up.

"I was wrong. The man who led that other group is dangerous. He's smart and ruthless. Keep an eye on him."

Kelsey smiled a little. "One good thing to come out of this is that you don't have to worry about him anymore. He didn't precisely want to come peacefully. I'm afraid that he died resisting."

That wasn't precisely the truth, but it was close enough for this conversation.

"I don't have time to go into the details of what happened to them or what's happening now. Events are in progress that give us a very narrow window to escape some very unfortunate consequences.

"Hopefully, we'll be able to get clear of the situation in about five hours. If things work out, we'll have plenty of time to talk. Mother, no matter what happens, I love you. That will never change."

Of course, Kelsey wasn't actually certain that she liked her mother. That was a stretch. Also, there was an all-too-real chance that her mother would revert to her old behavior.

Well, if that happened, it happened. She'd deal with it.

Kelsey rose to her feet. "I've got to go. There's still a marine outside your hatch, but it's not because you're under arrest. If you need to go anywhere, he'll make sure you get there safely. There are a lot of dangerous areas aboard a warship. I don't want you walking into something you're not prepared for."

Justine rose to her feet and pulled her daughter into another hug. "This isn't going to be easy. Not for me and not for you. I'm absolutely certain that I'm going to fall short. People don't change in a day. Or a week.

"But no matter what happens, I don't want us to ever stop talking. I don't want to ever see you hate me."

"I'll never hate you, Mother. I'm sorry, but I've got to get going."

Kelsey kissed her mother on the cheek, let herself out, and headed back toward her quarters. If she was going to get any sleep before they arrived at the multiflip point, she had to get it now.

She'd been awake long enough that she was starting to feel the effects of exhaustion. Her mind needed to be sharp when she made the final throw of the dice.

Besides, it had been over a week since she'd seen her husband. When he finally finished with the prisoners, she had no doubt that he had a very special welcome in mind for her.

* * *

FOUR HOURS LATER, Kelsey was back on the bridge, and *Persephone* was approaching the multiflip point. She felt better than she had since they'd kidnapped her mother. Things might still go to hell, but she was going to pray they didn't.

Her new friends Jacob and Derek sat in spare chairs against the bulkhead. They watched everything with wide eyes. She was certain that they'd wanted to be on the bridge during the battle, but she couldn't afford to take that risk.

The readings from the FTL probe in the Clan system indicated the enemy task force was a little more than an hour away from the flip point. The readings were still sketchy, but she felt confident that there were at least half a dozen capital warships. Possibly more.

She'd dropped a second FTL probe on this side of the flip point to watch their emergence. Once she was ready to take *Persephone* through the multiflip point, she'd send the destruct signal to the one in the Clan system. She couldn't take the chance that they'd find it later.

True, it supposedly had a self-destruct package that would take it out if an unauthorized ship came close, but she wasn't in the mood to risk it. They'd never tested that feature, and all it would take was one failure for someone else to get the FTL technology.

Angela turned. "Incoming signal from *Audacious*. It's Commodore Anderson."

"On screen."

The display of deep space cleared to show the flag bridge of the carrier. Zia Anderson sat in the center seat.

"We're about as ready as we're going to be, Highness. We've already sent the freighter through. Carl and his team have installed some type of modulator for us, but he won't give me any kind of odds about how it's going to work out. He says he just doesn't know enough to guess."

"What happens if it doesn't work? Is it going to burn out the flip drive?"

The commodore shrugged. "Probably. It's not as if we have a choice."

Kelsey nodded. "We're coming up on you right now. Cross your fingers and press the button."

"One roll of the dice coming up. No snake eyes."

The com channel closed, and Kelsey watched the image of the carrier floating in the darkness. The longer it sat there, the more worried she became that the flip drive had failed. Then, with a flicker, it vanished.

"Did you see that?" she asked.

Angela grinned. "I sure as hell did! They made it!"

Kelsey held up her hand. "No, not that. They didn't just vanish. They kind of flickered before they were gone."

Angela brought up the playback and watched it again. Then she slowed it down a great deal and played it for a third time.

The carrier had definitely disappeared and then reappeared before disappearing again. Not just once, but three or four times in the space of a fraction of a second.

"I've never seen anything like that," the marine said quietly. "I've never even heard of anything like it."

"Drop an FTL probe and let's get to Pandora," Kelsey said. "We need to make sure they made it. They could have gone to any of the potential branches. If they went to Archibald, we're totally screwed."

The helm officer touched his console. "Probe away. We're ready to flip at your order, Colonel."

"Take us across."

A moment later, they flipped into the Pandora system. To her relief, *Audacious* sat just ahead of them, and the freighter was a ways off to the side. They'd all made it.

"Incoming signal," Angela said. She threw it up onto the screen.

Zia appeared, frowning. "I've got good news and bad news. Obviously, we made it. The problem is that the flip drive burned out. It's completely nonresponsive. We're trapped here."

Kelsey sighed. "Well, that beats being trapped on the *other* side of the flip point or going to Archibald. Maybe you'll be able to repair it."

"I suppose anything is possible," Zia said. "I wouldn't hold my breath, though. What do we do now?"

Kelsey looked toward Jacob and Derek. "I believe we have some visitors to take home. It seems we'll be staying longer than we'd anticipated, so we might as well make as many friends as we can while we're doing it.

"Continue monitoring the FTL probes we left in the other system. We need to know what the Clan task force does. From what I understand, even if they suspect we've gone through the multiflip point, the default destination isn't this system. We should be safe here."

"What do we do if the drive is beyond repair?" Zia asked.

"That's a little more complicated. We know the multiflip point can get us to Archibald. If push comes to shove, we may have to insert a team into that system and acquire the parts we need."

The commodore didn't seem convinced. "We don't have a lot of experience dealing with the Rebel Empire. Even if we did, those kinds of parts are going to be difficult to obtain. Perhaps impossible."

Kelsey smiled. "We always seem to find a way. Don't count us out of the fight."

"Whatever you say, Highness. If you'll excuse me, I'm going to get us headed toward Pandora."

"Pandora?" Jacob asked. "What's that?"

"The name we decided to use for your planet. We had no idea what you called it, so we had to have a name. What name do you use?"

He shrugged and deferred to Derek.

The alien shook his head. "We have no name for ourselves or our planet that would make sense when referred to by someone not from here. Pandora will suffice. Does that make me a Pandoran? You'll have to explain what that means at some point when we have more time."

Kelsey nodded and sat back in her seat. No matter how good a face she put on this situation, they were in a real bind. One that might be impossible to solve.

She didn't know what she was going to do if that were the case, but she had the best people in the universe to work the problem. They'd find an answer. Or die trying.

The hatch slid open and Lieutenant Commander Clark Malone came onto the bridge. The medical officer gave Jacob and Derek an odd look before walking over to her chair.

"Might I have a few minutes of your time, Colonel? Outside?"

That was unusual, but she assumed he wouldn't have asked if it wasn't important. She excused herself and stepped into the corridor.

Once the hatch had slid shut, she raised an eyebrow. "What is it?"

The doctor licked his lips. "I was examining some of the medical waste left over from treating the aliens. I didn't have much of a chance to look them over while they were aboard. Things were a bit tense, as you recall."

She nodded. "That they were. I understand the injured only had relatively minor cuts."

"That's right. I didn't want to look the dead over very closely at the time. Their living comrades were already on edge. I finally had a chance to test some of the tissue and blood samples, though. I found something bizarre."

"They're aliens. That isn't shocking."

He shook his head emphatically. "What's shocking is how recognizable their DNA is. And I use that term with the specific meaning for deoxyribonucleic acid. Colonel, they might look alien, but their genetic markers are not only the exact same material that organisms from Terra have, but they are more than ninety-six percent identical to human DNA."

Kelsey frowned. "What? That's impossible."

"I thought so too. I checked the results a dozen times. Pandoran DNA is derived from human DNA. There is no mistake. It's obviously been modified at some point in the past, but the roots are crystal clear."

She opened her mouth to argue but stopped herself.

"I see," Kelsey said after a moment. "That's unexpected. Can you tell how long ago the modification took place?"

The medical officer shrugged. "A long time ago. Tens of thousands of years, probably. Perhaps even longer than that."

That really was impossible. That almost certainly meant the modification had happened before the formation of the Terran Empire. Hell, before humans had ventured into space at all. Definitely before they'd had that kind of skill with genetic manipulation.

"Find out everything you can," she finally said. "Take the samples over to *Audacious* for further testing with Doctor Zoboroski. Keep this quiet. Only tell Commodore Anderson."

He nodded. "Will do, Colonel. I'll let you know if we make any headway on figuring this out."

Kelsey rubbed her face as the officer left. What did this mean? Was there some other player they didn't know about? It would have to be another alien race.

Considering that the Old Empire had never found any evidence of nonterrestrial sentient life, this was getting ridiculous. Worse, how did she and her people keep stumbling across them? What would happen when they found a more advanced species?

She had no idea, and ignorance might kill them.

* * *

WANT to get updates from Terry about new books and other general nonsense going on in his life? He promises there will be cats. Go to TerryMixon.com/Mailing-List and sign up.

DID YOU ENJOY THIS BOOK? Please leave a review on Amazon. It only takes a minute to dash off a few words and that kind of thing helps Terry make a living as a writer and gets you new books faster.

WANT the next book in this series? Grab *The Terra Gambit* today or buy any of Terry's other books, which are listed on the next page.

VISIT TERRY's Patreon page to find out how to get cool rewards and an early look at what he's working on at Patreon.com/TerryMixon.

ALSO BY TERRY MIXON

You can always find the most up to date listing of Terry's titles on his Amazon Author Page.

Note: the links below (ebook only, obviously) redirect you to my website where you can click a button to go to Amazon. This allows me to participate in Amazon's associates program and earn a little more. Sorry for any inconvenience.

The Last Hunter

The Last Hunter

Bonds of Blood

Alpha Strike

The Enemy Revealed

Command Authority

The Grand Conspiracy

Shield of Humanity

Fog of War

Ships of the Line

Operation Liberty

The Empire of Bones Saga

Empire of Bones

Veil of Shadows

Command Decisions

Ghosts of Empire

Paying the Price

Recon in Force

Box Sets

The Empire of Bones Saga Volume 1

The Empire of Bones Saga Volume 2

The Empire of Bones Saga Volume 3

The Empire of Bones Saga Volume 4

Humanity Unlimited Publisher's Pack 1

Humanity Unlimited Publisher's Pack 2

ABOUT TERRY

#1 Bestselling Military Science Fiction author Terry Mixon served as a non-commissioned officer in the United States Army 101st Airborne Division. He later worked alongside the flight controllers in the Mission Control Center at the NASA Johnson Space Center supporting the Space Shuttle, the International Space Station, and other human spaceflight projects.

He now writes full time while living in Texas with his lovely wife and a pounce of cats.

TerryMixon.com

- amazon.com/author/terrymixon
- facebook.com/TerryLMixon
- patreon.com/TerryMixon
- bookbub.com/authors/terry-mixon
- goodreads.com/TerryMixon

www.ingramcontent.com/pod-product-compliance
Lightning Source LLC
Chambersburg PA
CBHW072054020726
47501CB00003B/590